HELLCHASER

**A Novel by
J. Wesley Buck**

HELLCHASER

1

Dr. Fred Samms was a stoutly built man with blue-gray eyes and dark brown hair. Although a practicing psychologist, he had also trained as a medical assistant. He hadn't asked for this particular assignment, but as the detention center medic, he was the only one who could perform it. He felt uneasy as he walked with the guard along the light gray corridor that held a slight antiseptic odor. Their steps were muffled on the tile, and the silence of the place seemed ominous. Their pace was purposeful, confident, yet he kept recalling what the psychiatrist had told him.

'Garnet is a heartless, cunning man. You must be very alert when you enter the cell to inject the transponder into him.'

When they stopped in front of the cell door, Samms felt intimidated at the thought of facing this particular felon. He was aware of Jovan Garnet's brutality, and it made him uneasy. He moved the small case from his right to his left hand, looked at the guard and nodded.

"You can wait here," Samms said. "This won't take long." The guard slipped the key card into the slot, they heard a click, and the door opened.

Stepping into the matt white cell, with sunlight falling through the barred window, Samms faced a hard looking man with hazel eyes and black hair sitting on the bunk. Samms opened the case and took out the injector.

"Time for your implant, Garnet," he said, trying to sound authoritative. Garnet just stared at him without getting to his feet. His inaction annoyed Samms and he shook his head.

"Don't make me call in guards and do this by force," Samms said, in a firm tone.

Garnet got slowly off the bunk and pulled up his sleeve. Samms stepped forward and pressed the injector to his bare arm and heard a slight hiss. He looked away from Garnet as he returned the injector to its case. In that instant of carelessness, Garnet smashed his fist against Samms' face and slammed him against the wall. He quickly had his arm around Samms' throat and began to slowly choke him.

"Now tell that fucking guard to open the door or I'll break your goddamn neck." He increased the pressure on Samms as he pushed him to the door.

"Guard," Samms said, trying to keep a steady tone. "Open up." There was a click and the door opened. Garnet used Samms to slam into the door. It swung out and impacted against the guard, knocking him down, stunned. Garnet grabbed the guard's weapon, shoved Samms to the floor, and fled down the corridor.

Coming to the main entrance, Garnet fired twice, taking out the guards. He quickly shorted out the electronic lock, pushed the door open, and stepped out. He headed for the nearest alley, knowing he would have to stay off the streets. Garnet felt good about himself for having quickly taken advantage of the chance the doctor had provided.

Jovan Garnet had been a respected, top rated chemist who had taught at a university. When he had been accused of plagiarism, papers had been found in his lab that seemed to verify the accusation. Unable to prove his innocence, Garnet was dismissed and blacklisted. Unable to find work, he drifted until he got the idea of synthesizing exotic narcotics. He set up a lab in his apartment and was soon a small time drug dealer, until he was entrapped by a sting operation.

During his two years in prison, knowing he had been incarcerated unjustly, Garnet turned hard, and decided that when he was released he would do as he damn well pleased, and to hell with anyone who got in his way. He was to live up to what he had decided as he became a masterful predator. Friend and foe alike would grow to fear him. But while he was in prison, he also decided to be a model prisoner, and give no one any suspicion about how he would act after his release.

Having escaped, Garnet knew where to go. He had friends that would help him get away from Earth. He was also aware that the transponder wouldn't become active for thirty-six to fifty hours. He was in no hurry, and would go when he was ready. He would now go where he wanted and do as he pleased. Garnet stepped into a shadowed alley, and made certain he wasn't being followed. He was cooled from the afternoon heat as he moved along to a door and knocked.

"It's Jovan," he said, and the door opened. He quickly stepped inside and turned to face the woman.

After closing the door, she came to him, slipped her arms around his neck and kissed him. When she pulled away, she smiled and shook her head. She was blonde with light blue eyes and a slim figure. The apartment was small, bright, and smartly furnished.

"I'll never understand how you're able to get out of those confinement installations," she said. Garnet smiled.

"I'm always looking for opportunity, Adele. When it comes, I take it. That's why they can never hold me for long." She gave him another kiss.

"I'll get you some clothes so you can get out of that jail suit," she said. "What are you going to do now?" Garnet got a thoughtful look as he regarded her, wondering that himself.

"Anything more I can do to help?" she asked, taking clothes from a closet. He shook his head.

"No. What I have to do, I have to do alone. I don't want to involve anyone. I've got to get to my ship and get the hell away from Earth.
"Well I can, at least, fix you a good meal before you go," Adele said. Garnet gave her a nod.

"That sounds good after what I've been fed the past three days."

Warden Grant Howell's office was sparsely furnished, but sunlight couldn't hide the grim expressions. He paced, turning angry glances at a bruised Samms and the guard.

"Goddamnit, Doctor! You knew Garnet's record and had been warned by Dr. Jacobs. Why did you go into that cell alone? Had you temporarily taken leave of your reason?" Howell spoke in an angry tone. Samms looked at him with a beaten expression.

"I didn't think he would be foolish enough to try anything in the cell," Samms replied, defensively. "I assumed he was aware there was no way he couldn't get away."

"Well he can't get out of the building," Howell said. "We'll have him back in a cell in no time." Captain Langford came into the office with an angry look.

"Well?" Howell asked. Langford turned a hard look to him.

"Garnet escaped," Langford replied. "He killed one guard and wounded another. He shorted out the lock and was able to get out of the building." Howell's lips twisted in disgust.

"Alert the patrol," Howell ordered. "Put a guard on Garnet's ship. I don't want that bastard getting away."

"Yes, sir," Langford said, and left the office. Howell slowly turned his face to Samms.

"Now there will have to be an official inquiry," Howell said. "As for you, Doctor, you'll just have to explain your action to the board." Samms looked down and inhaled. He knew he was responsible for Garnet's escape, and what he had inflicted on the guards.

Garnet waited at Adele's until dark. He now had had a good meal, was dressed in fresh clothes, and felt a burning determination to get as far away from Earth as he could. He turned to Adele with a pleased look as he stuck the guard's weapon in his belt.

"Adele, you're a darling. You've fed me, given me decent street clothes, and your loyalty. I won't forget you. Now I have to go." She stepped to him and gave him a long kiss.

"Be careful, Jovan. And take care of yourself." He caressed her cheek.

"That's one thing I always do." He went to the door, opened it, and looked over his shoulder at her.

"Be seeing you, Adele." He went out and disappeared into the night. He felt good with a full belly and the scent of freshly laundered clothes in his nostrils. Garnet stayed on dark back streets as he made his way to the landing park. He moved cautiously, not wanting to encounter an officer and give himself away by killing him.

Garnet moved quietly among the shadows of the ships, avoiding the lights that illuminated the parking area. When he saw two officers standing by a small ship, he stopped to assess the situation. Garnet got a wicked smile and moved closer to the ship. The officers were talking, not suspecting he was so close. He raised his weapon and fired twice. Bright flashes impacted the officers' chests and they crumpled to the ground. Garnet went to the ship, opened the hatch, and went on board. He quickly powered up the ship's systems and lifted off from the pad. As he looked at Earth dropping away, he got a cynical smile.

"You'll never take me again, you bastards," he said, and glanced at his arm. "Now I've got get this transponder removed or neutralized." He took the ship into orbit, fired the main engine, and sped away from the Earth.

Three days after Garnet's escape, Les Camden and Eliot Neil sat in a booth drinking beer. The bar was quiet, with only four other patrons sitting at the bar. The place was modestly furnished, but comfortable. They glanced at each other, knowing the same thing was on their minds.

"What do you think they will do about Garnet?" Les asked. Neil took a drink, put his glass down, and shrugged.

"They're going to have to send someone after him," Neil replied, regarding Les with a grim expression.

"And it won't be easy taking him – alive anyway," Les said, leaned back, picked up his glass, and took a drink.

"They never should have let the doctor go into that cell alone," Neil said. "That was really stupid." Les nodded.

"Especially since they knew how violent Garnet is," Les added. The bartender came to the booth and stopped beside Neil.

"There's a call for you, Eliot," he said. "You can take it at the bar." Neil followed him to the bar and turned the audio unit around. Neil got a sinking feeling when he saw Drydon on the screen. The conversation was short, and he returned to the booth.

"I've got to report to the chief," Neil said. Les regarded him with a grim expression.

"What was the call about?" Les asked. Neil frowned and got an odd expression.

"Looks like I'm the marshal they're sending after Garnet," Neil replied. "I hope the asshole gives me an excuse to kill him. That will be a lot easier, and more preferable, than bringing him back alive." Neil patted Les' shoulder.

"I'll see you later," Neil said. "I won't be leaving right away."

"I hope you're wrong, Eliot," Les said. "Anyone going after Garnet is putting their life on the line." Neil nodded and left. Les watched him go out the door and decided to go over Garnet's record. One could never tell what might happen with that sort of man.

Filtered sunlight reflected off the brass nameplate on the desk: CHIEF MARSHAL CHARLES F. DRYDON. He regarded Neil with a somber look as he stood in front of the desk.

"Neil, I'm sending you with two rangers after Garnet. He killed the two men at his ship," Drydon said, shaking his head. "Neither had a chance." Neil inhaled deeply.

[8]

"When do I leave, sir?" Neil asked. Drydon got an uncomfortable look.

"Tomorrow. Garnet's been reported seen on Inader Four."

"Yes, sir." Drydon frowned and got a hard look.

"Don't take unnecessary risk, Neil. Garnet is a felon. A killer! Don't forget that."

"Yes, sir." Neil turned and went to the door. Drydon stood.

"Take every precaution," Drydon said, emphatically. "The implant should tell you when you're close to him." Neil glanced over his shoulder.

"Yes, sir," Neil said, and opened the door. A worried look from Drydon followed him out.

Stepping out of the office, Neil saw Drydon's receptionist coming toward him. She held an envelope in her hand. She locked her green eyes on him.

"Marshal Neil, this is an introduction to Ranger Commander Conrad Helm," she said, holding out the envelope. "It will explain your mission." He took it, gave her a nod, and left.

Neil was back with Les in the booth. Neil turned an uneasy look to him.

"So I meet with Helm in the morning," Neil said. "He's going to assign two rangers to accompany me in the search for Garnet." Les shook his head.

"Even with two rangers, you're going to have to be damn cautious, Eliot. Garnet is dangerous and cunning as they come. And he never seems to care about the number of men after him, he just kills them and evens the odds." Neil frowned and nodded.

"You don't have to remind me about that, Les." Les regarded him with a knowing look.

"Be sure to keep it in mind. It just might save your ass," Les said. "How are you going to track Garnet?"

"By sightings, at first," Neil replied. "He has a transponder implant but it has limited range. I'm just going to have to follow his trail until I can localize him. There's nothing else I can do."

"I hope you get lucky," Les said. "And put that bastard back in lockup where he belongs. Just watch how you move on Garnet."

Reading over Garnet's record, Les began to see a pattern to his thinking. It would be useful for anyone going after Garnet. Knowing what was in the record should give one an edge over Garnet. Les felt it was too bad Eliot hadn't been able to read it before leaving. Should give one an edge, he thought. That didn't mean it would prove viable. He hoped Eliot would be all right, and accomplish what he was being sent to do. But from his new insight into Garnet's mind, Les felt Eliot was going to be at greater risk than he realized.

On being shown into the office, Neil saw a tall, muscular man with black hair and gray eyes.

"I'm Marshal Eliot Neil," he said, handing the envelope to him.

"I'm Conrad Helm, Marshal. Please have a seat." Neil took the chair indicated. Helm retook his seat behind the desk. He took the single sheet of paper from the envelope, unfolded it, and read. Helm slowly raised his eyes and regarded Neil with a grim look.

"It isn't the usual job of rangers to aid in chasing down criminals," he said. "They usually intervene in local disputes and help to settle them." Neil shrugged.

"All I know is what I was told," Neil said. Helm nodded with an understanding look.

"In this case," Helm said. "I'll make an exception. Knowing Garnet's reputation, it's essential that he be recaptured as soon as possible. I'll assign Ryan and Sutton to accompany you."

"I appreciate that, Commander," Neil said. "It would be really dangerous to go after Garnet alone." Helm got a studious look.

"Maybe so," Helm said. "But someone alone would attract less attention. That could, possibly, lead Garnet into a false sense of security. Now I'll introduce you to the rangers who will accompany you."

After introducing the rangers to Neil, Helm began his briefing. Sutton was of medium build with brown hair and eyes. Ryan was a bit taller, stockier, with light blue eyes and sandy hair. Both were surprised when Helm told them what the mission was.

"That sounds a bit out of our league, Commander," Ryan said. Helm nodded.

"I know," Helm said. "But Garnet is a special case. He's a brutal killer. The sooner he's back in custody, the safer everyone will be. I can only caution you to use extreme caution when you approach him." Helm looked to Neil, extended his hand, and Neil gripped it.

"Good luck to you all," Helm said, also shaking each ranger's hand. The men filed out of the office.

They had been following a twisting trail from planet to planet, always arriving after Garnet had left. Neil and the rangers were frustrated at their luck. When the ship was on automatic, Ryan and Sutton looked at Neil as he took a PDA from his pocket. He glanced at them.

"I want to give you a better idea as to what sort of person Garnet is. This is all from his record," Neil said, and proceeded to fill them in. When he finished, the rangers looked unnerved.

"That man is going to be a tough customer," Ryan said. Neil nodded.

"How are we going to nail this guy?" Sutton asked. Neil frowned.

"Very carefully," Neil replied. "He'll take a person out quickly and without being provoked. So we're going to have to be alert, and cautious, when we come across him. Surprise will be our only advantage." Ryan paled.

"Landing this ship close to him will be anything but subtle," Ryan said. Neil nodded.

"Then we'll have to play it as it comes," Neil said. "Hopefully, we'll be able to take him without much trouble."

"I wouldn't count on that, Marshal," Sutton said. "From what you've told us about Garnet, he's going to be a whole lot of trouble."

As Ryan took the ship into orbit, Sutton kept his eyes on the scanners, and Neil took out the implant indicator and saw it emitting a faint glow. He knew he was just at the limit of its range.

"He's down there," Neil said. Sutton and Ryan glanced at him.

"About damn time," Sutton said.

"Yeah," Ryan agreed. "We've been on this bastard's trail for over a month now." Neil turned a grim look to them.

"Let's go get him," Neil said, in a cold tone. They pulled their straps tight and turned to the instruments.

Ryan took the ship into the atmosphere, fired its thrusters to break its speed, and set it down in an open area. They released their straps and Sutton went to a bulkhead locker, took out side arms, and handed one to Neil and one to Ryan, and held one for himself. As they strapped them on they glanced at each other.

"I feel I should remind you that we have to be careful," Neil warned. "Garnet won't hesitate to kill.
So if you get the chance, kill the son of a bitch." Ryan pressed the release and the hatch began opening. Neil kept his eyes on the implant indicator.

[12]

Going down the ramp, Neil noted an odd look from Ryan.

"What?" Neil asked.

"He couldn't have missed seeing our landing," Ryan replied. Sutton got an alarmed look.

"That means he could be waiting to ambush us," Sutton said. Neil knew he had to calm them down.

"There are three of us," Neil said. "We're after him, not the reverse. As long as we stay alert, he can't put anything over on us." They still had uneasy looks as Ryan nodded.

"Okay," Ryan said, "Let's go." Neil led off using the implant indicator.

Even though a bright sun was shining, the environment they found themselves in was cool, but not uncomfortable. They went along slowly until they came to a stop at the base of a wide hill with a copse on it. Behind was a dark, mist filled forest that gave Neil a chill. He turned the indicator around as Sutton and Ryan pulled their weapons from the holsters and looked around. Neil held up the indicator and glanced at them.

"He's in this area," Neil said, grimly. Sutton quickly glanced around.

"How are we going to find him in there?" Sutton asked, nodding at the forest. Neil shook his head.

"The indicator can't quite get a lock on him," Neil said, and pointed to the right. "You circle around that way, Ryan. See if we can flush him out." Ryan nodded and cautiously started away. Neil pointed to the left.

"You go that way, Sutton," Neil said. "I'll go straight over and we'll meet on the far side of the hill. And stay alert." Sutton moved off at a slow pace. Neil watched him for a moment, frowned, shook his head, and started up the hill with his weapon leveled.

Ryan moved slowly along the side of the hill, turning his head, but not far enough to see Garnet coming from among trees holding a large rock. A small branch snapped under his foot. Ryan spun quickly, his eyes widened as he raised his weapon. Garnet moved fast and slammed the rock against the side of his head. Ryan dropped without a sound.

"One down, two to go," Garnet mumbled, as he tossed the rock aside and moved back among the trees.

Sutton moved with caution, looking around, walking quietly as he wiped sweat from his face. He was afraid of running into Garnet alone, and wished they had stayed together. He kept his weapon moving in an arc in front of him, and glancing over his shoulder. He came around the hill and saw Neil. A surge of relief flooded him as he stopped beside the marshal. They looked around with puzzled expressions.

"Where the hell is Ryan?" Neil asked. "He should have gotten here before us." Sutton glanced around with an alarmed look.

"We are going to look for him?" Sutton asked. Neil turned a disgusted look to him.

"Damn right we're going to look for him," Neil replied.

Alert, they quietly moved along the way Ryan should be coming. Sutton suddenly grabbed Neil's arm and pointed. They saw Ryan lying on the ground, his head bloodied, and they rushed to him. As they knelt beside his body, Garnet stepped from behind a tree and fired twice. One charge hit Sutton in the groin, dropping him. The second hit Neil on his right side, spun him around, and he fell to the ground. Garnet came over to them and looked down. Neil looked up, his mind fuzzy from pain, and he knew he had screwed up.

"You lawmen! Always so damn stupid." He turned his back to them and walked off.

An elderly man came across the bodies and wondered what had happened. He checked them, kept his fingers against Neil's throat for a moment and lifted his eyelid.

"At least you're still alive." He took hold of Neil's arm, pulled him to his feet, and moved off.

Picks and shovels leaned against one wall of the crude shack. An electric lantern lit the place from a wooden table. Neil lay on a flimsy wooden bunk. The man came and checked him as Neil moaned. He gently patted Neil's shoulder.

"Don't worry, young man, I'll have you fixed up in a week."

The room had a slight perfume odor, exotic furniture, and artwork of alien landscapes hanging on the walls. Garnet sat in a plush armchair and watched the slim blonde by the wall working the panel keypad. The wall opened and two drinks slid out on a tray. She picked them up, turned, and locked her brown eyes on him. She sauntered across to the chair and handed him a drink with a slight smile. She sat down on the sofa facing him.

"It took balls and smarts to escape from confinement on Earth, Jovan." He took a drink and smiled.

"It's not hard when you're dealing with idiots."

"What are you planning now?" Garnet finished his drink and put the glass on the stand beside the chair.

"I've heard about a new narcotic, Marna. Quite potent, or so I've been told. I figure on getting a sample, synthesize it, and retire." She got a dubious smile.

"Of all the narcotics around, what makes this one so special?" He laughed, leaned forward, and took her hand.

"Sutain, supposedly, gives one contact with their cosmic soul." She leaned toward him.

"I prefer this kind of cosmic soul," Marna said, and kissed him. When they parted, they looked into each other's eyes.

"Marna, you are the most potent narcotic I know of." She smiled and caressed his cheek.

"I'm glad you like this bad habit." Garnet laughed.

[15]

Drydon sat at his desk going over reports as filtered sunshine filled the office. He heard the door open and looked up to see his receptionist coming toward him with a distraught look.

"I just heard from Ranger HQ, Chief," she said. "Their ship, with Marshal Neil aboard, has failed to make contact for the last three days." Drydon got a pained look.

"Do they know where it last was?" he asked. She shook her head.

"They have only an approximation of its location, but they're searching for it."

Drydon rose and came around the desk and stopped regarding her with a concerned look.

"I wouldn't worry just yet," Drydon said. "Let the rangers conclude their search and see what they come up with." She regarded him as a tear ran down her cheek as she nodded. Drydon patted her arm.

"Let me know if they come up with anything new," he said. She turned and left the office.

2

Neil sat on the cot looking as weak as he felt. Sunlight filled the one room shack through its only window. The man handed him a cup of coffee and Neil gave him a grateful nod.

"I don't know how to thank you, Tom," Neil said. The man took a drink from his cup.

"I was glad to help. But I didn't much care for burying your friends. That's something

I hope I never have to do again." Neil drained the coffee from the cup and put it on the table.

"I've got to be going," Neil said. "The son of a bitch who done the killing is going to pay." Tom got a doubtful look.

"Sure you feel up to it? You still look a might peaked." Neil regarded him as he nodded.

"I'll be fine. Can you take me to the ship?" Tom put his cup down and stood.

"Sure can."

As Neil and Tom walked through gently rolling countryside, Neil took deep breaths, enjoying the fresh air and feeling lucky to be alive. But he was haunted by the deaths of Sutton and Ryan, and knew it had been his fault. They should have stayed together. Neil had now learned, the hard way, how Garnet operated, and silently vowed not to let him get anything over on him again. Tom glanced at him with a concerned expression.

"How are you going to find the man who killed your friends?" Neil turned a grim look to him.

"It won't be hard to find Garnet," he replied. "He leaves bodies wherever he goes." Tom got a sad look and put his hand on Neil's shoulder.

"This Garnet sounds like a real bad person. You're going to have to be mighty careful when you catch up with him." Neil stopped and leaned against a tree. Tom got an alarmed look.

"You okay?" Neil got a weak smile.

"Yeah. I'll be all right." They moved on.

They stopped in the clearing where the ship sat. Neil turned to Tom and extended his hand. Tom smiled and took it.

"Is there anything I can do for you before I go?" Tom shook his head.

"Nothing for me, Marshal. But get Garnet! I don't like seeing people like him running loose." Neil smiled, went to the ship, activated the hatch and went on board.

As Neil traveled through space, he couldn't shake his guilt over the rangers' deaths. He knew there was nothing he could do about it, but he kept going over what he might have done that would have turned the situation out differently. It was hard, but he could see nothing he might have done that would have prevented Garnet from killing them seperately or as a group. Neil had learned a lesson he would never forget.

Neil reported to the nearest ranger station.

"We've been searching for the ship," the commander said.

"I'm sorry. I was wounded and unable to activate the emergency transponder," Neil said, and went on to relate what had gone down. The commander then put him through to Drydon. He related, again, how the event had unfolded, and asked what he should do. Drydon's brow wrinkled as he thought for a moment, blinked, and replied.

"Remain where you are. I'll see if I can get a lead on Garnet. Neil, I don't feel right sending you after him alone. So just wait until you hear from me." Neil nodded.

"Yes, sir," he said, but knew he now had to go after Garnet alone, if only to redeem his self-respect. The ranger commander regarded him with a sad look.

"If you can give me an approximate location of their graves, I'll have them brought back for proper burial." Neil nodded and began describing the area they had been killed in.

Neil walked along the crowded, brightly-lit street. As he passed an alley, a hand grabbed his arm and pulled him into the shadow. He couldn't see the man's face.

"Garnet's on Lindun," he said, in a low voice. "He'll be there awhile conducting his dirty business. The details are with the bartender at the Bone Yard."

"Thanks," Neil said, wondering if this guy was for real.

"Tell the bartender someone left a message for you. He'll know what you mean." The man vanished into the shadows. Neil started down the street toward the bar.

As Neil went into the rundown bar, all conversation ceased, and all eyes turned to him. He went to the bar and leaned against it, hoping to get out quickly and away from the strong odor of the place. The bartender came to him with a hard look.

"Someone left a message for me," Neil said, in a low voice. The bartender nodded, reached under the bar and took out an envelope. He handed it to Neil, who stuck it in his pocket and walked out.

The next morning, Neil reported to the commander and showed him the contents of the envelope. The commander read over the paper and quickly looked up at Neil.

"There's nothing I can do about this," the commander said. "You'll have to return to Earth and show this to Chief Drydon." Neil nodded.

"Yes, sir," Neil said, turned, and walked to the door.

"I'll contact the chief and let him know you're on your way." Neil glanced over his shoulder and gave a nod.

Les heard about Eliot being wounded when he got to the office. Dave met him at the door and told him what he knew.

"He's damn lucky to be alive," Dave said. Les turned a puzzled look to him.

"Why he isn't dead is something to make one wonder," Les said. "I would have thought Garnet wouldn't leave a live witness to a double murder behind." Dave got an angry look.

"He probably thought he would die," Dave said, and got an odd look. "You know how Eilene is going to take this." Les nodded.

"I can handle that," Les said. "I've just got to be firm, and not give in to what she wants."

Drydon stood when Neil came into the office and stopped in front of the desk.

"It's good to have you back, Neil. Your report was quite disturbing. Please, have a seat." Neil sat down with his lips set in a grim line.

"I underestimated Garnet, sir. I'll not do so again. And I'm very sorry it cost those rangers their lives." Drydon nodded with a hard look.

"He was just as cold-blooded when he killed a guard during his escape," Drydon said.

"And the officers at his ship. Are you all right?" Neil nodded.

"Yes, sir. Just anxious to get after Garnet as soon as possible. And from here on, sir, I prefer to operate alone." Drydon gave him an understanding look. Neil took the envelope from his pocket and handed it across the desk to Drydon.

"That was given to me by an informant, sir. I don't know how reliable it is, but it seems Garnet is making his way to Varian

Four to get a sample of the narcotic sutain." Drydon's chest expanded as he inhaled, frowned, as he read the information in the note.

He lowered it and looked at Neil.

"I want you to have a doctor take a look at your wound," Drydon said. "There may be complications."

"But I'm fine, sir." Drydon got a stern look and shook his head.

"You're not going anywhere, Neil, until I hear from the doctor. Clear?" Neil felt annoyed as he nodded.

"Yes, sir."

"Any idea where Garnet is now?" Neil shook his head.

"He was gone when I got to Lindun. But from the information in the note, I would guess he would be stopping at Alphin Three, sir." Drydon nodded.

"Very well," Drydon said. "After you're cleared by a medical checkup, you can head there." Neil stood.

"Yes, sir. I'll go see the doctor now." Neil turned and walked from the office.

As Neil pulled his shirt on, the doctor made notes on his PDA. Neil turned to him with a questioning look. The doctor noticed his expression.

"Well, Doc, am I fit for duty?" The doctor shook his head.

"The man who treated you certainly knew what he was doing," the doctor said. "I see no reason you can't return to duty. I'll inform Chief Drydon." Neil got a slight smile and nodded.

"That old man saved my life, Doc. And I don't know anything more about him other than his name was Tom and he's a miner." The doctor glanced at Neil with a smile.

"Well if he should ever come into medicine, he won't have any problem getting into med school.

"I'll be waiting for that call from the chief, Doc."

"I'll have my nurse inform him immediately."

Neil and Les sat in their usual booth having a beer, and Les was curious.

"What's Garnet like?" Les asked. Neil got a hard look.

"I only saw him after I was wounded. He holds law enforcement people in contempt.

He didn't hesitate to kill those rangers. He probably thought I would die, or maybe he only wounded me so I could spread the word about what he did."

"Why would he do that?" Les asked. Neil shrugged.

"To try and intimidate anyone else coming after him. Who knows how a mind like Garnet's works? The man is definitely a psycho." Les looked down at his glass, feeling he knew how Garnet thought.

"You going after him again?" Les asked. Neil nodded.

"I have to. I have a good idea of how he operates," Neil replied. "That makes me an expert on the bastard. As I told the chief, I won't underestimate him a second time." Les had reservations about his last statement, but couldn't deny his experience.

"You better be damn careful, Eliot. Read over his psych file before you leave, it could help you. I don't want to see you dead." Neil looked into Les' eyes and got a grim frown.

"I've got a score to settle," Neil said, with cold determination. Les nodded, understanding how he felt.

[22]

"Don't let it blind you to the point where you put yourself in danger."

"I'm going to be a lot more careful when I catch up with him next time." Les didn't mention that he had gone over Garnet's record and felt he might be more of an expert than Neil.

After leaving Earth, Neil put the ship on automatic. This time he was alone and glad of it. He didn't want to feel responsible for anyone, other than himself, again. All he wanted was to get Garnet – dead or alive, and he preferred the former to the latter. He leaned back and began running through his mind how he might take Garnet by surprise. But he knew the chance of that happening were slim to nonexistent. Neil wanted to come up with some idea of what he might be able to do knowing full well he would have to roll with events. Yet he had to have some sort of plan, even if it was only an expedient.

Neil took the ship in orbit around the pearl-colored world, reached to the control panel, and pressed a switch.

"This is Marshal Eliot Neil. Code Pi Two Seven Beta. Request permission to land." A male voice came from the speaker.

"Pi Two Seven Beta, permission granted. Use pad 6A." He pulled the straps tight around him, moved his hand across the controls, pressed another switch, and took hold of the manual control and turned the ship into the atmosphere.

Exiting the ship, Neil found the port moderately busy as he walked toward the administration building. He found the office he was looking for and went in. It was cluttered with files, and the young woman behind the desk looked haggard. But she was pretty, with auburn hair and brown eyes. Neil stopped in front of the desk and she turned an impatient look up to him.

"I'm Marshal Eliot Neil. I'm in pursuit of a felon named Jovan Garnet. I need your permission to go armed while I search for him." Her eyes widened in surprise.

"Unfortunately, Marshal, we're familiar with Garnet here. You have permission to wear your sidearm." Neil gave her a pleased look and nodded.

"I'll try to take him out of your hair – permanently." She relaxed and smiled.

"It would be a relief knowing he was where he couldn't do anymore harm." Neil went
to the door, glanced over his shoulder, and smiled.

"I'll do my best for you," he said. She gave him a nod as he opened the door and stepped out of the office.

Garnet opened the door and faced a very attractive woman with light brown hair and hazel eyes. She frowned as she regarded him and tilted her head.

"Come in, Larisa," he said, and pulled the door open. She stepped past him into the suite and looked around.

"Please, sit down," he said. She went to the sofa and sat down. He noted her light blue blouse and green skirt as he took the chair facing her.

"Want a drink?" Garnet asked. She shook her head.

"What do you want me to do?" she asked, wasting no time. He smiled and took her hand.

"There's a marshal at the Roadside Inn," Garnet said. "I want you to contact him and tell him you have information he needs." Larisa got a suspicious look.

"What sort of information?" Garnet smiled.

"I want you to tell him where I am." She got an incredulous look as he patted her hand.

"Don't meet with him before tonight. I want to have a surprise ready for him when he comes for me." She gave him a wary look.

"I don't know, Jovan. I know your kind of surprises. They're usually fatal." He released her hand, stood, and went to the window.

"Meet with him where no one will see you," he said, and glanced at her. "You won't be involved in any way." Larisa stood, went to him, and he turned to her.

"What the hell," she said. "I never could say no to you, Jovan." She leaned forward and kissed him.

Despite the bright sunlight, Neil lay dozing on the bed. The audvid unit sounded. He reached over and pressed the comlink. The caller wasn't sending an image, only audio.

"Marshal Neil?" a female voice asked.

"Yes."

"Be on North Eider Street at the intersection of Selton at eight o'clock. I have information you need."

"Who are you? How will I know you?"

"I'll know you, Marshal." She disconnected. Neil stared at the blank screen with an uncertain look. He knew it could be a trap, but if she had information about Garnet he would have to take the chance and meet with the woman.

Neil walked along the semi dark, empty street. He was feeling uneasier with each step he took. A woman stepped from a dark doorway and he stopped facing her.

"Glad you could make it, Marshal." He regarded her with a frown for a silent moment.

"What's this about?" She glanced around with a nervous look and back to him.

"Garnet's at the Norcroft Inn, room 501." She started past him and he took hold of her arm. She turned her face to him.

"Why are you telling me this?" She took his hand from her arm with an angry look.

"I've hated Garnet since he raped my sister," she said, and hurried off down the sidewalk.

Neil moved along the brightly-lit hallway, stopping in front of room 501. He put his ear to the door and listened. He drew his weapon and reached for the door release. The door swung open to reveal a well-lit, empty room with an odd chemical odor. Neil moved cautiously in and looked around. He took another step and felt a sudden pressure on his ankle release. He looked down and saw it had been a trip wire. It dawned on Neil that he had again underestimated Garnet. Alarmed, he began backing out of the room when it exploded.

3

Les Camden had two older brothers he saw finish college, get married, and settle into mundane jobs and begin families. That had little appeal for Les, so he looked around for a more attractive profession. He found an interest in law enforcement, and seemed to have an aptitude for it. When he became a marshal, he felt he had found the career he wanted.

He had met Eilene Cole through her brother, David, who was also a marshal. After dating for some months, Eilene and Les began living together. Except for vague hints, she had held her opinion until Les' friend, Eliot Neil, was wounded and the two men with him killed. She then began pressing him to give up law enforcement. He stubbornly kept putting her off. Now he had more bad news and felt he knew exactly how she was going to react.

As he expected, she didn't take the news of Eliot's death well. Les felt ill at ease as he stood in the comfortable living room regarding Eilene, and hoping she wouldn't start harping again for him to give up his job. With a look of disbelief, she slowly sank down on the sofa. Les knew he needed to try to explain to her, hoping she would be reasonable.

"Eliot was killed doing his job, Eilene. I just can't let it go. I've got to do something about it." She turned a concerned look to him. She held her blue eyes on him as she nervously brushed at her short cut, black hair.

"Do something? This is all the more reason for you to give up law enforcement, Les." He frowned and got a hard look. She was reacting the way he had expected, and it annoyed him that she wouldn't even try to understand what he had to do.

"Eliot was my friend. I'm going to ask Drydon to let me go after his killer." She quickly stood, grabbed his arms, and regarded him with a horrified expression.

"No, Les! You can't." He looked at her with a softer expression.

"I understand how you feel. But consider how I feel. Damnit, Eilene, someone has got to stop that madman." She embraced him and turned her face up to him.

"You're right, Les, he has to be stopped. But let someone else do it. Someone who wasn't a friend of Eliot."

"I'm the only one qualified to go after Garnet. I've studied his record, his psych file. I know him as well as anyone. That's why I have to be the one to go after him." She pushed away from him with a pensive look.

"Please don't do this. Think of me." He turned his face from her, knowing she was always thinking of her wants, and nodded.

"You win," he said, to avoid further argument." But I won't forget Eliot, or that Garnet murdered him. And I'm not giving up law enforcement." She got a relieved look.

"As long as you're here with me, I won't mind." She kissed him, they embraced. His expression said the opposite of what he had told her. Les only wished she would try to understand his motive instead of pressuring him to quit his job. He was becoming very annoyed with that.

The filtered sunlight illuminated the assorted display of weapons on the wall behind the desk. Drydon was pacing, his hands clasped behind his back. He was a stocky built man with sandy hair and blue eyes. He stopped and turned his face to Les.

"Garnet is an unfeeling killer, Camden. I don't like sending anyone after him, especially after what happened to Neil." Les nodded.

"I'm volunteering, sir. I've studied Garnet's record and psych file and have a good idea of how he thinks." Drydon's expression became dubious.

"No one can know how that bastard's mind works," Drydon said, in a cold tone. "He doesn't think like a normal person." Les frowned and straightened his posture.

"That's what I understand, sir. That makes me the only person able to carry out this assignment." Drydon regarded him with a solemn look.

"Are you forgetting what happened to Neil? He was a good, cautious marshal. Yet, somehow, Garnet was able to lure him into an ambush and kill him." A look of anger flashed briefly over Les' face.

"I'm not forgetting anything, sir. Especially Eliot Neil. He was my friend. That's another reason why I should be the one to go after Garnet." Les regarded him with a calm look. Drydon scowled, leaned on his desk, palms flat.

"I'm not sure there is any person who is right to go after Garnet. He's dangerous. Damned dangerous!" Les regarded him with a determined look.

"Someone has to go after him, sir. A man like Garnet can't be allowed to remain free to kill again." Drydon gave him an annoyed nod.

"I'm aware of that, Camden," he said, his eyes narrowing. "Do you really think you have a chance to nail Garnet?" Les nodded.

"Garnet is, after all, only a man. I just have to keep the idea of what he might try in mind. I've done a thorough study of him, sir. I feel I know him very well just from his record." Drydon pushed away from the desk and regarded Les critically.

"In his case, the term 'a man' is strictly ersatz." Les got a confident look.

"I can bring him in – or kill him, sir." Drydon didn't look convinced.

"Very well, Camden. But take pains to cover your ass. You can leave on a ranger ship tomorrow. I'll make the arrangements."

"Yes, sir." Les stood and turned toward the door with a cold, grim expression. He was aware of the challenge facing him, but he was determined to get Garnet. From now on, that would be his sole focus. That and making sure he remained alive and able to carry it out as a priority.

Eilene opened the door and faced her brother, David, who had a grim look.

"David! What are you doing here?" He stepped in and she closed the door and turned to him.

"Thought I would drop by and see how you are," he said. "Going to miss Les while he's gone?" She gave him a puzzled look.

"He's leaving?" she asked. Dave nodded.

"He volunteered to go after Garnet." Eilene's expression turned to one of surprise.

"He what?" Dave's eyes narrowed and he got a questioning look.

"He hasn't told you?" She shook her head.

"No." He frowned and looked away from her.

"Shit! I should have known better."

"Why wouldn't he tell me what he was going to do?" Eilene asked, a tremor in her voice, but quickly realized Les had told her what he intended to do.

"He probably didn't want you to worry about him," Dave replied. Her expression turned to one of anger.

"He told me he wouldn't do this," she said, choking back a sob. He took hold of her arms and regarded her steadily.

"I can't believe he lied to me." Dave dropped his arms to his sides and got a stern look.

"What do you expect after the way you've been ragging his ass to quit his job?" Her mouth fell open and she gave him an angry glare.

"I'm sorry," he said, turned, and left the apartment.

After he had gone, Eilene began thinking about how she could stop Les from going after that man. But she finally concluded that there was nothing she could do.

Wanting to get ready, Les came into the apartment in the early afternoon. He gave Eilene a light kiss and went to the bedroom, she followed. He took his travel bag from the closet and began to pack, he glanced at her.

"I've got a new assignment," Les said. Eilene remained silent and Les turned his face to her. The dark walnut furniture stood out against the pastel blue walls. She began to pace, her arms folded, an angry expression flashed to him.

"How long will you be gone?" Les shrugged and continued packing. She stopped pacing and grasped his arm, causing him to turn his attention to her.

"Who is this Garnet?" He frowned as he regarded her.

"The man who killed Eliot, two rangers, and a lot of other people." She got an alarmed look.

"And you're going after him alone! Why?" Les exhaled slowly, trying to control his temper.

"I'm not going alone. I'm being accompanied by two rangers. Besides, someone has to stop him. That's my job." She gave him an angry look and turned away from him.

"That's not what David told me." Les narrowed his eyes and got a hard look.

"What did he tell you?" Eilene tilted her head and frowned.

"That you volunteered for this assignment." Les' expression didn't change. She gripped his arms with a pleading look.

[31]

"You promised me you wouldn't do this." Les shook his head

"I made no promise, Eilene." An intense, angry expression came to her.

"Resign," she said, emphatically. He stared at her in silence, not certain how his response would sound.
"Let some other damn fool go after him and get himself killed," she added. "Anyone but you."

"I have to do this. Can't you understand that?" She got a hurt look but regarded him steadily.

"I'm not going to sit and wait for a call telling me you're dead." Les turned and closed his bag.

"I don't intend getting killed."

"Those people Garnet murdered, do you think they expected to die?" Eilene asked, desperate. Les kept his back to her.

"Damnit, Eilene! Apprehending people like Garnet is my job. It's what I'm good at." She got a defiant expression.

"It's time you made a drastic career change." He turned to face her.

"I can't quit because I have a difficult assignment." She waved her arm in a frustrated gesture.

"If I walk away from this, Eilene, I'll walk from every difficult decision I ever have to make." Her eyes widened as he grabbed his bag and headed for the door. Her anger erupted quickly.

"Damn you, Les! Why won't you listen to reason?" He glanced over his shoulder.

"I told you, it's what I do. It's my job," he replied, and walked out.

As Les was shown into the office, Helm stood and extended his hand. Les shook it.

"I'm sorry about what happened to Marshal Neil. I knew he felt bad about what happened to Ryan and Sutton," Helm said. "Have a seat." Les sat down.

"I read Neil's report on what occurred. I don't intend on making the same mistake Eliot did," Les said. "I've studied Garnet's record closely and have a pretty good idea of how he thinks." Helm nodded.

"The rangers who will accompany you are on the way to this office." Les leaned forward.

"I also don't intend letting them put their lives in jeopardy needlessly." Helm's eyebrows lifted.

"Well I'm glad to hear that." The door opened and the two men came in. Helm stood, came around the desk, and stopped beside them.

"Marshal Camden, this is Ranger Barton." Les shook the hand of a man of average height with dark brown hair and green eyes. Helm waved his hand to the other man.

"And this is Ranger Flint," Helm said. "This is Marshal Les Camden." Les shook his hand. Flint was solidly build with auburn hair and brown eyes.

After being introduced to the rangers, Les felt he had to tell them what sort of man they were going after.

"I assume you both know that Garnet killed two of your fellow rangers?" Les asked.

They both nodded.

"The man is an unfeeling killer," Les continued. "In escaping custody, he killed three officers without a thought. We can't take the risk of underestimating him. He's smart and ruthless. So let's track him down and put him out of circulation."

"Good luck, Marshal," Helm said. "And to you two also." He shook each of their hands.

Their time was spent following leads to where Garnet had been seen; but always arriving after he was gone. Les was getting frustrated when they got a break. Flint turned his seat and regarded Les with an expectant look.

"It's just been confirmed by one of our ships, Marshal. Garnet has been seen landing on Lantro." Les nodded and looked relieved.

"How long will it take to get there?" Les asked, calmly.

"About three hours," Barton replied. Les pulled the straps around him.

"Let's go," Les said. Flint and Barton pulled their straps snug and Flint glanced at Les.

"Ready, Marshal?" Flint asked. Les nodded and was pushed into the seat by the sudden acceleration.

They looked at the green planet on the screen and Flint moved his finger to the control console when he saw a yellow light start blinking.

"I got a lock on his ship," Flint said. Les glanced at him.

"See someplace to set down?" Les asked.

"I've put landing coordinates into the computer," Flint replied. They watched the screen as the ship descended through clouds.

The ship dropped toward the surface, fired its thrusters, and landed easily. Les quickly

loosened his straps and stood.

"What the hell is he doing on a planet with no civilization?" Barton asked. Les glanced at him with a knowing look.

"He probably learned we were after him," Les replied. "He wants a place of his own choosing for an ambush." Flint turned an alarmed look to Les.

"Do you want us to come with you?" Barton asked. Les shook his head.

"I'll handle it," Les replied. "No sense in risking more than one of us now."

"That's dangerous, Marshal," Flint said. Les glanced at him with a frown.

"I'm remembering Ryan and Sutton," Les said. The rangers exchanged surprised glances.

"Do you think going after him alone is a wise move, Marshal?" Barton asked. Les strapped his weapon around his waist and looked at him.

"Wise or not, it's the safest play right now. Marshal Neil took the rangers with him. Garnet surprised them, and that cost those rangers their lives. I'm not about to make the same mistake." Les went to the airlock, activated the hatch, and left the ship.

Les stood outside looking around. He heard the odd sounds of alien animals as a slight breeze ruffled his hair. He took the implant indicator from his pocket as occasional clouds blocked the sunlight and quickly passed. He looked at the indicator as he drew his weapon. Les walked over open ground toward a thin line of trees with large boulders scattered among them. He moved cautiously until a sudden flash erupted from a tree just in front of him. He ducked and moved behind a tree and slipped the indicator back in his pocket. He had located Garnet, and he had been waiting for him just as Les thought he would be.

Les tensed, then made a dash for a boulder and pressed against it. He peered around its edge. A flash hit the boulder and a rock splinter cut Les' cheek. He dropped to one knee and wiped the small trickle of blood from his face. Les tried to get a good look at where the pulses had come from. He saw no movement, and made a dash to another boulder. Les pressed against it, his finger on the trigger, hoping for a shot at Garnet.

"Give it up, Garnet." Harsh laugher erupted in the quiet landscape.

"Not a chance." Les glanced around the boulder but still saw no movement. He slipped to the other side and looked again.

"There are two rangers with me. You can't get away."

"Rangers don't worry me. They're dumber than you, Marshal."

"Is that what you thought of Neil?"

"He was stupid enough to walk into a trap. He should have minded his own business and left me to mine."

"You were his business, Garnet. Now you're my business." Les leaned toward the side of the boulder, and a flash on his side dropped him to the ground. He raised his hand and pressed a tiny switch on his badge. He heard footsteps, looked quickly around, but saw no one.

From his left, Garnet stepped from behind a tree smiling. Les grabbed for his weapon and Garnet kicked it away.

"You're too slow, Marshal," Garnet said, in a hard tone, looking down at Les and shaking his head.

"Give up on me, Marshal. You'll live longer." Garnet holstered his weapon, squatted beside Les, and held up a finger.

"You hesitated," Garnet said. "You gave me one second. In that second, I got you." He got an arrogant smile.

"You haven't made a very good first impression with me, Marshal." Les passed out. Garnet stood, looked at Les with a sneer, and walked back among the trees.

Barton's eyes were drawn to the upper console as a red light began flashing.

"We're getting an emergency signal from the marshal." Flint turned his seat and saw

the blinking signal.

"You got a firm lock on his position?" Barton nodded as he got to his feet.

"Yeah." Flint got up with an uneasy look.

"Let's go find out why he needs help," Flint said. They strapped on sidearms and hurried from the ship.

Barton and Flint moved among the trees, their weapons in their hands ready for use. They looked around as they moved along until Flint pointed.

"There he is." They hurried to Les. Barton holstered his weapon and knelt beside him. He took a small first aid kit from his belt and began treating the wound. Flint stayed alert, looking around, turning slowly. Barton stood.

"Let's get him to the ship," Barton said. Flint holstered his weapon and they each took one of Les' arms, pulled him up, and started for the ship. They moved as fast as possible with their burden.

"It was foolish of him to come after Garnet alone," Barton said. Flint turned a surprised look to him.

"He didn't want us risking our lives," Flint said. Barton gave him a hard look.

"What does that make him – brave or stupid?" Flint got a puzzled look.

When they got to the ship, each took hold of Les' weapon belt, lifted him, and carried him up the ramp. In the ship, they put him on a bunk and strapped him in. Flint went to the pilot's seat and began a preflight check. He glanced at Barton.

"How's he doing?" Barton glanced over his shoulder.

"I think he'll be all right, if we can get him to a hospital."

"Don't worry about that. Better give him an injection of painkiller. If he regains consciousness, he'll be in a world of hurt." Barton took the injector from the ship's first aid kit and pressed it against Les' wrist.

"Strap in, Barton, we're ready for lift off."

Flint took the ship into orbit and made his call.

"This is ranger ship Alpha One Eight. Request emergency landing. We have a wounded Marshal on board and need a med team standing by." A female voice came back.

"Alpha One Eight, you can land at pad 2A. I'll get a med team there as soon as possible."

"Thanks," Flint said, broke contact, and started taking the ship down.

The med team brought Les off the ship on a gurney, put him in the emergency vehicle, got in and drove off. Flint and Barton watched it fade into the distance.

"I guess we're lucky," Barton said. Flint turned a surprised look to him.

"How so?" Barton glanced at him.

"The marshal didn't take us with him," Barton replied. "So we were luckier than Ryan and Sutton." Flint thought for a moment and nodded.

"Well I guess we owe him for that," Flint said.

In the ER, they got Les stripped down and the doctor made a close examination of the wound and glanced at the nurse.

"I can only treat him temporarily," the doctor said. "Better make preparations for his transport to Earth. That's the only place he can get proper treatment."

"I'll see to it right away, Doctor," she said, and hurried from the ER.

4

It was quiet in the room with off white walls surrounding the hospital bed. The monitor, above Les' head, showed his vital signs were stable. Eilene stood on one side of the bed, her hand over his, and Les' brother, Ben, stood on the other side. Les loudly sucked in a deep breath, stirred, and opened his eyes. Eilene got a relieved look and bent down and kissed him lightly. Ben put a hand on Les' shoulder.

"Ready to give up law enforcement?" Ben asked. He was tall, muscular, with dark blond hair and blue eyes. Les got a weak smile and shook his head.

"Can't," Les replied. "I've got a score to settle now. It will take more than Garnet to kill me." Ben got a dubious look.

"He came pretty damn close to doing just that," Ben said.

"Garnet got lucky," Les said. "That's all." Eilene got a surprised expression.

"Damnit, Les! I want you alive," she said. He raised his arm and cupped her chin with his hand.

"And I intend to stay alive, despite Garnet." Her expression turned to one of frustration.

"Give up this line of work, Les," she pleaded. "Find a safe job." Les turned his head and looked up at Ben.

"There's no such thing as a safe job. Right, Ben?" Ben looked annoyed and nodded.

The doctor came in, saw Les was conscious, and got a satisfied look. He glanced at Ben and Eilene.

"You'll have to leave now," the doctor said. "He needs to rest." Ben gave Les' shoulder a pat as Eilene kissed him on the forehead and they walked from the room together.

When they stepped into the corridor, Eilene turned to Ben with an anxious look.

"We've got to find someway to convince him to get out of law enforcement," she said. Ben regarded her with an understanding look.

"I don't know how," Ben said. "He's too damn stubborn to listen to reason." Eilene put put a hand on his arm and regarded him with a plaintive look.

"You're his brother, Ben. There must be something you can do." He showed a trace of annoyance at her presumption.

"After what happened to Steve, Les feels that as long as what he's doing is right, he'll stick with it. And with Eliot murdered – "He slowly shook his head.

"He's driven to get Garnet. So what do you think I can do?" After a slight pause, he continued.

"I know what he's planning to do as soon as he's able." Eilene got a wide-eyed alarmed look.

"No! He wouldn't go after Garnet again, would he?" Ben remained silent and nodded.

"Then he's got to be stopped," she said, emphatically. "Before he gets himself killed." Ben shrugged.

"If you can't stop him, Eilene, no one can. He certainly won't listen to me." She got a beaten look as she regarded Ben.

"Nor me," she said, softly, in a pathetic tone. He took her arm and they walked off down the corridor.

The doctor stepped beside the bed and regarded Les with a studious look.

"You were lucky you got your beacon on." Les closed his eyes.

"I've always been lucky, Doc." The doctor frowned as he looked at the monitor and checked the IV.

[41]

"If the rangers hadn't gotten to you when they did," the doctor said, shaking his head.

"You would have died." Les kept his eyes closed and pulled the sheet up over him.

"I don't die easy, Doc." The doctor grunted and left the room.

Les was sleeping when the audvid sounded. He sat up on the side of the bed, turned on the lamp, and looked at the clock. Eilene turned on her side but didn't wake up. Les pushed the switch for audio only.

"Yeah?" Ben's voice came from the speaker.

"It's Ben. Steve's been killed in a lab explosion." Les couldn't believe what he heard. His brother was dead! How could this have occurred?

"What happened?"

"We can't be certain until the investigation is complete," Ben replied. "But it seems likely it was caused by an oxygen leak."

"What about Sally and the kids?" Les asked, concerned.

"They'll be taken care of." Les got a sad look.

"I never expected a brother of mine to die before me." Les awoke with a start. That dream again! Les wished it would never recur again.

After a week, Les was being released from the hospital.

"You need to take it easy for a month or so," the doctor said, as Les dressed. He nodded knowing he couldn't lounge around for a month. Eilene came in with a smile, thinking she was going to have him to herself for some time.

"Ready to leave?" she asked.

"Ready as I'll ever be," Les replied.

In front of the hospital, Les decided to pay Drydon a visit. Eilene pulled the vehicle up and Les got in. He regarded her for a moment.

"I want to stop by HQ," he said. "I've got to let the chief know I'm all right." She turned a horrified look to him.

"You need time to regain your strength," she said, pleading. He gave her hand a gentle squeeze.

"I've been flat on my back for over a week. I'm not going to get any stronger. You drop me off and I'll see you at the apartment later." He could tell she strongly disagreed with the action he was taking, but remained silent and pulled away from the hospital. For her silence, Les was glad.

The receptionist opened the door and Les stepped into Drydon's office and went to the desk. Drydon motioned for him to sit down. They faced each other across the desk.

"The doctor says you're not quite fit for duty." Les nodded.

"Yes, sir. But I know my condition better than the doctor does. And I'm ready to get back to duty." Drydon got a cool expression as he regarded Les.

"All right," Drydon said, nodding. "You still have Garnet's case. You proved, the hard way, that you know how the son of a bitch thinks. And those rangers are praising your action for not leading them into danger, as Neil did." That made Les feel good.

"I made a slight miscalculation, sir. That gave Garnet an edge he used with alacrity."Drydon got a stern look.

"No qualms about going after him again?" Les got a confident look.

"None, sir. As a matter of fact, I'm looking forward to our next encounter." Drydon wagged a finger at him.

"I want Garnet alive, if at all possible. I want to see him stand trial, found guilty, and sent to Forten. Is that clear?" Les nodded.

"Yes, sir." Drydon's expression softened.

"Don't take unnecessary risk, Camden. Not with a killer like Garnet."

"I have no intension of being careless, sir." Drydon got a pleased look and nodded.

"You've been assigned your own ship. Don't give Garnet a moment of rest until you take him into custody." Les sat up straight and nodded.

"I don't intend to let him rest, sir. I certainly won't be getting any." Drydon stood and Les did also. Drydon stretched his arm over the desk and Les gripped his hand.

"Good luck, Camden." Les turned and left the office.

Les sat at his desk in the light gray cubicle with a flourescent light overhead. Dave stuck his head in.

"Good to see you back, Les. Pull a new assignment yet?" Les turned his face to him.

"Hi, Dave. I do have an assignment." Dave stepped in as Les pressed a key on the compac and turned the monitor. Dave paled when he saw Garnet's face. He looked at Les with a disbelieving expression.

"Sure glad it's not me going after him." Les turned the monitor off.

"Does Eilene know about this?" Les shook his head.

"How do you think my sister is going to take this?" Les frowned and shrugged.

"She will understand." Dave got a cynical look.

[44]

"After the way she's been pressuring you to quit? Of all people, I wouldn't count on her understanding." Les regarded Dave with a serious look.

"Garnet's going to screw up, Dave. When he does, I'm going to be there and put an end to him." Dave put his hand on the desk and leaned forward.

"You're doing this for Eliot, aren't you?" Les got a grim look.

"Garnet has got to be stopped. His killing brought to an end." Dave got a pronounced frown.

"Garnet came from hell." Les nodded.

"He has no feelings," Dave continued. "He kills without any provocation." Les kept a steady gaze on him.

"You're right, Dave. But he's still only a man. A man who has to be taken out of circulation." Dave got a concerned look as he shook his head.

"You just got out of the hospital, Les. It was Garnet who put you there." Les stood with a confident look.

"And I'm going to return the favor as soon as I can." Dave frowned and pushed away from the desk.

"Man, you must be crazy! You're lucky he didn't use a frag bomb on you, like he did Eliot." Les stood and patted his shoulder.

"I didn't give him time to make one, Dave." Dave shook his head.

"He likes putting a lot of holes in people," Dave said, with a hard look. "Garnet doesn't like certain people to die easily." Les nodded, knowing what he was talking about.

"The chief wants Garnet brought in alive," Les said, calmly. "I intend complying with the chief's order." Dave looked shocked.

"There's no way you'll bring Garnet in alive." Les got a self-assured look.

"There's always a way to accomplish anything, Dave."

Les came into the apartment, quietly closed the door, and watched Eilene as she set the table for dinner. He came up behind her, slipped his arms around her waist, and kissed her neck. She put a plate down and turned her face to him with an uneasy look.

"What is it, Les?" she asked. He kept his arms around her and looked away.

"I've got an assignment."

"But the doctor said you needed a month to heal properly."

"I'm as healed as I'm going to get. Besides, I would go crazy just sitting around for a month." Eilene got an irritated look.

"How long will you be gone this time?" she asked, in an annoyed tone. He glanced at her and shook his head. She turned, embraced him, and put her head against his shoulder.

"Give up this kind of work, Les. Find a job here on Earth." She lifted her head and looked at him.

"Ben said he could get you a job at the lab." Les put his hands on her cheeks and looked into her eyes.

"Please, Eilene, try to understand. I can't stop now. Not after what's happened." She got a hard, determined look.

"If you take this assignment, we're through. I mean it, Les." He regarded her with a neutral expression and said nothing. His expression quickly turned to one of impatience and he took his hands from her face.

"I just can't walk away, Eilene. You know me better than that. I always finish what I start, and I intend to finish Garnet." She got an alarmed look.

"Is that what this assignment is?" He quickly rubbed his chin.

"Yes. I'm going after him again." She jerked her arms from around him and stepped back. She folded her arms in an angry gesture.

"It's more than the job this time, isn't it?" Les gave her a puzzled look.

"What do you mean?" Eilene got a hard frown.

"I remember that remark you made in the hospital, about having a score to settle." Les regarded her with a frown.

"And?" he asked, in a cold tone. Eilene tilted her head in a defiant gesture.

"You're going after Garnet for revenge because he got the better of you." He held a stony expression on her. Her eyes widened and her mouth fell open in disbelief at the look she was getting.

"Come on, Eilene, you can't believe that. Drydon wants Garnet alive, and I intend to follow through with his order." Her expression hardened.

"I'm not waiting this time," she said. Les remained silent. She drew her shoulders back in a defiant posture.

"Make your choice, Les. Me or that damn badge." He got a cold look.

"I'm going after Garnet, and that's that," he said, in an emphatic tone. "I owe Eliot, and myself, that much." He walked away from her, never looked back, and went out the door. Eilene looked beaten as her arms dropped to her sides.

The hangar was brightly lit with a few small ships setting around in various stages of repair. A man stood looking at his PDA as Les came up to him.

"Is my ship ready?" Les asked. The man looked at him and nodded.

"All checked out, Les. How did Eilene take your assignment?" Les got a disgusted

look.

"She gave me a choice – her or the job." The man whistled and shook his head.

"Some choice."

"Yeah! I just want to get the hell away from here." The man pointed to a ship on the

landing park.

"Your ship is fifth on the right."

"Thanks," Les said, and headed out of the hangar. As he walked toward the ship, he became curious as to why he didn't feel bad about breaking up with Eilene.

"Because I don't like the idea of someone trying to force me to do what I know is wrong," he mumbled.

5

The saloon was a crude structure, smelled of spilled drinks, and noisy with conversation and the tinkling of glasses. Garnet sat at a round table with a scruffy looking man sitting opposite him. A young man with curly dark brown hair, baggy pants and white shirt, was waiting on tables.

"I'm ready for a drink, Carson," Garnet said. The man nodded and waved his hand.

"Bring us drinks, Andy," Carson said. Andy got a lopsided grin, nodded, and went to the bar. Garnet looked at Carson and nodded at Andy.

"What's wrong with him?" Garnet asked, curious. Carson tapped his finger against his head.

"Feebleminded." Andy came to the table with the drinks on a tray. He sat one in front of Carson and one in front of Garnet. As he turned away, the tray knocked Garnet's drink over, spilling it onto his lap. Garnet quickly stood with an angry look.

"Clumsy bastard!" Andy turned frightened light blues eyes to Garnet, took a towel from his back pocket and mopped up the liquid from the table.

"I'm sorry, Mister, real sorry," Andy said, turning uneasy glances to Garnet, who gave him a cold look and patted his shoulder.

"No harm done," Garnet said. Andy looked at him and grinned.

"Thanks, Mister." Andy put the towel on the tray and walked toward the bar. Garnet drew his weapon and fired. A flash impacted Andy's back knocking him forward onto the floor. Garnet held his weapon level and looked around the now silent saloon with a menacing expression.

"Anybody got anything to say?" Garnet asked. The place remained quite as everyone turned their eyes to Andy's body.

"I didn't think so," Garnet said, holstered his weapon, and retook his seat. Carson was staring at him in amazement. Two men came from the rear of the saloon, picked up Andy, and carried him away. Subdued conversation began. Carson shook his head.

"There wasn't any call for that," Carson said. "Andy was a good kid." Garnet leaned forward, put his arms on the table, and gave Carson a hard look.

"You want what the feebleminded got?" Garnet asked, in a cold tone. Carson's eyes widened in fear as he shook his head, picked up his drink and downed it.

The ship was cramped but not uncomfortable. Les sat in the pilot's seat looking at the stars on the monitor. He noted his reflection as he recalled Eilene's words.

'Ben said he could get you a job at the lab.' He leaned back, locked his hands behind his head, and relaxed.

"No thanks. Too dangerous," he said, aloud, just to hear a voice. He could now see his destination on the monitor and took the ship off automatic.

The ship dropped toward a desert-like planet, kicked up dust when the thrusters cut in, and landed. As the dust settled, Les came down the ramp. The place was hot, dry. He saw no one on the streets as he walked to a dilapidated building with SHERIFF over the door. He turned his face down as the wind blew dust around him. Going into the rundown office, Les saw that dust covered everything. He stopped in front of a desk and regarded a stocky, weather beaten man who was staring at him in surprise.

"What can I do for you, Marshal?" Les took the photo from his pocket and handed it to him.

"Have you seen this man?" Les asked. The sheriff spit out a curse.

"Garnet!" He looked up at Les.

"You after him?" the sheriff asked. Les was mildly surprised at the man's reaction to the photo as he nodded.

"I take it you've seen him," Les said. The sheriff handed the photo back.

"The son of a bitch was here. He left a couple of days ago." Les remained silent as the sheriff leaned back and looked out the window.

"He killed a retarded boy for spilling a drink on him." He turned his eyes back to Les.

"He killed three other men while he was here. I don't know what, if any, reason he had for killing them." Les got a puzzled look.

"You just let him go?" The sheriff got an angry look.

"I couldn't do a damn thing."

"Why not?" The sheriff got a scowl.

"Garnet got friendly with the Prosser brothers." The sheriff tapped his chest.

"I'm only one man, Marshal. I have no deputy, and those brothers are the same breed as Garnet." Les got a sympathetic look.

"Can't say I blame you for not doing anything." The sheriff got a hard look.

"Garnet was nothing but trouble while he was here." Les nodded, understanding what he meant.

"Any idea where he was headed?"

"Casin Three, I heard. But I can't vouch for the truth of that." Les rubbed his ear.

"Others have told me that was where he was headed, too," Les said. The sheriff stood and nodded at the door.

"Let me buy you a drink, Marshal. I don't get much chance to talk with a fellow lawman out here on the fringe." Les nodded.

"Sounds good." They left the office, the sheriff pulling the door shut behind them.

As they walked, the blowing dust made them turn their faces down. When they looked up, they saw two rough looking men come out of the saloon and stand watching them. The sheriff stopped and turned an alarmed look to Les.

"It's the Prosser brothers! Garnet must have anticipated your arrival."

"I'm not looking for trouble, Sheriff." The sheriff got a grim look as he backed away from Les.

"Well you got it. And there's nothing I can do to help." He turned and hurried back to his office. Les looked at the brothers and mumbled.

"I see there's no way to avoid this." He put his hand on the butt of his weapon.

They stepped into the street and walked slowly toward him. Les glanced around and saw a nearby alley and quickly formed a plan. The brothers stopped about six feet from him and dropped their hands to the butts of their weapons.

"You Camden?" the one to Les' right asked. Les regarded them coolly. They looked so much alike Les wondered if they were twins.

"Yeah. Where can I find Garnet?" Both got sneers.

"Why do you want to know?" asked the brother on the left.

"That's my business." The brothers laughed as Les broke for the alley. They drew their weapons and fired at him.

As Les made it to the alley, pulsar charges exploded against the corner of the building and splinters showered his back. The brothers glanced at each other and nodded. One headed for the far end of the street and the other went to the opposite end. Les stopped by a building and peeked out, looking in both directions. Seeing no one, he stepped back out into the empty street and dashed across into another alley.

The brothers stepped from the cover of buildings, their weapons leveled. They moved toward each other, converging on the alley they thought Les was in. They stopped and took quick glances around the corner of buildings. When they saw it was empty, they exchanged puzzled looks.

"Where the hell did he go?" asked one brother.

"We got to find him," said the other. "We told Garnet we would take care of the son of a bitch." They moved into the alley and toward the street.

As Les pressed against the building watching the alley he had come from. He drew his weapon, set it for stun, and waited. He saw the brothers step cautiously into the street, each protecting the other's back as they turned around with confused looks. Les tensed and stepped into the street.

"Looking for me?" They spun, raising their weapons. Les fired twice, dropping them in the dusty street. Les went to them and kicked their weapons away and holstered his weapon. The sheriff came up beside him and glanced at Les.

"Let's lock these bastards up," Les said.

Les and the sheriff stepped from the cell and Les noted the sheriff avoided looking at him.

"Sorry I couldn't help." Les gave him a sympathetic look.

"You got a family?" The sheriff gave him a puzzled look and nodded.

"A wife and two kids. Why?" Les smiled.

"You did what you had to do. Considering your family, you were in the right." Les nodded toward the cell.

"What will you do with them?"

"A neighboring system has warrants out for them. I'll notify their authorities and they can come and get them." The sheriff looked relieved and Les patted his shoulder.

"How about that drink now?" The sheriff smiled and they walked from the office.

When they went into the saloon, all eyes turned to them. It was apparent that word had gotten around as to what Les had done, and everyone had a pleased smile. The sheriff led the way to a table, made a signal with two fingers, and the bartender nodded.

"Looks like you're the hero of the day," the sheriff said, taking the chair opposite Les.

"Nobody around here likes the Prosser brothers." The bartender brought two large glasses of beer and placed them before Les and the sheriff. He looked at Les and smiled.

"Thanks, Marshal. Your drink is on the house." They sat at the corner table drinking their beer.

"You going after Garnet?" the sheriff asked. Les took a drink and put the glass down.

"I have to. Someone has to take him out of circulation, stop his killing." The sheriff looked down and raised his eyes back to Les.

"He'll have more Prossers waiting for you, Marshal." Les frowned and turned the glass.

"I don't have a choice. He killed a close friend of mine." The sheriff stretched his arm across the table and they shook hands.

"Good luck, Marshal. You're sure as hell going to need it."

Les had just taken his ship into orbit around Casin Three. He glanced at the photo of Eilene, picked it up and rubbed his thumb over it. He wondered why he still didn't feel bad about the break up with her. He knew it was because of her pressuring him to give up his job, so the break up was easy.

"You should have waited. Garnet's the last one I'm going after." He put the photo face down on the console and pressed a switch.

"This is Pi One Eight Delta, Marshal Les Camden. Request permission to land." A male voice replied over the speaker.

"Pi One Eight Delta, permission granted. Use landing pad seven."

"Roger, and thanks." Les took control of the ship and turned it into the atmosphere.

Les stood regarding the man sitting behind an ancient wooden desk with two chairs in front. He was overweight and looked at Les through rimless glasses. He drummed his fingers on the desk and he held a peeved expression.

"I'm sorry, Marshal, but our law is clear. Only our law enforcement people are permitted to go armed." Les felt his frustration rise.

"The man I'm after is armed and dangerous. He's already killed a number of people."

The man leaned back with a frown.

"There's no way he could have gotten a weapon through security," he said. "And he can't purchase weapons here." Les kept his annoyance from showing.

"You don't know Garnet. He could have brought a disassembled weapon through and no one would be the wiser." The man got an uncertain look and shook his head.

"I don't believe that's possible." Les inhaled deeply.

"It would look like accessories, decoration on his luggage. He's done it before." The man turned an annoyed look to Les.

"I am sorry, Marshal, but I can't authorize you to go armed."
Les showed his disappointment and nodded.

"I understand," Les said, turned, and walked from the office.

Les came out of the building, looked both ways, and headed
down the street. As he walked among the people, he didn't notice
a man watching, then following him. Les turned into a cool,
green, neatly trimmed park and sat down on a bench to try and
figure out his next move. No one was close by as the man
approached slowly. Les paid him no attention until he sat down
beside him.

"Something I can do for you?" Les asked. The man licked his
lips and glanced around, obviously nervous.

"Are you the marshal that's after Garnet?" Les nodded.

"Then what you can do for me is kill that son of a bitch." Les'
eyes narrowed as he regarded the man closely.

"I don't know where he is," Les said. The man got an uneasy
look.

"He's at Ruby's, over on Webster." Les was getting
suspicious.

"Why are you telling me this?" Les asked, not quite trusting
the man.

"Garnet killed my sister," he replied, stood, and walked
quickly away. Les couldn't quell his suspicion, but decided to
check out the man's story.

Garnet came through the door into a room that was lavishly
furnished and held the scent of the vases of exotic flowers on two
stands. No one was in the room, so he went to the wall and
pressed the code on the pad. A beep sounded as a tray slid from
the wall with a drink on it. He picked it up, went and sat down in
a plush chair, and made himself comfortable. Another door
opened and a redhead in a light blue dress came in. She closed
the door, turned her light gray eyes on him and smiled, not
seeming to be surprised to see him.

"Well. Well. It's been awhile, Jovan. What brings you here?" He finished the drink and put the glass on a stand beside the chair. He stood, went to her, pulled her to him and kissed her. She pulled away from him with a knowing look.

"I should have guessed," she said. "You're in trouble and want me to help you out."

Garnet held her hands and smiled.

"You're as perceptive as ever, Ruby." She stepped back and regarded him with a raised eyebrow.

"I heard you were going after a new narcotic." Garnet stood in a relaxed pose.

"I got sidetracked. I'm on my way to Varian Four now." Ruby put her hands on her hips and gave him a dubious look.

"I've got a business stop to make before I go there." She frowned and tilted her head.

"What do you want me to do?" she asked, with resignation. Garnet rubbed the back of his neck.

"You still got that video setup in the bar?" he asked. Ruby nodded.

"Good. There's a hardass marshal after me and he'll be coming here." Her eyebrows rose in surprise.

"How will he know to come here?" Ruby asked. Garnet took her hand, lifted it, and kissed it.

"I sent him an invitation," Garnet replied. She narrowed her eyes and took her hand from his.

"What do you expect me to do with him?" she asked. Garnet rubbed her arms and smiled.

"Distract him. I didn't realize he was so close on my tail. I need time to get to my ship and get away from this planet." She got an annoyed look.

"And just how am I supposed to do that?" Ruby asked. Garnet got a confident look.

"You have your ways, Ruby. You'll think of something." She gave him a hard look.

"Are you suggesting that I seduce him?" Garnet smiled.

"That wouldn't be hard for you to do, but I prefer he be incapacitated for awhile." She smiled and gave him a light kiss.

"That shouldn't prove difficult," she said. Garnet laughed.

"One more thing, Ruby. I got a transponder implant in my arm. Can you neutralize it?" She smiled, cocked an eyebrow, and nodded.

"No problem."

After dinner, Les went to Ruby's. He had never been in such an exotic bar. It had dark paneling all around, and a long wooden bar that gleamed. He felt the paneling and bar had to be polished daily for it to hold such sheen. But more surprising, it was the first bar he had been in that smelled clean. Les went to a table and sat down. Subdued conversations filled the place with a low din. A cute young woman came to the table and smiled.

"What's your pleasure?" she asked, paying no attention to his dark blue uniform and silver badge. Les relaxed and smiled.

"A local beer," he replied. She gave him a nod and headed for the bar.

In Ruby's suite, Garnet quickly pointed to the TV screen.

"That's him," he said. "Can you handle him?" Ruby laughed and slapped his shoulder.

"There isn't a man I can't handle, Jovan. I've handled you haven't I?" He laughed and kissed her.

"I'll need a couple of hours to get a head start on him." She caressed his cheek.

"I'll get you more time than that." She gave him a light kiss, went to the door, and glanced over her shoulder.

"See you the next time you come this way, Jovan." She smiled, opened the door, and went out of the room. Garnet went out the back door and into the darkness.

As Les drank his beer, he noticed an attractive redhead coming downstairs. She stopped at the bottom of the stairs and looked around. Her eyes locked on Les and she came toward his table. She stopped and smiled.

"You're a stranger on this planet," she said. "We don't see many marshals around here."

"Just passing through," Les said, looking up at her.

"Mind if I join you?" He waved her to a chair and she sat down giving him an odd look.

"How come you're only passing through?" Ruby asked, as the woman from the bar came over.

"The usual, Ruby?" she asked. Les narrowed his eyes on Ruby. She glanced at the woman and nodded.

"Yeah," Ruby replied. As the woman went back to the bar, Ruby reached over and ran a finger over his badge.

"I take it you have business here, Marshal." He took a drink and nodded. Ruby got an annoyed look.

"Will you talk, goddamnit!" Les put the glass down, leaned forward, and rested his arms on the table.

"What would you like me to say?" She moved her chair closer to his.

"It's rare for a marshal to show up in these parts. I'm just curious as to what brought you here." Les smiled

"I'm looking for someone." Ruby put her hand over his, leaned close to him, and got a sexy smile. The scent of her perfume reminded him of Eilene.

"A real badass, I bet," she said. Les shrugged, not quite trusting her.

"I wouldn't call him a badass," Les said. He regarded Ruby as the woman returned with the drink and put it in front of her. She lifted the glass and took a drink as she kept his eyes on him.

"What do you call him?" she asked. Les lifted his glass and looked over the rim at her.

"Jovan Garnet." Ruby got an innocent look and tilted her head.

"Should I know the name?" she asked. He gave her an apprasing look.

"I guess not." She leaned close to him and gave his hand a squeeze.

"I have more to offer than a man," Ruby said. Les laughed and got an indignant look from her.

I've no doubt of that," Les said. "And definitely more pleasant then Garnrt could offer. Ruby relaxed and smiled.

"Garnet is a real special case," Les added, watching her reaction. He leaned toward her and glanced around.

"I've got a special score to settle with that son of a bitch." She leaned back and smiled.

"Does that mean you never take time for pleasure?" Ruby asked. Les got a surprised look, and his suspicion was growing.

"Well –"She stood and took his hand.

"Let's go upstairs," she said. "It's private and you won't have to pay for the drinks."

Les stood and regarded her with an uncertain look.

"You know someone who might know Garnet?" Ruby flashed her sexy smile on him.

"Maybe. But we can discuss that in private." She went to the stairs and looked back at him. Les was hesitant, but followed her.

Coming through the door, Les was impressed at what he saw. The floral scent was the first thing he noticed. He looked around until his eyes came to rest on Ruby.

"You have got good taste," Les said. She got a mischievous smile.

"In more ways than you can see, Marshal. Would you like a drink?" Les nodded.

"Anything weak." Ruby went to the wall panel and worked the keypad. A tray slid from the wall with drinks on it. She picked them up, came to Les, and handed him one.

She took a drink from her glass.

"This Garnet, why are you after him?" Les took a sip, looked surprised, and glanced at her.

"This is good," he said, tapping the glass. Ruby tilted her head and smiled.

"I have liquor brought in from all over." Les took a hefty drink.

"Tell me about this fugitive you're after." Les lowered the glass as an odd expression came over his face.

"He's a coldblooded killer." Ruby sat her glass on a stand and stared at him.

"Then why aren't you dead?" she asked, sharply. He pinched the bridge of his nose and shook his head. The glass fell from Les' hand and he staggered to a chair and flopped down. He frowned and turned a hard look to Ruby.

"You know Garnet." She stepped in front of him and put her hands on her hips.

"You're quite right, Marshal. He's on his way to Masun Four by now." She put her hand under his chin, lifted his head, and put her face close to his.

"It's going to be sometime before you'll be able to follow him, Marshal." She jerked her hand from his chin and Les' head slumped forward on his chest. He slid from the chair and sprawled on the floor. Ruby went to the door, opened it, and motioned with her hand. Two tough looking men came in. She waved her hand at Les.

"Get him out of here," she said. Each took an arm and dragged him across the room and out into the hallway. Ruby watched with a satisfied look and pushed the door shut.

The men pulled Les along to a backdoor leading to a dark alley.

"Let's put him where it won't be easy to spot him," one said. The other turned, bumped into a trash container and cussed. At the mouth of the alley, they shoved Les into a pile of trash and hurried back inside.

Garnet moved stealthily along the line of parked ships. The lighting along the landing park revealed three officers at his ship. He stopped and looked over the situation.

"Damn!" he mumbled. He knew Camden had to be responsible for this. Another annoyance in his column, Garnet thought. He drew his weapon and moved toward the ship. He halted across from it and watched the officers moving around the ship. Garnet smiled, aimed and fired. Without a sound, the closest officer dropped. The second screamed as the flash hit his leg and that alerted the other officer, who came running from the rear of the ship. Garnet vaporized his arm below the elbow. The man lay moaning in agony. Garnet came over and looked down at him.

"You're lucky," Garnet said. "One had to die so I could let you two live." He went to the ship, opened the hatch and went onboard, and was quickly lifting off from Casin Three.

6

Susan Burns was an attractive woman with black hair and brown eyes. Her father had wanted her to be educated so she could go into the business world. But she had wanted a more interesting vocation and had chosen law enforcement. She was patrolling in a hover car when the headlights fell on an arm lying on the alley floor. She stopped, got out, and went to the arm. She bent down, moved trash away, and rolled the man over. She was surprised to see he was a marshal. Susan pressed her fingers against his throat and found a pulse. She went back and opened the car door. She returned to the man, pulled his arm over her shoulders and pulled him up. She dragged him along to the car and got him in on the seat. Susan closed the door, hurried around, got in and lifted the car from the street.

As Les opened his eyes, he saw indirect lighting reflected off white walls. He heard footsteps, slowly turned his face to the door, and saw a woman wearing a light green smock come in. He turned his head and winced at the pain. The woman stopped beside him and looked down.

"I'm Dr. Grant," she said. "You really shouldn't drink so much." Les blinked his eyes and focused on her.

"I didn't drink that much. It was what was in it that hurt. I was drugged." She patted his shoulder.

"I know," D. Grant said. "I gave you something to make you feel better." Les looked around and back to her with a perplexed look.

"How did I get here?" he asked. The doctor got a slight smile.

"Officer Burns brought you in. She found you lying in an alley." Les pushed himself to a sitting position.

"I would like to thank her. No telling how long I would have been there if not for the officer." The doctor patted his arm.

"She's waiting. I'll send her in." She went out of the room.

Burns came in, stopped beside the gurney, and gave him a slight smile.

"You need to choose your friends more carefully, Marshal."

"I want to thank you for your help," he said. She gave him a nod. Les had something else on his mind.

"Do you know a woman named Ruby?" Susan got a knowing look and nodded.

"No wonder you're here. She's a vixen. We've never been able to get anything we could prosecute her on." Les stretched out his arm.

"I'm Les Camden. Thanks again for helping me." She took his hand and they shook.

"Susan Burns. What brought you here, Marshal?" He took the photo from his pocket and handed it to her.

"This man. Jovan Garnet." Susan looked at the photograph and glanced at Les.

"You need to see my watch commander," she said. Les got a somber look.

"How many victims?" he asked. She got a sad look and handed the photo back.

"Sergeant Farrel will tell you. Do you feel up to coming with me?" Les nodded.

"I'm feeling better by the minute." The doctor came in and Susan turned to her.

"Can he leave?" Susan asked. The doctor looked at Les and smiled.

"Yes," Dr. Grant replied. "My medical advice for the marshal is to keep away from bad company." Les regarded her with a grim expression, sat up, put his feet on the floor and stood.

"In my line of work, Doctor, that's not possible."

As Susan drove, she glanced at Les.

"I don't suppose you would be willing to file charges against Ruby?" He glanced at her and shook his head.

"I can't wait around for a trial. I'm too close to Garnet." Les rubbed the back of his neck and frowned.

"Whenever I get some place Garnet's been, I know there are victims." She looked at him and nodded.

"You're right about that," Susan agreed.

The room was freshly painted in a pastel yellow. A plaque on one wall held the names of officers killed in the line of duty. Les faced a tall man with light brown hair and sad blue eyes.

"After what you said at immigration," Farrel said. "We got an alert to put a guard around Garnet's ship. That cost the life of one officer and the wounding of two others."

Les got a hard look and nodded.

"What else has he done?" Les asked, eliciting a surprised look from Farrel.

"How do you know he's done more?" Susan asked. Les glanced at her.

"I know Garnet," he replied. "He's hell in a man's body." Farrel nodded.

"He tried to rape a young woman, and beat her," Farrel replied. "Then wounded the two officers who came to her aid." Susan regarded Les with a hard frown.

"He must have been at Ruby's," she said. Les nodded.

"He must have pointed me out to her," Les said. "She came straight to me. And I fell for her line." Susan got a scowl.

"I've been told she's hard to resist," she said. Farrel turned a hopeful look to Les.

"You still going after him, Marshal?" Farrel asked. Les nodded. Farrel got an enraged look.

"I hope the bastard resists," Farrel said. "At his ship, the three men were down and

Garnet gone before anyone could get there."

"I'm sorry about your loss," Les said. Susan got a cold look as she regarded Les.

"When you catch up with him, Marshal," she said, in a hard tone. "Have a weapon malfunction. A person like Garnet doesn't deserve a trial. He never gave any of his victims a chance."

"You don't know how tempting that sounds," Les said, and glanced from Susan to Farrel. "Garnet put Ruby in my way to slow me down. But he didn't count on her telling me where he was going, and I'm still close on his tail, thanks to Officer Burns." Susan gave him a nod.

"Glad to be of service," she said. "Want a ride to your ship?" Les smiled and nodded.

"I would appreciate it," Les replied. "Thanks." Farrel leaned over the desk with a look of rage.

"Get that son of a bitch, Marshal," Farrel said, in an angry tone. "Anyway you can."

Les gave him a nod and left with Susan.

As they drove along the street, Les sat quiet.

"How long have you been after Garnet?" He turned his face to her.

"A little over six months. The first time I caught up with him, he wounded me. That was his first mistake." Susan got a concerned look.

"You're lucky he didn't kill you." Les got a slight smile.

"So I've been told." She glanced at him with a frown.

"Isn't it risky going after him alone?" Les gave her a long look as he thought about her question.

"Garnet doesn't want me dead – yet. I think the risk is minimal, until I have him cornered."

At the ship, Les activated the hatch and turned to Susan.

"Sorry I wasn't early enough to stop Garnet." Susan shook her head.

"What could you have done? You were denied permission to carry a weapon. It's not your fault. You had no idea where Garent was." Les regarded her with a serious look.

"How do you think I ended up at Ruby's?" he asked. "A man tipped me off that was where Garnet was. And, like a young rookie, I walked right into the trap he had set."

Susan puckered her lips and shook her head.

"He should have been more thoroughly checked by security when he came through."

Les stretched out his hand and she took it.

"Thanks again," he said. Susan smiled.

"Maybe we can get together sometime under better circumstances." Les smiled and released her hand.

"I would like that," he said, turned, went through the hatch into the ship. Susan turned and walked back to the car.

"I'm now on my way to Masun Three, still close on Garnet's tail. That concludes my report." Les absently took his finger from the key and got a reflective look.

"Sooner or later, I'll catch up with Garnet. And when I do…" He leaned back and frowned.

"I don't know what I'll do."

Garnet made his way cautiously along a country road in the twilight. He was headed toward a shack with one window showing light. He stopped by the window and peered in. He smiled wickedly and drew his weapon. He stepped to the door, kicked it open, and rushed in. The place was shabby with a lantern setting on a rickety table and a gray haired old man sitting on a dilapidated cot. He reached for crutches, but Garnet grabbed them and flung them over by the door. The man had a terrified look, and kept his brown eyes on Garnet.

"I heard you were complaining to the law about me, Webb." The old man stared with wide, fear-filled eyes.

"I was only talking. I didn't mean for it to sound like I was complaining." Garnet lowered the weapon and stepped closer to him.

"In that case, I won't kill you." Garnet raised his weapon and vaporized the man's legs below the knees. The man cried out in pain. Garnet then took his right arm off at the shoulder. He bent forward, getting in Webb's face.

"I don't like anyone talking to the law about me," Garnet said, in a harsh, threatening tone."That really pisses me off." The old man grimaced and moaned. Garnet spun, went to the door, and looked back over his shoulder.

"You better hope someone comes looking for you," Garnet said. "Or you could die." He walked into the darkness laughing.

Les walked among people in the bustling spaceport. Different ships sat along the side with techs working to maintain and repair them. He was headed for the main building when a stocky man stepped in front of him.

"You Marshal Camden?"

"Yeah," Les replied, wondering what the man wanted.

[69]

"I'm Martin Fowler. I know Garnet and that you're after him." Les was curious.

"And?" Rage exploded on Fowler's face.

"The bastard murdered my brother." Les remained silent, regarding him, recalling the man on Casin Three.

"I want to help you get him," Fowler added, in an angry tone.

"You know where he is?" He handed Les a small sheet of paper.

"He'll be at that address around seven tonight," Fowler replied. Les looked at the address.

"Can you show me where this place is?" Fowler shook his head.

"I'm getting the hell off this planet before he finds out I talked to you. I don't want to end up prematurely dead." Les' suspicion was up, but the man sounded more truthful than the first man had.

"How could he know that?" Les asked. Fowler looked around as he spoke.

"He's got people everywhere who tell him what's going on." Les got a dubious look.

"Really?" Les asked. Fowler turned a grim look to him.

"How do you think I knew you would be landing here today?" Les' eyebrow lifted.

"Impressive," Les said, and glanced back at the paper.

"You're certain he'll be at this address at the time you said he would?" Fowler nodded with a determined look.

"A package from a fringe world came for him. He prefers picking up packages after hours so no one can ask any questions." Les put the paper in his shirt pocket.

"I appreciate the help. Thanks." Fowler got a hard look.

"The only thanks I want is that bastard dead." He turned and walked off leaving Les staring after him.

As Les had dinner, he went through scenarios of confronting Garnet. But reality quickly sunk in and knew he would have to react to events as they unfolded. The waiter came to the table to refill his cup. Les took the paper from his pocket and held it out.

"Can you tell me how to get to this address?" Les asked. The waiter bent forward and looked at the paper and nodded.

"Sure. It's not far from here," the waiter replied, and gave Les directions.

Les walked along the deserted, semidark street lined with warehouses. His footsteps echoed loudly in the narrow street. He stopped at the number he was looking for and saw that the door had been jimmied open. Les pushed it all the way open, drew his weapon, and cautiously entered the building. The security lighting gave dim illumination that contrasted with shadows. Les moved from one shelf lined with packages to the next. He glanced around a shelf and saw movement and quietly went toward it. The figure hurried away.

"I know it's you, Garnet," Les said.

"That's obvious," Garnet said, in an annoyed tone."How did you know I would be here?"

"That's my job." Les heard Garnet hurry off. Les moved cautiously, looking quickly around. He dropped to one knee and tried to see Garnet in the shadows.

"Give it up, Garnet. You can't get past me."

"That line is wearing thin, Marshal. Can't you come up with something original?" Les ignored what he said.

"I've got you this time," Les said. "Now toss out your weapon." Garnet moved again.

Les went after him and his arm broke a tripwire. A bright flash and roar to his right showered Les with metal splinters. The burning pain was couldn't be ignored. He fell to the floor, semiconscious, his right arm and side bloody. Feet appeared beside him. He looked up and saw Garnet looking down at him, smiling.

"You're not very damn smart, Camden. You gave me that second again – and I got

you again. You need to work on your technique, or develop a new one." Garnet holstered

his weapon and squatted

"This is the second time I'm letting you live. You're a real challenge. I like that." Les

passed out.

7

The ER had pale green walls with an LED monitor above the gurney Les lay on. AnAsian doctor removed a metal fragment from Les' arm. The Afro-American nurse held the tray the doctor dropped the fragment in. He laid the instrument aside and nodded to her.

"That's the last of them," the doctor said, and she took the tray to a table. After putting it down, she went to a cabinet, took out bandages, and returned to the gurney. The doctor stepped aside as the nurse began dressing Les' wounds. An officer stood by the door with his arms folded.

"How long before he comes around?" the officer asked. The doctor glanced at him and shrugged.

"He's stabilized," the doctor replied. "He should come around anytime now." The officer got a dour frown.

"Will I be able to question him?" The doctor glanced at Les.

"I don't see why not," the doctor said. "His wounds aren't that serious, but I'm going to keep him overnight for observation."

Les rolled his head, opened his eyes, and looked around.

"Not again," Les moaned. The nurse stepped aside as the doctor came to Les' side.

"I removed eleven metal fragments from you, Marshal. You're lucky. None penetrated any organ." Les got a frustrated look.

"Luck had nothing to do with it.. That's the way Garnet likes it," Les said. The officer stepped to the opposite side of the gurney and looked down at Les.

"Want to tell me what happened?" the officer asked. Les nodded.

"Yeah. Maybe you can figure out a way to keep Garnet from leaving." The officer nodded.

"I'll do what I can," the officer said.

The room was a matt light blue with a small light over the head of the bed. Les was dozing when an orderly opened the door, glanced up and down the corridor, and quietly came to the bed and spoke in a low voice.

"Marshal?" Les opened his eyes and started to sit up. The orderly put a hand against his chest.

"No, no! Lie still.

"Who are you? What do you want?" The orderly glanced nervously at the door and back to Les.

"Who I am isn't important. I borrowed these clothes so I could talk to you." Les gave him a suspicious look.

"Why?"

"Garnet's headed for Varian Four. I don't know why, and I don't give a damn." Les heard the suppressed rage in his voice.
"I just want that worthless fuck dead." Les wasn't surprised at his attitude. It seemed that Garnet had as many enemies as friends.

"You're not the only one. What did he do to you?" The orderly got a despondent look.

"The bastard sent me on an errand. While I was gone, he raped and beat my wife. She died from that beating."

"I'm sorry. Is Garnet already off the planet?" He nodded.

"He left on a transport about four hours ago," the orderly replied. Les was surprised.

"A transport? Why didn't he take his ship?" The orderly shrugged.

"I don't know.

"How do you know where Garnet is going?"
"One of his cronies told me." The door opened and a pretty nurse came in and gave the orderly a stern look.

"What are you doing in here?" she asked. The orderly and Les exchanged glances and looked back to the nurse.

"I asked him to talk for awhile," Les replied. "I'm having trouble sleeping." The orderly nodded and and the nurse gave him a suspicious look.

"I'll get you something that will help you to sleep," she said, and frowned at the orderly. "You should have said something earlier, Marshal." Les gave her an innocent look.

"It didn't occur to me," Les said. She got a disgusted look, shook her head, and walked from the room. The orderly turned back to Les.

"Kill him, Marshal! Kill that worthless piece of shit." He walked out of the room before the nurse returned. Les wasn't surprised that the authorities had failed to find Garnet before he left. That was just as well, or there might have been more people killed. The door opened and the nurse came in with a pill cup. She got a puzzled look as she came to the bed.

"Where did your pal go?" she asked.

"To attend to his duties," Les replied.

Garnet stopped at the mouth of an alley, glanced around, saw he was alone and quickly stepped into the shadows. He came to a door, glanced back at the street, took a lever from his pocket and jimmied the door open. He went in, found the stairs and went up. He pushed the door open and peered out. Seeing no one, Garnet stepped into the hallway, and moved past doors and stopped in front of room 308 and knocked.

Fowler glanced at the door when he heard the knock. He quickly slipped the weapon he held under the mattress and went to the door.

"Who is it?"

"I have a message for Mr. Fowler." Fowler got a puzzled look as he hesitantly unlocked the door. When he opened it a crack. Garnet slammed his shoulder against it eliciting a loud curse from Fowler as he fell to the floor. Garnet stepped inside and pushed the door shut. He regarded Fowler lying on his back. Fear surged through Fowler, unable to take his eyes off Garnet. He slowly got to his feet.

"When I heard you were here, I thought I would drop by and see how you've been,

Martin," Garnet said. Fowler looked confused as Garnet smiled in a friendly manner.

Fowler's lip began to twitch.

"Don't worry," Garnet said. "I don't have a weapon. I couldn't have gotten one on this planet." Fowler looked relieved and glanced at the bed.

"That marshal, he –" Garnet's expression turned cold as he quickly interrupted.

"He talked to you?" Garnet asked, in a menacing tone. "Or did you talk to him? Your brother was stealing my money. That's why I killed him." Fowler went to the bed and satdown.

"I know what my brother did. But –"Again, Garnet interrupted.

"I don't like buts or any excuse. When I discover someone is crossing me, I take action." Fowler shoved his hand under the mattress. Garnet pulled a hypo from his pocket and jabbed it into Fowler's shoulder. A strong chemical odor began to fill the room. Fowler stiffened, turned his face to Garnet as he pulled the hypo from his shoulder and fell to the floor. Garnet looked down at him as he picked up the hypo and put it back in his pocket.

"You're going to be paralyzed until you die," Garnet said, smiling. "And you're not going to enjoy dying, Martin." He went

[76]

to the door, opened it, and peeked out. He glanced back at Fowler whose face was contorted with pain. Garnet pulled the door open and stepped out.

The ship was in orbit around a blue-green planet similar to Earth. Les stared at Varian Four with a grim, determined look.

"You gave me one second, and in that second I got you," Les mumbled. He reached to the control panel and hesitated before pushing the key.

"This time, Garnet, your ass is mine." He pressed the key.

"This is Marshal Les Camden. Code Pi One Eight Delta. Request permission to land."

"Pi One Eight Delta, permission granted," a female voice replied. "Use pad Two Alpha." Les pulled the straps tight around him, pressed a switch, took hold of the guidence column and turned the ship into the atmosphere.

Coming out of the ship, Les was surprised to find the port quiet, with no one hurrying around. He stood at the bottom of the ramp, then headed for a building with IMMIGRATION above the door. He went in and saw a clerk standing behind a long counter. When he stopped before the counter, the clerk looked at Les' offered ID and turned a curious look to him.

"What brings you here, Marshal?" Les took the photo from his pocket and handed it to him.

"Have you seen this man?" Les asked. The clerk took the photo, looked at it, and tapped it with a finger.

"Yeah. He came in a few days ago. Don't recall his name though." Les frowned.

"No doubt he used an alias," Les said. The clerk handed the photo back.

"You here after this guy?" the clerk asked. Les nodded.

"That's right. I need to get permission to wear a sidearm." The clerk got a broad smile.

"Then you need to see Chief Corey," the clerk said. "She's the law around here." Les got a surprised look.

"She?" Les asked. The clerk leaned against the counter and nodded.

"Don't let her pretty face fool you, Marshal. Corey's a hard one to deal with if you find yourself on the wrong side of the law." Les gave him a nod.

"How do I get to her office?" Les asked. The clerk gave him directions.

Early on, it didn't appear likely that Angelena Corey was destined for a career in law enforcement. But as she grew through her teens, and better understood, she became proud of the work she saw her father doing. This decided her to follow him into his chosen profession.

After graduating from the police academy, with top honors, her father had helped her to secure the chief constable's job on Varian Four. People there were quick to learn that Angel was a stickler for the letter of the law. They also learned she was compassionate when she learned that someone hadn't meant to break the law. So she earned a reputation as a person who was stern but fair.

Les stopped in front of a door with ANGELENA COREY CHIEF CONSTABLE painted on it. He opened the door and stepped into the office. The place was neat with white walls and a couple of chairs in front of a desk where a stocky deputy sat. He looked up when Les came in.

"Can I help you?" the deputy asked.

"I'm Marshal Camden. I would like to see Chief Corey on official business." The deputy turned to an audvid unit and pressed the comlink. The pretty face of an auburn haired, green-eyed woman appeared. The clerk had been right, Les thought.

"There's a marshal here to see you, Chief."

"Show him in, Ed," she said. The deputy got up and went to a door at the far end of the room, followed by Les. He opened the door and glanced at Les.

"In here, Marshal."

The office was the same color as the anteroom. Sunlight spilled through a window at the back of the room. Angelena stood and extended her hand. Les stepped to the desk and they shook hands.

"I'm Angelena Corey."

"Les Camden." She got a humorous smile.

"Call me Angel. Everyone around here does, though I doubt I'll ever be one. Now how can I help you?" He took the photo from his pocket and handed it to her.

"That's Jovan Garnet. I've been after him for sometime." She took the photo and motioned for him to sit. She retook her seat and studied the photo.

"He looks like a ruthless bastard," she said. Les nodded.

"He's a coldblooded killer. He has no conscience and shows no mercy." Angel turned a surprised look to Les.

"Garnet's here?" Les nodded.

"That he is, Angel." She got an annoyed look.

"Then why aren't you armed?" Les leaned back and relaxed.

"Regulations. I have to get local authorization to be armed." Angel nodded.

"You got it," she said, without hesitation.

"Thanks." Angel got a curious look.

"How do you know Garnet is here?" Angel asked.

"From a tip. And the clerk at immigration identified the photo. He told me Garnet came in a few days ago." She handed him the photo and he slipped it back into his pocket.

"You have a place to stay?" she asked. Les shook his head.

"Not yet. I came directly here." Angel leaned back and wagged a finger at the window.

"The Crawford Inn is across the street. They have decent rooms and a good restaurant."

"Sounds good." Angel gave him a nod.

"In the meantime, I'll see what I can find out about your fugitive." Les stood and turned toward the door.

"I'll meet you in the restaurant in an hour," Angel added.

Back on the ship, Les opened a locker on the bulkhead and took out a belt with a holstered weapon on it. He strapped it on and smiled as he patted the weapon. He also took out his travel case and left the ship.

Les walked back into the immigration building. The clerk smiled and pointed to his weapon.

"Looks like you and Chief Corey hit it off," the clerk said. Les nodded and put his hand on the butt of the weapon.

"Yeah. We got a lot in common – law enforcement."

8

When Les walked into the lobby, he saw modest furniture grouped around a large TV screen on the wall. The sofa and chairs didn't match in color or style, and Les smiled at this. As he came to the desk, he noted the desk clerk nervously kept glancing at his weapon. Les leaned against the desk and regarded the clerk with a serious expression.

"Don't worry. I only shoot bad guys. Now I need a room."

The room was clean with pale yellow walls and sturdy furniture. Les put his travel case on the bed, opened it, and took out a clean uniform. He went to the bathroom and turned on the shower, came back, pilled off his uniform and stuck it in the case. After being in space, Les took great pleasure as the water sprayed over him. It was what he missed most on the ship. After the shower, a shave, and a fresh uniform, he was ready to head to the restaurant.

Les sat at a table in the modest restaurant that had no showy decorations. Angel came in and toward the table. Les started to stand, but she motioned him to stay put and sat down across from him. A waiter came to the table and placed drinks before them. Les looked surprised as Angel smiled.

"I often eat here," she said. "They know what I like." Les gave her a nod and took a drink from the glass.

"Learn anything about Garnet?" She took a drink and nodded.

"He arrived four days ago. Used the alias Arthur Green. He was thoroughly checked by security and wasn't in possession of any weapon." Les got a dubious look.

"What about his luggage?" Angel shrugged.

"It was thoroughly checked, too. There wasn't any disassembled weapon on or in it."

Les got a puzzled look.

"That doesn't sound like Garnet," he said, and got an odd look from Angel.

"What do you mean?" Les leaned forward and kept his voice low.   "Since I've been on his case, I've never known him to go unarmed. There are too many people who want him dead."

"Any particular reason for such a list of enemies?" Les chuckled.

"A long list of complaints," Les replied. "From beating someone's wife to killing someone else's brother." She leaned close to him.

"Well he wasted no time getting armed, Les." This brought an uneasy look to him.

"The records I found showed that he purchased a pulsar rifle and assorted chemicals the day after he arrived." Les frowned.

"I wish to hell I knew what he was up to." Angel looked puzzled.

"What's he do with chemicals?" she asked. Les took a drink from the glass and lowered it.

"Makes bombs," Les replied, and saw the alarmed look she got.

"Christ! You mean he could blow up part of the city?" Les regarded her with a grim look, as he almost still felt the pain in his right side.

"He doesn't make that kind of bomb." Angel got a perplexed look, put her arms on the table, and leaned forward.

"Please explain what sort of bombs he makes," she said. "You have me confused." Les inhaled deeply.

"The bombs Garnet makes fill you with lots of fragments. That way it takes a long time to die. That's what amuses him." Angel leaned back and let her arms drop onto her lap.

"I see what you mean by no mercy," Angel said. Les rolled up his sleeve and stretched out his arm. Angel looked at the four small scars from his wrist to his elbow.

"Mementos from my last encounter with Garnet." She looked from his arm to him.

"Any idea why he came here?" Les pulled his sleeve down as he shook his head.

"Not an inkling, Angel," he replied. She began patting her lips with a finger as she thought for a moment.

"A man was found dead two days ago," she said. "No ID on him except the card he used to come here. We'll go to the morgue later." Les gave her a puzzled look.

"What for?" She regarded him with a raised eyebrow.

"Maybe you can tell if Garnet done the killing." Their dinners were served.

"What name was on the ID card?" Les asked.

"Frank Tilton," Angel replied. "But I doubt that's his real name."

As they ate, Angel turned a curious look to him.

"How did you get to be a marshal?" She shook her head and smiled.

"I guess I mean, why did you become a marshal?" Les put his fork down and locked his fingers.

"I had two brothers who have families and steady jobs. That looked very boring to me." Angel took a drink.

"Not the family type, huh?" Les got a disgusted look.

"I wanted adventure. So I applied for law enforcement." Angel put her glass down and regarded him with a look of interest.

[83]

"Did you get what you wanted?" she asked. Les got an annoyed look.

"Hell no! I get shot at, wounded, and spend most of my time chasing an asshole like Garnet across the galaxy." Angel smiled.

"That doesn't sound boring." Les picked up his fork and waved it in the air.

"The times of being scared shitless are few and far between. The rest of the time I'm traveling, alone and bored." Angel laughed and they resumed eating.

The morgue was dim with a cream colored wall at the far end and had a slight chemical odor about it. The other two walls were lined with refrigerated units. Angel, Les, and the ME's assistant came in. The assistant stopped at one of the units.

"This is the one," the assistant said, opened the door, and slid the tray out. He lifted the sheet from the corpse's face.

"Damn!" Les exclaimed, sharply. Angel and the assistant looked at him.

"You knew him?" Angel asked. Les glanced at her with a scowl.

"His name is Martin Fowler," Les replied. "He's one of the men who put me on Garnet's trail." She noticed Les' confused expression.

"What's wrong?" she asked. Les nodded at the corpse.

"He was on the run from Garnet. So what the hell was he doing here?" Angel shook her head.

"We may never know the answer," she said. Les rubbed on his ear as he thought.

"Check with immigration, Angel," Les said. "Find out when he arrived. Maybe we can trace his movements." Les turned to the assistant.

"How did he die?" Les asked. The assistant looked at him with a grim visage.

"Slowly and very painfully," the assistant replied. "But what he died from we haven't been able to figure out yet."

"Why not?" Angel asked. The assistant pulled the sheet back over the face.

"His insides are a mass of jelly," the assistant replied. "Can't tell anything from that."

Angel glanced at Les and saw his brow furrow.

"It's Garnet's doing," Les said. "He's a first class chemist as well as a killer. A slow, painful death is what he likes to inflict on his special victims."

"But is this why Garnet came here?" Angel asked. Les thought for a moment.

"What have you got here that would be valuable off world?" Les asked. Angel's eyes widened.

"Sutain!" she exclaimed. "A very potent narcotic." She glanced at the assistant and back to Les.

"So far, we've been successful in keeping it isolated here," she added. "A few ounces could mean a lot of money." Les nodded.

"The narcotic is why Garnet is here," Les said. "Finding out Fowler was here was a bonus for him."

"How can you be sure?" Angel asked. Les rubbed his cheek as he considered the question.

"With a small sample of the narcotic, Garnet can symthesize it and sell it." He got a puzzled look and rubbed the back of his neck.

"I've always had a problem with one regulation, Angel."

"Which one are you referring to?" He turned a hard look to her.

"The one that prevents me from shooting people like Garnet unless I'm in fear for my life, or protecting the lives of citizens." The assistant slid the tray back in the unit and closed the door. Angel and Les turned and walked to the door.

In the corridor, outside the morgue, they stopped and faced each other.

"Is there a local address for this Arthur Green?" Les asked. Angel puckered her lips.

"We'll have to go to my office and check." They walked to the exit in silence.

"I'll put extra people in immigration." Les shook his head.

"It's a waste of time," he said. "He wouldn't risk being seen after a murder. No,

Garnet's got another way off this planet." Les had an idea and got a smug look.

"If Garnet knew I was here," he said, thoughtfully. "He might not be in such a hurry to leave." Angel turned a puzzled look to him.

"I don't follow you." Les regarded her with a plan forming in his mind.

"He's wounded me twice," he said, and rubbed his chin. "But he hasn't killed me.

With him, I'm a game he's confident he can win."

"So?" Angel asked, still not getting what he was inferring. Les got a cynical smile.

"If he knows I'm here, he'll realize that killing me is the only way to get me off his back." Her eyes widened.

"You mean use yourself as bait?" Les got a sullen look and nodded.

"It may be our only chance to get him." Angel got a dubious look.

"He might just use that chance to kill you, Les." He nodded.

"It's a risk I'm willing to take. No! It's a risk I have to take." They walked toward her office in silence.

In the office, Les sat silent as Angel worked the computer. She looked from the monitor to Les.

"His address is listed as one of the prefab units on the far side of town," she said. "Do we go after him?" Les considered the element of surprise, but decided to pass on it. He didn't want to endanger innocent people. Besides, he was curious as to how Garnet would react when he learned Les was in the same place with him, and limited in his options as to where to run.

"No. There's no telling how he might react. And the last thing I want is civilians getting killed. Let's see what he does when he finds out I'm here." Angel got a doubtful look.

"I agree with you about civilian casualties, Les. But with surprise, we might just be able to take him with little trouble." Les shook his head.

"There's no chance of that with Garnet, Angel. He'll do what he has to to escape." She nodded.

"I hope you know what you're doing, Les." He frowned.

"If I don't, he'll kill me. So let him know I'm here, Angel." She leaned back with a disapproving look and frown.

Angel faced the camera with a serious expression.

"I have a short announcement to make. Today, Marshal Les Camden arrived in the city. Should he request anyone's help, I expect every citizen to cooperate with him.

Thank you." As she stood, Les came to her with a slight smile.

"That should shake him up," Les said. Angel gave him an incredulous look.

"I think you're wrong, Les. We should have used surprise to nail Garnet." He shook his head.

"Maybe so. But him knowing I'm here may give us a better advantage. Here he has no where to run."
Garnet's mouth dropped open as he heard Angel's announcement. He leaned forward

in the easy chair as her image faded from the screen.

"Son of a bitch!" He stood, went to the desk, and opened the drawer. Taking out an envelope and sheet of paper he began writing. He had just decided to put an end to the interfering marshal. He mentally chided himself for letting Camden live this long. But Garnet felt confident that he would soon be rid of the pest. Then he would be free to carry out his plan with interference from any one. And it would give him peace of mind knowing that no marshal would be dogging his ass.

9

In the lobby of the hotel, the following morning, the desk clerk was watching the TV screen.

"Last night, Chief Corey announced the arrival of a marshal," the newscaster said.

"But she gave no reason for his visit. The questions on everyones mind is, who is this marshal after? And how dangerous is this fugitive?" The clerk saw Les come out of the elevator and start across the lobby.

"Marshal," the clerk called, motioning for him to come to the desk. Les glanced over his shoulder, turned, and went to the desk.

"This was left for you," the clerk said, handing Les an envelope. He tore it open, took out the sheet of paper, and read it.

'I know why you're here, Camden. I'm leaving the city, and I want to be finished with you. I know you won't refuse to come after me because you're not that smart." It was signed Garnet. Les looked at the clerk with a curious expression.

"When was this left here?" Les asked. The clerk shook his head.

"I don't know. It was here when I came to work." Les nodded.

"Thanks," Les said, and headed for the entrance.

Les sat quiet as Angel read the note. She looked up and regarded him with an uncertain look.

"You certainly got a quick response from him," she said. Les leaned forward and rested his arms on his legs.

"I expected it would. What have you learned about Fowler?" Angel put her arms on the desk and spread her hands.

"It appears that he came here to kill Garnet." Les frowned.

"What leads you to that conclusion?" She tapped a finger on the desk.

"He arrived here the day after Garnet," Angel replied. "Apparently he followed Garnet because his photo was identified at the places Garnet went to."

"Did Fowler have a weapon?" She shook her head.

"And he didn't purchase one either," Angel said. This puzzled Les.

"Then how the hell was he going to kill Garnet? Wish him dead?" She leaned back and tapped a pen on the palm of her hand.

"I had a deputy go back over Fowler's room." Les leaned forward with a feeling of anticipation.

"Did he find anything?" Angel nodded.

"His luggage hadn't been checked closely enough," Angel replied. "The deputy found an assembled weapon under the matress." Les leaned back with an understanding look.

"And Garnet somehow got word that he was here and struck first. He's not one to wait for someone to try and kill him." Angel tossed the pen on the desk.

"That's the way it seems to me, Les." He got a thoughtful look.

"I guess Fowler didn't trust me to kill Garnet." Les stood and rubbed his hands on his legs.

"I think it's time we paid a visit to that address," he said.

"Okay," Angel said, standing. He gave her a determined look.

"If Garnet gets out of the city, I'll have to go after him." Angel got an uncertain look.

"You really think he'll leave the city?" she asked. Les nodded.

"He has to. He can't get off the planet any other way." She tilted her head.

"I see your point, Les. But it's not going to be easy for him." Les frowned and his brow furrowed.

"How can he get out of the city without being seen?" Angel raised an eyebrow.

"The only other way out, except immigration, is the access tunnel under the city." She got a doubtful look.

"But there are at least a dozen exits." Les got a confident look.

"That's his escape route, Angel. You can bet on it."

"What makes you so certain?" Les spread his hands.

"He wants to avoid attention, and he also wants to make sure I know which way he went." Angel got an uneasy look.

"But there's nothing outside the city but jungle," she said. "And no one knows much about the animals that inhabit it." Les shrugged.

"I still have to go after him." She got a resolved look as she came around the desk and faced him.

"If that's the case, I'll have to come with you. After all, it is my jurisdiction." Les smiled.

"I wouldn't know where to start without you," he said. Angel frowned and went to the door, Les followed.

The street looked like any neighborhood, with kids playing in yards. There was little or no traffic. As Angel drove, the flatbed vehicle moved with a soft hum. She pulled to a stop across from a single level house. She nodded at it.

"That's the place," she said. Les took a long, hard look at the house. He couldn't imagine Garnet living in such an environment – he was just too violent. He glanced at her.

"I'll go in first," Les said. "There's a good chance he's boobytrapped the place." Angel gave him an anxious look as she got off the vehicle, came around beside Les, and they started toward the house together.

As they went up on the porch, Angel noticed the windows were covered by heavy drapes. Les reached out and pressed the door release, and the door swung open. Angel glanced inside then to Les.

"Doesn't look like anyone's here," she said. Les nodded.

"He was probably gone before I got that note." She got an irritated look.

"Why didn't you tell me that?" He turned a surprised look to her.

"I wasn't sure, Angel – until now." Les pushed the door open until it bumped against the wall. He slowly shook his head.

"I don't like unlocked doors. They usually mean trouble," Les said, and drew his weapon. He moved cautiously in with Angel following.

The drapes made the place dark as Les moved slowly with his eyes turned down.

Angel regarded him with a puzzled look.

"Why are you looking down?" He turned an uneasy look to her.

"Tripwire. It's sort of Garnet's trademark. Remember those scars I showed you?" She nodded.

"I got them when I broke a tripwire." He looked around the room and holstered his weapon. They crossed to a closed door. Les turned an edgy look to her.

"Something wrong?" Angel asked. He nodded at the door.

"This is probably the trap." Les put his finger against the release, pressed it, and heard

a loud twang as the door opened. He grabbed Angel's arm.

"Let's get the hell out of here." They ran for the door.

Halfway across the street, the house erupted with a loud roar, and a flash of heat knocked them off their feet. They rolled under the vehicle as debris rained down around them. After a moment, they crawled out, stood, and looked at the burning ruin. Other people had come out to gawk at the fire. Les looked at Angel with a puzzled look.

"He usually don't make his bombs so big," Les said, awed. "I guess he's serious about killing me this time." She pointed to the flames.

"Do you have any idea of his reason for this?" Angel asked. Les shrugged.

"None at all," Les replied, shaking his head. "On second thought, I don't think that bomb was meant for me." Angel's eyes widened.

"You're sure?" Les bit his lip and nodded.

"He wouldn't have invited me to come after him and then planted a bomb to kill me." He turned his face to her.

"Garnet doesn't want me to have a clean death." She got a questioning look.

"What makes you so certain about that?" Angel asked. Les kept his eyes on her.

"Garnet's consistent in how he kills. This bomb was meant for someone he really fears, and that's not me." She glanced back at the burning ruin.

"This was meant for someone else?" she asked. Les nodded.

"That would be my guess." They looked at the dazed people who stood silent, staring at the flames and smoke.

"Doesn't look like anyone is hurt," Les said. Angel glanced at him with a frown.

"A lucky coincidence," she said. Les shook his head.

"When it comes to Garnet's bombs, there's no such thing as a coincidence. This bomb was waiting for anyone looking for him – except me." She took a mike from beside the seat and lifted it to her face.

"This is Chief Corey. I'm at Fifth and L Streets. There's been an explosion. Send the firefighters." They got back on the vehicle, Angel started it, and turned back the way they had come.

A deputy stood facing Angel across her desk as Les stood beside the door.

"You'll be in charge while I'm gone, Ed," she said. He handed her a belt with a holstered sidearm.

"Your packs and rifles are on the vehicle," Ed said. Angel strapped the sidearm around her waist.

"Let's go. Ed, you drive." They walked from the office with Les following.

The overhead lights were spaced to keep a continuous glow along the tunnel. The flatbed moved along with flashes of sunlight hitting it when they passed a gate. Ed pulled the vehicle to a stop beside an open electrical box. He got off the vehicle and checked the electrical connections and glanced over his shoulder.

"The magnetic field for this gate has been shut down, Chief." Les and Angel exchanged looks.

"A magnetic field surrounds the lower part of the city," she explained, as Les nodded.

"That's what keeps the animals out."

"Of course," Les said, with a confident look. "I told you Garnet would show me the way he went." Angel didn't look convinced, but nodded.

"Then we might as well get moving," she said.

They got off the vehicle, slipped their packs on, adjusted the straps and picked up the rifles. Angel turned to Ed.

"Keep a high altitude track on us," she said. Ed nodded.

"Better check those transponders," Ed said. Angel stepped to Les and pressed a small metal band on his pack strap. A beep came from it. Ed stepped to Angel and done the same. Ed nodded, satisfied when the beep sounded.

"Don't mention us in any communication," Les said. Angel and Ed turned questioning looks to him.

"Why not?" Ed asked.

"It's a sure bet Garnet's monitoring the police channels. I want to keep him guessing as long as possible." Angel pointed to the electrical box.

"Get a tech out here and get this gate up and running.

"Sure thing, Chief," Ed said, got on the vehicle and drove off.

As they moved out into the jungle, Les glanced at Angel.

"Just out of curiosity," Les said. "Why did they build a city in this jungle?" She got an amused smile.

"It's set on the largest aquifer on the planet," Angel replied. "It's the only convence this world offers." They started by brushing past wide, waxy-looking green and yellow leaves on trees with bark that looked like gray scales. A myriad of animal sounds surrounded them.

As they pushed on, Angel unslung her rifle, cocked it, and carried it at the ready. Les gave her a lost look.

"Why did you arm your weapon?" he asked. She glanced at him and looked around at the jungle.

"I have no idea of what we might run into out here. So I'm going to be ready for anything." Les quickly took the rifle from his shoulder and armed it, while looking around with an uneasy expression.

Moving on, Angel turned a curious look to him.

"How can you be sure Garnet came this way?" she asked. He stopped and pointed to a small branch that had been freshly broken, hanging free.

"He doesn't want me getting lost." Angel gave him a respectful look.

"I would have missed that," she said. "You know Garnet pretty damn well." Les turned a frown to her.

"Not as well as I would like to, now that he wants me dead." Angel got an alarmed look.

"We're dealing with a psychopath?" Les shrugged.

"He gets his enjoyment from the suffering of his victims. Garnet's not one to give you a quick death, unless you scare the hell out of him, or piss him off." He adjusted the rifle

on his arm and smiled grimly.

"Guess that's why I'm still alive." Angel's eyebrows shot up and she got a dubious look.

"You've never pissed him off?" Les shrugged.

"Oh, I've pissed him off – but only slightly. I haven't done anything to cause him to be afraid of me." Angel shook her head.

"Well it seems to me you finally got him really pissed, Les." He got an irritated look.

"He's a pain in the ass! I want him put away so I can get some rest." She couldn't help smiling at that as she started to step ahead of him. He grabbed her arm and pulled her back. Angel turned an annoyed look to Les.

"What the hell are you doing?" she asked, sharply. Les dropped to a knee and pointed to a tripwire.

"Keeping you from this." Les moved his finger along the tripwire to its end. He stood, turned his rifle and used the butt to break the tripwire. A whiz followed the small dart to

its impact in a tree. Angel stepped to the tree, worked the dart loose, and sniffed the tip.

"Amphorine," she said, looking at Les. "It's a local poison and quite lethal." He pointed to where it had lodged in the tree.

"It would have got you in the leg," Les said. She gave the dart a disgusted look and dropped it.

"How did you know that wire was there?" Angel asked. Les brushed a hand on his

pants with an uneasy look.

"Garnet made it obvious with that broken branch. He wants to see how alert I am," he replied, and looked at her. "He won't do so again." She got an alarmed look.

"There's going to be more?" Les nodded. A loud roar from the jungle distracted them and Les raised his rifle. Something flashed past his face as Angel fired her rifle. Les stared at what looked like a lump of gelatin with tentacles lying at his feet. He slowly turned his face to her.

"Thanks," he said, and poked it with his rifle. "What is this thing?" Angel glanced at the creature and shook her head.

"Call it whatever you like, Les. I've never seen one of these things before." He glanced back at the thing.

"We better keep moving," he said.

Les slowed his pace, then stopped. Angel stepped beside him and glanced around.

"Something wrong?" she asked. He narrowed his eyes as he took in the jungle. She saw he was tense.

"We should have come across another boobytrap by now," Les replied. A branch above their heads was vaporized by a pulsar charge, and they dropped to the ground.

"I could have killed you, Camden," Garnet said, loudly. "But I'm a sportsman." Les looked in the direction of the voice but couldn't see Garnet.

"I've never heard a killer describe himself that way before," Les said, as he turned an angry look to Angel.

"You're making it too damn easy to kill you," Garnet said. "And I don't want you dying without a lot of pain, Marshal. Pain like you've been causing me lately." Angel moved her face close to Les.

"I'll circle around behind him." Les put a hand on her arm and shook his head.

"No. It's too dangerous. Besides, he'll be gone by the time you get there."

"Better sharpen your wits, Camden," Garnet said. "I don't want you disappointing me." Angel glanced in the direction of Garnet's voice.

"So much for keeping him guessing," Les said, in a frustrated tone. He looked in

Garnet's direction and shook his head.

"He's right," Les said. Angel gave him a questioning look.

"About what?" He glanced at her and looked down.

"All that time and no surprise," he replied, and slammed his hand against the ground.

"I ignored his warning, goddamnit." She got an understanding look.

"Don't be so hard on yourself, Les. We all have our bad days." He turned a frustrated look to her.

"Maybe so," he said. "But a bad day, with Garnet around, can get us killed."

"I think he's gone," Angel said, standing and slinging her rifle onto her shoulder. Les stood and loosely held his rifle.

"He was also making sure I didn't lose his trail," he said. She patted his shoulder.

"What really pisses me off," Les continued. "Is that as long as I've been after him, he can still surprise me." Angel tilted her head.

"Psychopaths are unpredictable," she said. "What more can be said?" Les shook his head.

"We're going to have to be more alert," he said. Angel gave him an uncertain look.

"That will slow us down," she said. "He might backtrack, take us from behind."

"I doubt that. He's in a hurry to get somewhere. He'll depend on his traps to slow us down, or stop us." Les arced his rifle around.

"And he doesn't know this jungle any better than we do."
They moved on.

Late in the afternoon, they came to a small stream and Angel
noticed a cave on the other bank. She pointed with her rifle.

"We can stay in there tonight," she said. They waded across
the stream and entered the cave. Les took the electric lantern
from his pack and turned it on.

"Rather cozy," he said, looking around. "Let's get settled in
and eat."

Sitting on their sleeping bags, they finished eating, put the
cans in a plastic bagand

Angel stuck it in the pack. Now they could relax.

"How long have you been a marshal, Les?" He glancecd at
her with a slight frown.

"Almost ten years."

"My father was in law enforcement before he retired," Angel
said. "I think he was disappointed when his only child was a
girl." Les became curious.

"What's he think of his little girl now?" She got a contented
look.

"He's very proud of my work." Les got a sour look.

"I'm not very damn proud of my work," he said. "I've been
after Garnet for what seems like forever." Angel gave him a
confident look.

"We'll get him, Les." He leaned against the rock wall and
rubbed an ear.

"Three times I've caught up with him, and screwed up each time. I gave him the advantage, and each time I ended up in a hospital." She got an understanding look.

"You can't anticipate what a psychopath will do," Angel said, as she moved beside him with a mischievous look.

"How long has it been since you were with a woman?"

"Huh?" he asked, puzzled.

"When was the last time you got laid?" Les was surprised and at a loss for an answer.
"Hell, I don't know. I've been preoccupied with Garnet. Besides, I never seem to have the time." She tilted her head and put her hand over his.

"I never have the time either. That's why there's no one in my life." Angel leaned forward and kissed him. She put a hand on his cheek, looked into his eyes, and smiled.

"We have the time now, Les," Angel said, softly. Les put an arm around her.

"I always cooperate with the local law," he said.

10

They were on the trail early the next morning, moving cautiously. They used their rifles to push aside broad leaves and thick yellow-green vines, some so congested they had to detour around them.

"I got a bad feeling," Les said. Angel turned her eyes from side to side, alert for any movement.

"I'm feeling uneasy, too," she admitted. Les was looking for any sign that Garnet had set a trap for them.

"Garnet should have left a trap for us before now," he said. She glanced at him.

"You said he was in a hurry." Les turned his face to her.

"Maybe so –" He stopped abruptly and aimed his rifle at the underbrush. The sound of

It rustling as something was moving their way. Angel quickly raised her rifle at a loud grunt. A black furred animal, as large as a male lion, came into view. It stopped, regarded them for a moment with bright yellow eyes, growled, exposing long, hooked teeth and went on its way. They exchanged glances.

"This is unreal," Les said. Angel lowered her rifle. Les wiped sweat from his face and they moved on.

They sat on a fallen tree eating when something caught Les's eye. He put the can down, went to the underbrush and pushed it aside with his rifle. Angel came beside him, curious.

"Find something?" she asked. Les reached down and pushed the brush aside revealing a metal cylinder tied to a tree.

"A homemade frag bomb," he replied. She stared at it with an alarmed look.

"He's certainly determined to kill you, Les." He tapped the cylinder with a finger as he shook his head.

"This is powerful enough to put a lot of frags in you," Les said. "But not powerful enough to kill." He leaned close to the cylinder and moved his hand carefully around it.

"I found the tripwire," he said, and looked over his shoulder to where it crossed their path. They went to the spot and Les knelt and parted the undergrowth. He looked up at

Angel.

"We're damn lucky," Les said. "I never would have spotted this wire until it broke."

He stood and looked around.

"Let's give Garnet a thrill," he said, and got a bewildered look from Angel.

"What do you mean?" He raised his arm and pointed to a tree.

"Let's get behind that tree," Les said, and they quickly slung their rifles. Angel was giving him a confused look as they went to the tree.

"What are you going to do?" she asked. Les glanced at her and smiled.

Thick vines made it hard to stand behind the tree, but it was good protection. Once there, Les raised his rifle and fired. A bright flash erupted from where the cylinder was, followed by a roar and gush of white smoke rising into the air. As Angel looked on, they heard excited sounds from animals in the jungle. She looked at Les.

"Do you think Garnet was close enough to see that?" she asked. Les nodded.

"You can bet on it, Angel. He likes to see how his tricks work."

"Is it possible he now thinks we're wounded?" Les glanced at her, and shook his head.

"He probably heard the shot. So it's not something he'll take for granted." They went back to the fallen tree, picked up their packs, and moved on.

As they passed a wide lake, a large retilian beast, with gray-green scales and a long, narrow head, emerged and began to pursue them. They dove into the undergrowth and the beast charged past them. Les looked at Angel.

"I've never been in a situation like this before," he said. Angel slowed her breathing and leaned her head against his arm.

"Neither have I," she said, and got a weak smile. "But you have to admit, it is rather exciting." Les frowned.

"This kind of excitement I prefer to do without." She regarded Les with a perplexed look.

"How does Garnet get past these beasts?" she asked. Les got a cynical smile.

"They probably sense he's like them," he replied. Angel shook her head.

"If we only had some idea of where he was going," she said. That set Les to thinking.

"He must have a ship coming for him," he said. "And it can't land in this jungle." Angel pointed her rifle in the direction they had been going.

"There's open country some miles ahead," Angel said. Les bit his lip as he pondered the chance of getting ahead of Garnet.

"That has to be where he's headed," Les said. "But we can't get around him in this jungle." She got an excited look.

"Can we catch up with him before that ship gets here?" Les frowned as he regarded her.

"I hope so. I'm damn tired of chasing this bastard." Angel adjusted her pack straps as she looked at Les with a serious expression.

"We're going to have to move faster," she said. Les got a wary look as he adjusted his pack.

"Faster, yes," he said. "Carelessly, no. I've no doubt he has other surprises waiting for us."

They camped that night in a grove of close-cropped trees. The light from the lantern could not be seen from the outside. Angel lay on her sleeping bag with her head propped on her arm.

"I wonder why he hasn't tried anything after dark?" she asked. Les raised an eyebrow.

"Garnet isn't stupid, Angel. Would you go wandering through this jungle at night?"

She got an uneasy look and shook her head.

"Do you think we'll catch up with him tomorrow?" she asked. Les glanced at her and shrugged.

"That or he'll get us." She sat up with a disbelieving look.

"You think that's possible, Les?" He frowned and rubbed his hands on his legs.

"He might get lucky. He almost did with that last bomb." Angel moved beside him with a serious look.

"Then we had better take advantage of tonight," she said, leaning close to him.

The jungle had thinned when they stopped before a clearing. Les looked it over carefully.

"It looks safe," Les said. They moved into the clearing and heard a pulsar fire. A loud blast blossomed behind them knocking them to the ground. Garnet came from among the trees, his rifle aimed at them. He stood looking down at the two unconscious people.

"You still gave me one second, Marshal." He looked at Angel and smiled.

"Pleased to meet you, Chief." He knelt beside her, removed her pack and sidearm, lifted her to his shoulder and walked off, leaving Les lying in the clearing.

Les rolled over, sat up and shook his head. He looked around and saw Angel's rifle, sidearm, and pack beside him. With an angry look, he got to his feet.

"Goddamnit!" He shrugged off his pack, picked up his rifle, and started out of the clearing. He stopped, went back to his pack and cut the transponder loose. With a grimly determined look, Les hurried from the clearing.

Garnet shoved Angel to keep her moving. Her hands were tied behind her and she felt utterly helpless. They were moving through open country, with an occasional tree breaking the level landscape.

"What do you want with me?" she asked, turning an angry glare to him.

"You're insurance." This brought a puzzled look to her. Angel stopped and turned to face him.

"What are you talking about?" Garnet pushed her and she resumed walking.

"The marshal will certainly come after you. When he does, I'll have the pleasure of killing him." Angel glanced at him and shook her head.

"Is his death that important to you?" Garnet frowned and nodded.

"You're damn right it is. I'm tired of Camden dogging my ass. And killing him is something I'm looking forward to now." He took hold of her arm to hurry her along.

Angel tried walking slow, but he gripped her arm so tight she winced at the pain.

"It won't do you any good trying to slow us down. Camden can catch up with us where I'll be waiting to put an end to his life." Angel turned a questioning look to him.

"I know exactly where we're going," Garnet said. He pointed to a low, rocky hill with a natural opening in its side.

"That's where we'll wait for Camden." He pulled her along toward the hill.

On arriving at his destination, Garnet pushed Angel down on a flat rock and stepped behind her. He took a cylinder from his pack and tied it to her back. He stepped in front of her with a look of satisfaction.

"That will give the marshal something to think about before he makes any move."

Angel regarded him with an angry scowl.

"You won't get off this planet a free man," she said. Garnet laughed and jerked the cord sharply across her back, causing her to wince.

"You should know by now Camden's no match for me."

"That's where you're mistaken," Angel said, defiantly. "He's a capable marshal. And he's determined to get you once and for all." Garnet slipped his hand under her chin, turned her face up to him, and smiled.

"You're siding with a loser, pretty lady."

Just before dark, Les came across a pool of water and saw footprints pointing in the direction he was going. He had his first evidence that he was heading in the right direction. He hurried on, hoping to catch up with Garnet before it got dark. But as he hurried on, that hope faded into darkness. The rising of two moons provided some illumination. He stopped when he saw a light ahead. Les moved cautiously toward the rocky hill.

Arriving at the natural opening, he took a quick look in. He saw Angel sitting on a rock on the far side, her hands tied behind her, an electric lantern beside her. Les couldn't see Garnet, but he heard him.

"Doesn't look like the marshal's coming after you." Les saw Angel turn a hard look in Garnet's direction.

"And you certainly look good enough to come after." This brought a defiant look to her.

"Maybe your damn bomb killed him," Angel said, sarcastically.

"It wasn't that powerful," Garnet said. "Besides, if it had killed Camden, it would have killed you, too." She glared at him and remained silent.

"Maybe one of those beasts had him for lunch," Garnet said, and laughed. Angel turned her face away from him.

"I like that idea," Garnet said. "Camden ending up as a meal for a jungle beast."

Les pulled the rifle up on his shoulder and mumbled.

"You're in for a surprise. That second is mine this time, you son of a bitch." Les moved slowly away from the opening over loose rocks. He hurried along until he was a good distance from the opening. Les started to climb, slipped on the loose rocks and fell, got back on his feet and kept climbing. Slipping on stones, he struggled to the top.

Les slid down the opposite side of the hill, got to his feet, and headed back toward the opening. Carefully, he climbed to the top, raised his head, and saw Garnet sitting in shadow, his back against the rock wall. He moved so he could look down at Angel.

"Shit!" he exclaimed, in a sharp whisper. She had a bomb tied to her back. Looking back at Garnet, Les saw he held a detonator.

"I'll be off this planet tomorrow," Garnet said. "And Camden will be here permanently." Angel tilted her head and gave him a curious look.

"Why did you come here?" she asked. Garnet reached in his shirt pocket and took out a small plastic bag and held it up.

"This small amount of sutain will provide me with an income for life." He stuck it back in his pocket and smiled.

"You knew it would get off this planet sooner or later, Chief."

"It hasn't gone anywhere yet," Angel countered. Les pulled his head down, frustrated. He lifted his arm and illuminated his watch dial. There was nothing he could do until daylight. But Les had no idea what he would do when a new day arrived.

As light gradually filled the sky, Les peered over the crest and saw Garnet pacing. He inhaled deeply, knowing it was time to confront his nemesis.

"Garnet," Les shouted. Garnet started and looked around with a frown.

"So you finally made it," Garnet said. "I'm slightly disappointed, Marshal. I was hoping you had been a jungle lunch."

"Let the woman go. It's me you want." Garnet shook his head.

"As long as I have her, I've got your attention."

"I can drop you, Garnet." He held up his hand with the detonator.

"I think not, Camden. My thumb comes off this trigger and the lady dies."

"Goddamnit, Garnet, what do you want?" Garnet got a cold look as his lips drew into a tight line.

"I want you dead. I'm tired of you showing up and trying to screw up my plans. But this time you can't interfere." Les kept silent as Garnet looked around with a nervous expression.

"Make conversation, Camden." Les took his sidearm from the holster, adjusted the setting, and laid it in front of him. He took the transponder from his pocket and activated it.
"This time, Garnet, the second is mine," he mumbled, and shook his head. "I've got to stop talking to myself."

Garnet looked uneasy until he was distracted by a sound in the sky. As Garnet looked up, Les aimed the rifle and fired. The detonator, along with Garnet's hand, was vaporized. Garnet stared in disbelief at where his hand had been. Les dropped the rifle, grabbed his pulsar, leaped to his feet and fired. Garnet dropped, unconscious.

Les climbed over the crest and came down behind Angel. She tried to turn to see him.He stopped behind her and laid the pulsar aside.

"That was pretty fancy shooting, Les."

"Don't move. I've got to disarm this bomb." Slowly he worked the firing mechanism loose, removed it, and carefully put it down. He removed the bomb and untied her. They stood and embraced. Les looked at her with an expression of relief.

"As for the fancy shooting, Angel, it was an act of desperation." She looked at him as she pressed against him smiling.

"If I ever get in another predicament like this, I want you there – and desperate." They looked up and saw the aircraft descending.

A deputy was applying first aid to an unconscious Garnet. Les looked from him to Angel.

"He won't be feeling any pain soon," Les said. "I hit him with a full stun charge." She folded her arms and regarded Les with a satisfied look.

"It hasn't been such a bad day after all," she said. They lifted Garnet into the small cabin, and then squeezed in with Angel sitting on Les' lap. The craft lifted into the air with the engine straining under the weight.

Les entered the cell and regarded a sullen Garnet sitting on a bunk with his handless right arm in a sling.

"If it wasn't for Eliot Neil's death, you would have probably gotten away," Les said. Garnet sneered.

"He was just like you – stubborn as hell." Les couldn't help the smile that came to him.

"Looks like Ruby is going to have to visit you on Forten." Garnet gave him a hard look and remained silent.

"By the way," Les said. "They'll give you a new hand on Forten. Everybody there works for a living." Garnet shook his head.

"They won't keep me there long," Garnet said. "No dumb son of a bitch like you is going to best me." Les shook his head.

"Then you better do what I did." Garnet got a puzzled look.

"What was that?" Les held a confident look on him.

"Learn from your adversary. That second was mine this time, Garnet." Les stepped to the door and looked back over his shoulder.

"I hope there's not too many people on Forten who have old scores to settle with you."

He saw Garnet pale and his mouth fell open. Les knocked on the door and the guard opened it.

Les walked into Angel's office and took a chair in front of the desk. She smiled.

"The extradition papers have been cleared," she said.

"What about the ship coming for Garnet?" She stood and came around in front of the desk, leaned against it, and folded her arms.

"We got it in orbit," Angel replied. "And that takes two more wanted felons out of action." He stood and regarded her with a serious expression.
"I'm resigning after I take Garnet back." Her arms dropped to her sides and her eyes widened in surprise.

"You're a law enforcement officer, Les. What will you do?" He stepped forward and kissed her.

"I'm hoping you could suggest something." She put her arms around him, pressed against him, and turned her face up to him.

"I could use a forensics expert here," she said.

"I was hoping you might say something like that," Les said, and kissed

11

In his ten months on Forten, Garnet's hatred, and thirst for revenge, against Les Camden had grown. It became an obsession as he planned his escape. The authorities had kept him isolated, knowing there were many there who would kill Garnet, if given the chance. This isolation worked to Garnet's advantage by not distracting him from his plotting.

He slowly worked out a plan to escape from the prison planet. He knew it would call for a lot of luck, but he felt he had it. He worked with a guard watching over him for his protection. Garnet knew he would have to kill the guard for his plan to work, and he had no compunction about that. He just had to choose his time carefully, so he bided his time until the guard felt comfortable with him. Now he just had to select the right time and place to kill him.

The cell door opened and a guard came in.

"I've been assigned to guard you," he said. Garnet was surprised to see they had changed his guard. This was the opportunity he had been waiting for.

"Let's go, Garnet." He meekly got off the bunk and walked to the guard. The man was young and cocksure, until Garnet's new hand flashed out and gripped his throat. It was quickly over. Garnet stepped to the door and looked into the corridor. Seeing no one, he pushed the door shut, stripped the guard and put his body on the bunk, covered him, and turned him so his back was to the door. Garnet put on the uniform and found it was a close fit. This, he thought, was going to be easy. All he had to do was walk to the landing park, get aboard a ship and he was out of there, free.

Using the guard's communicator, he reported that Garnet was sick and he had left him in bed. He knew it would be sometime before they could get in the cell as he had disabled the lock. He walked leisurely to the landing park, made his way among the ships, and chose the ship he would make his escape in. Garnet stepped to it, looked around, activated the hatch and quickly went on board. He powered it up and lifted off with a laugh of triumph. Now it was time to find out where Camden was and get his payback.

Angel and Les were no sooner through the door than Ed was out of his chair coming to them with a sheet of paper. He handed it to Angel, who read it, and passed it to Les. As he read it, he got a sinking feeling. Angel turned a worried look to Les.

"Do you think he'll come here?" she asked, in a troubled tone. Les thought for a moment and shook his head.

"I doubt it," Les replied. "He's going to have to be cautious, if he wants to remain free. I'm probably the reason he made such a daring escape. He wants me to know he's on the loose again."

"Well, at least, we can be ready in case he does come here," Angel said. Les felt there was no way for anyone to be ready for Garnet, but kept it to himself.

"The problem is, where will he go?" Les asked. "He's not going to do anything to attract attention to himself. That would be pushing his luck." Angel raised an eyebrow.

"How about the way he planned to get away from here?" she asked. Les shook his head.

"He knows we're aware of that," Les replied. "No, he's going to have to be very careful about what he does." Angel folded her arms and regarded him with a frown.

"Well what are we going to do?" she asked. Les had already considered what action to take.

"I'm going to Earth and meet with Chief Drydon," he replied. "Maybe together we can come up with a plan to trap Garnet." She stepped forward and embraced him.

"Be careful, Les," she said. "You know he can always surprise you." They kissed and he got a slight smile.

"As I recall, at our last encounter, it was me who surprised him." She pulled away from him and regarded him with an alarmed look.

[114]

"Don't do anything foolish, Les," she said. He patted her arms.

"Don't wory about that, Angel. I put him on Forten, and I intend doing it again, without getting myself broken in any way."

On his trip to Earth, Les reflected at how much more relaxed his relationship with Angel was compared to his relationship with Eilene. It had to be because they had so much in common. But he wanted to make certain Garnet knew he was on Earth, and keep him away from Varian Four, and Angel. After he had resigned as a marshal, he had returned to Varian Four and Angel. They had found an apartment to share and had been together almost eight months. Les also had feelings for Angel he had never felt for Eilene. For the first time in his life, Les was enjoying a domestic life,

Drydon stood and extended his hand when Les was shown into his office. Les stepped to the desk and took the offered hand.

"I've been expecting you, Camden, since I was told of Garnet's escape," Drydon said, as he waved Les to a chair. Les sat down and regarded Drydon over the desk.

"Sir, I feel somewhat responsible for his escape because he badly wants to get back at me. But I think I might know how to draw Garnet into a trap." Drydon nodded.

"Tell me about it."

"I know Garnet wants his revenge on me, sir. If it can be leaked that I'm working here in an administrative post, it just might bring him to where we can be waiting for him."

Drydon shook his head.

"Garnet is unpredictable, Camden. There's no way to tell if, or when, he might show up, and it would be putting your life at risk. Besides, I don't think he would risk coming here. That would be a stupid mistake on his part." Les nodded.

"I realize that, sir. But my life was at risk bringing Garnet in alive, as you asked."

Drydon frowned at the reminder as he regarded Les.

"It will mean you will have to be kept under surveillance for your own protection."

Les nodded.

"Getting Garnet back in custody is what's important, sir." Drydon was in agreement, but hesitant at risking another life to Garnet's brutality.

"Very well, Camden. I'll instruct those who need to know about your plan. Let's hope this can be done without anyone being killed."

Les sat in his cubicle, a place he had never expected to see again. He was lost in thought when Dave stepped in.

"Les! I never thought to see you here again." Les turned his chair and looked up at him.

"I'm back because of the same problem – Garnet. He's wanting to get back at me, and

I'm trying to think of a way to take him without a lot of trouble."

"Lots of luck with that. Going to see Eilene?" Les shook his head.

"Nope. She said it was over if I went after Garnet. I'm leaving her decision stand."

"She would probably be glad to see you." Les got a slight smile.

"I'm after Garnet again. How do you think she would react to that?" Dave frowned and nodded.

"I see your point," Dave said, and patted Les' shoulder. "Just be careful." Les gave him a nod.

"With Garnet, I'm always careful."

Ruby had just picked up her drink when she heard a light tapping on her back door. She put the drink down, went to the door, and opened it slightly. Her eyes widened in surprise.

"Jovan! How the hell did you get here?" He pushed past her. He hoped he hadn't been recognized on his way from the landing park.

"I'll tell you over a drink, Ruby." As he made himself comfortable, he told her about his escape from Forten. Ruby was impressed.

"That really took balls, Jovan."

"Not really. It was just knowing how to act as I went to the landing park. I never took a hurried step, just kept a confident pace."

"What do you plan to do now?" He lost his smile, replaced it with a grim, determined look.

"First, I want to get rid of this guard uniform," he replied. "Then I've got to figure out how to get to Camden. I think his lady on Varian Four is the lever I can use to bring him to me."

"Do you know where he is?" Ruby asked.

"I heard he's on Earth. But the woman who helped him is still on her planet."

"And you intend going to Varian Four?" Garnet shook his head and finished his drink.

"I'm not going myself. I'll get in touch with some people I know there." He got a savage look.

"If I can get her, I'll get Camden." Ruby said nothing, but felt trying to get the woman was a distraction from what he really wanted to do.

Sunlight filled Angel's office as she sat at her desk unable to concentrate on work. Les was on her mind, and she missed him. She decided it would be better to be with him than sitting and wondering what Garnet might try. Angel had vacation time coming and quickly decided to take a transport to Earth. The idea that Garnet would try to get to Les on Earth seemed ludicrous to her. But with a man like Garnet, one could never be certain

what he would do, especially if he was hell bent on revenge. So, Angel decided, it was time to get things in order and leave for Earth.

Angel pushed away from the desk, stood, and headed for the door. Stepping into the anteroom, she stopped facing Ed.

"I'm going to take some time off, Ed. You'll be in charge while I'm gone." He stood and gave her an odd look.

"You going to be with Les?" he asked. Angel nodded.

"Yeah. I want to be nearby if he has to face Garnet." He gave her a slight nod.

"I like Les," Ed said. "He's an all right guy. I would hate to see Garnet the upper hand over him."

"I know I can count on you to take care of things while I'm away," she said.

"I'll do my best, Chief."

"I'll finish up here and take the transport tomorrow," Angel said, feeling uneasy.

As Angel packed, she considered letting Les know she was coming. But she felt apprehensive about that as she thought Garnet might get wind of it and make a move on her before she left. She recalled Les telling her about how there were people all over that would get any useful information to him that mattered.

HELLCHASER

Angel decided not to tell Les in advance of her trip. It would be safer for her to travel without any word of her destination being revealed.

Angel had a pensive expression when Ed got her to the landing park about a quarter of an hour before the transport was due to lift off.

"Have a good trip, Chief." Angel got a wan smile.
"I hope to, Ed. I wish I could let him know I'm coming, but it's best to be discrete." Ed got a broad smile.

"He'll be really surprised to see you. He's probably missing you more than you're missing him." The boarding alarm sounded.

"I have to get on board, Ed. I'll be seeing you." She turned and hurried up the ramp and into the ship. Ed watched until she disappeared into the ship's interior.

Off Varian Four, Angel sat in the cabin feeling both relief and apprehension. She hoped she had gotten away without anyone who knew Garnet seeing her departure. She leaned back and tried to get some sleep, but her mind was bouncing from scenario to scenario. The one thing Angel was sure of was that she would be glad to be with Les again. That idea made her feel good.

The tall, stocky built man regarded Garnet with cold blue eyes as he took the drink offered. Garnet began to pace.

"I don't dare show my face in the city on Varian Four," Garnet said. "The law there knows me. But I need to know the pattern that woman chief follows. If I can get her, I'll

get Camden." The man took a drink and nodded.

"I want you to follow her," Garnet continued, after taking a drink from the glass he held. "If you get the opportunity to grab her, there will be a ship in orbit waiting to pick you both up. Just use the preselected code word." Garnet put a hand on the man's shoulder and smiled.

"Bring me that prize, Carl, and I'll reward you handsomely." The man finished his drink and put the glass down.

"I'll do my best, Jovan." He turned and left the apartment. Garnet rubbed his chin, feeling he had picked the one person that could get Corey for him.

The audvid unit on Les' desk sounded. He pressed the comlink and saw Drydon with an odd expression.

"Will you come to my office, Camden?" Les' brow furrowed as he got a puzzled look.
"I'll be right there, sir." Les stood wondering what Drydon could want.

Stepping into Drydon's office, Les took a few seconds before he recognized Angel. He had never seen her in a dark brown skirt and pale yellow blouse before. He was surprised to find her here.

"What are you doing here, Angel?" Drydon raised an eyebrow.

"Chief Corey has offered her help in apprehending Garnet," Drydon said. "Since she was instrumental in his capture, I've accepted her offer." Les looked from Drydon to Angel and nodded. He was elated to see her, as he had missed her a lot.

"We've had no clue as to his whereabouts, Angel," Les said. "Garnet is really covering his trail this time." She regarded Les with a serious expression.

"One of the reasons I came here," she said. "Was that I was concerned he might try to get me in his clutches again. I certainly don't want to find myself in that situation again, especially with you not around." Les nodded.

"I can understand that," Les said. "And I'm glad you're here, Angel. Maybe we can figure out what move he might make that would give us the advantage." Drydon looked pleased.

"I'm glad you two will be working together," he said. "You've had more contact with Garnet than anyone in law enforcement. If anyone can determine what he might attempt it's you two." Angel stood and went beside Les and turned her face to Drydon.

"Thank you, Chief," she said. "We'll do our best." She and Les left the office. In the corridor, Angel saw they were alone, leaned forward and kissed him.

"I don't have a place to stay," she said. "Can you recommend a place?" Les smiled.

"I know exactly where you can stay." She smiled, locked her arm through his, and they started down the corridor.

Carl spent his first two days on Varian Four keeping a discrete watch on the constable's office. He saw no woman going or coming from the office, and this puzzled him. He decided to take a more direct approach and went to the nearest tavern. Inside, he took a seat at the bar.

"What will you have?" the bartender asked. Carl told him and watched as the bartender filled the glass.

"I'm curious," Carl said. "I heard you have a hard nosed woman in charge of the law here. Is that true?" The bartender smiled.

"Corey's hard on lawbreakers all right. But she sure is a good looking woman."

"How does one go about seeing her?" The bartender shook his head.

"Can't. She's away on vacation. Rightly deserved since it's the only time she's taken off since become chief constable over a year ago." Carl finished his drink, stood, and paid for the drink.

"Enjoy the day," Carl said, and left the bar. As he walked along the street, he wondered if he could find out where she had gone.

As they had dinner, Les outlined his thoughts to Angel.

"I don't think Garnet would risk coming here," he said. "My concern is that he will get word to one or more of his flunkies to try and take me out." Angel regarded him with a serious look as she held her fork up.

"That means you don't know how, when, or where, someone might try to kill you." Les nodded and took a bite.

"I've been alert for anything out of the way," he said. "But I can't do so continually. It just takes too much out of me. That makes me thankful to Drydon for keeping me under surveillance." Angel took a bite as she thought for a moment.

"I'll try to watch your back," she said. "That makes my coming here worth it." Les put his hand over hers and smiled.

"I'm glad you're here, Angel. I was getting very lonesome." She smiled and leaned toward him.

"I was lonesome, too," she said. "I had to be with you,Les. I just didn't feel right being alone." He nodded.

"My greatest concern was that Garnet would try to get his hands on you to force me to come after him." Angel frowned and nodded.

"I had considered he might try that. Maybe I was lucky to get away from Varian Four when I did."

"Well we're a team again," Les said. "And I have confidence we'll put Garnet back where he belongs." Angel got an uneasy look.

"You don't think my staying with you will cause any trouble, do you?" Les gave her hand a squeeze and shook his head.

"No. That's our private lives and dosen't interfere with what we have to do. And remember, I'm not a marshal any longer." She smiled and leaned over and gave him a light kiss.

"I'm glad. I don't want to become the source of any conflict."

12

When Ruby came into the room, she knew immediately something was amiss.

"What's wrong, Jovan?" He was pacing, slamming his hands together with an angry look. He glanced over his shoulder and she could tell he was enraged.

"Corey isn't on Varian Four," he replied, in an angry tone. "She's gone on vacation, and Carl wasn't able to discover where she's gone." Ruby knew better than to press him about the woman, but felt what had happened was for the best.

"Want a drink?" she asked, going to the panel. He didn't answer for a moment, then nodded.

"Yeah. I can use a drink right now. I've got to figure out what to do now. It has to be a foolproof plan with a minimum of risk to me. But I've got to get back at Camden for what he did to me." Ruby pressed the order into the keypad and a tray slid from the wall. She took the drinks from the tray and went to Garnet and handed him one.

"Why not get word to someone on Earth you can trust?" Ruby asked. "Have them try to get Camden." Garnet stopped lifting his glass to his lips and looked at her with a raised eyebrow.

"Ruby, you just hit on what I've been trying to think of." He pulled her to him and kissed her.

Chico Perez was of average height with black hair and dark brown eyes. He had been surprised when he had gotten word from Garnet about what he wanted Chico to do. He owed him a lot of favors, but he never dreamed he would be asked to repay them by murdering a man. He couldn't refuse Garnet, but he didn't like the idea of committing a murder either. He was seeking out a friend he knew he could trust and he hoped he would help him.

As Chico walked along the sidewalk, in the fading light of the setting sun, he passed a bar and glanced in. He saw his friend,

Dan Howe, sitting at the bar. Chico stepped into the bar and went to his friend.

"What you been up to, Dan?" Chico asked, taking the stool beside him. The man had blue-gray eyes and short cut sandy hair.

"Not much. It's been awhile since I seen you, Chico." Chico nodded and raised a hand to the bartender.

"I'll have a beer," he said, and the bartender nodded. He turned his face to Dan with a grim look.

"I got a message from Garnet," he said, in a low voice. "He wants me to take out a guy called Camden." Dan's eyebrows raised.

"That's the guy who nabbed him," Dan said. Chico spread his hands on the bar as the bartender sat a beer in front of him. Chico handed the bartender a bill, who took it and walked to the far end of the bar and opened the cash register.

"Anyway, Garnet escaped from Forten. He can't risk coming to Earth, so he sent word for me to do it. I know you owe Garnet, too, and I need help. I've never thought anything about killing someone, and I don't want to start now."

"What do you think I can do to help you?" Chico shrugged.

"I don't know. I need advice so I can figure out what to do." Chico looked back to Dan.

"Will you help me out, Dan?" Dan turned his face to him.

"How do you want to go about it?" Dan asked. Chico took a drink and frowned.

"I have no idea where to begin. I have to try because I owe Garnet that much, and I certainly don't want him to think I might have crossed him. But I don't think I can kill a man for him."

"Then I just might have the answer you're looking for, Chico." The bartender returned and placed the change in front of Chico and gave him a nod, then returned to cleaning glasses.

"I don't want to let Garnet down, but I'm not the killer type. I don't know why I was picked when there's some real hard-nosed bastards who could take that guy out and think nothing of it." Dan nodded and took a drink.

"My solution should take care of your problem, Chico."

The audvid unit on the desk sounded. Les leaned forward, pressed the comlink, and saw a grim Drydon looking back at him.

"You need to come to my office immediately, Camden." Les raised an eyebrow and nodded.

"I'll be right there, sir."

As Les came into Drydon's office, he saw two men sitting in front of his desk.

"Camden, I would like you to meet Chico Perez and Dan Howe." They stood and shook hands with Les.

"Please sit down, Camden," Drydon said. "I want them to tell you why they are here."Les sat down.

He listened with a grim look as Chico and Dan related what Chico had been asked to do. Les wasn't as amazed that Chico had been asked to kill him as he was that they had done the one thing Garnet would never have considered they would do. They had brought the story to the authorities. There's still good people in this world, Les thought.

"It has to look like I've done something," Chico concluded. "Or Garnet will send someone after me." Les nodded and glanced at Drydon.

"This could be the break we've been waiting for," Les said. "Let's see if we can figure out how to exploit it." Drydon leaned back with a pleased look.

"You and Corey work on it, Camden," Drydon said. "You two know more then anyone about how Garnet operates." Les patted Chico on the shoulder.

"Don't worry," Les said. "We'll come up with something that will make it look like you came through for Garnet." Chico looked relieved.
"Thanks," Chico said. "I sure wouldn't want Garnet to know I had crossed him."

"Neither would I," Les said. "And I'm the one who should be thanking you."

Angel was astonished as Les related what happened. When he finished, he had only a vague idea of a plan.

"What are you going to do now?" she asked. Les shrugged.

"Try to work out a plan that will put Garnet back where he belongs and protect the man he ordered to kill me." He watched her breasts rise as she took a deep breath.

"You could go undercover and try to track Garnet down, Les. Drydon can get you an unregistered ship. It will keep you out of sight and put you in business." Les nodded.

"It would seem that's the only option I have, right now. I'll speak with Drydon in the morning." Angel smiled and embraced him. He thought of the contrast when Eilene had demanded he choose her or his job.

"Now let's have dinner," she said. Les held her for a moment with a thoughtful look.

"I'm going back to Casin Three, where Ruby is," Les said. "If Garnet is anywhere, it's got to be with her." Angel regarded him and nodded.

"That's probably the best place to start," she agreed.

Angel stood in the background as Drydon addressed the media.

"Les Camden, the marshal who captured Jovan Garnet, is missing," Drydon said. "We have no idea what's happened to him, but believe that Garnet is behind his disappearance. We can't prove that, of course, but it's the only logical assumption. Now I'll take questions." Angel was torn between concern and apprehension as Drydon answered questions. Les had left two days ago, and she knew they wouldn't hear anything from him until he had something to report.

When Susan Burns walked into Farrel's office, she couldn't have been more surprised to see Les sitting in front of the desk. Farrel smiled and nodded to her. She kept her eyes on Les as she approached the men.

"It's good to see you again, Marshal," she said. Les stood, smiled, and shook her hand.

"It's good to see you too, Susan. But I'm not a marshal anymore. I'm an authorized agent who has one job – find and take Garnet back into custody. With that kind of authority, your officials couldn't deny me permission to wear a sidearm." They released their hands.

"What are you doing here, Les?" Susan asked, with a puzzled look. "We've not had a homicide in some months." She and Les sat down.

"Garnet would have kept his killing in check after escaping from Forten," Les replied.

"But I've got a strong suspicion he's at Ruby's." Susan got a cynical look.

"Lots of luck getting in there," Farrel said. Les frowned and rubbed his chin.

"I couldn't get in because Ruby knows me. But I would like to find someone who can,

and tell me if I'm right about Garnet being there."

"I'll ask around and see what my informants can learn," Susan said.

"Tell them to be careful how they ask. It could prove dangerous," Les said. "I have to keep out of sight. I can't afford to let Garnet know I'm here – if he is at Ruby's. I wish there was someway to surprise him, and take him with the least amount of trouble. But the chance of that happening is nil." Farrel and Susan silently agreed with his assessment.

Ruby could tell Garnet was uneasy as he paced from wall to wall with short, quick steps. He glanced at her.

"Camden has disappeared," he said, almost to himself. "But is he dead? Or is this some kind of ruse?" Ruby went to him and stopped his pacing.

"How could it be a trick, Jovan?" Ruby asked. "Nobody knows you're here but me."

He regarded her with a pronounced frown.

"It might be a way to find out where I am. Until I know Camden is dead, and know it for sure, I won't feel safe." Ruby slipped her arms around him and embraced him.

"They will find his body in a couple of days, Jovan. Your people will come through for you. They've never let you down yet." He kissed her, pulled away, and his brow furrowed.

"I hope you're right, Ruby. I really do." His state of mind was beginning to worry her.

After the press conference, Drydon was putting his papers in order when he noticed the worried look Angel had.

"What's troubling you, Corey?" Angel clasped her hands and turned her eyes to him.

"I hope Les knows what he's doing. The idea that he knew where Garnet is hiding now seems a bit unreal to me." Drydon put his papers down and regarded her with a gentle look.

"I've never known anyone who knew their target as well as Camden. It's almost as if he can sense Garnet's thoughts. I've been in law enforcement for more than twenty years, and I've never known an officer like Camden. I, too, had doubt when he told me he knew how Garnet thinks. But he sure as hell convinced me that he did when he brought him in, and alive." Angel frowned and dropped her arms to her sides.

"I hope you're right, Chief," she said. "Les once told me that as long as had been after Garnet, he was still able to surprise him." Drydon nodded.

"This time, I believe, it will be Garnet who is going to be surprised. As you know, Corey, Camden has a knack of taking care of himself." Angel nodded, but kept her uncertainty to herself.

The man regarded Garnet with a pleased look. But Garnet didn't look convinced.

"Are you certain it's Camden?" Garnet asked. The man shrugged.

"The body was too mutilated for quick identification," the man replied. "But he hasn't been seen for the past week. We'll know in about two weeks when they release the DNA results. From the description of the body, it sure sounds like Camden." Garnet still wasn't convinced; he had to be certain before he moved into the open.

"I'm going to wait until his death has been confirmed," Garnet said. "I'm not taking any chance that it's not Camden." The man nodded.

"I understand your caution, Jovan," the man said. "But I believe that it was Camden's body. The height, weight, and everything else almost matches exactly the description of him.""Garnet nodded and patted the man's shoulder.

"Good work," Garnet said. "When you go downstairs, Ruby will pay you." The man turned and left the room. Garnet held a troubled look on the man until the door closed.

[129]

"I must be certain," Garnet said, to himself. "I have to know that Camden is dead."

Les was finding it difficult to remain out of sight, but few people on the planet knew him by sight. He spent his time between his apartment and Susan's apartment for dinner, and Farrel's office waiting for any lead that might give some indication that Garnet was at Ruby's. Susan's informants had come up with only second hand information, and Les couldn't move on that.

When Susan had told him about the body found on Earth, it gave him confidence that Garnet would soon move into the open. But waiting was boring, and Les knew he had to bide his time. The body had given him an unexpected edge, and protected the man Garnet had instructed to kill him. He sat watching Susan set the table and listening to what she was saying.

"I tell you, Les, when I saw the photo of that body, I would have sworn it was you if I hadn't known you were here." He now had one thought in mind: Who was the victim and how had it been mistaken for him? Les was curious as to why the body had showed up when it did. Questions with no answers. This disturbed him most.

"Earth Authorities have no idea yet who he is, or who killed him," Susan continued.

"In fact, they have very few clues to the crime." It seemed an awful coincidence to Les, but it also gave him hope that it would draw Garnet out. He knew he would have to be very cautious now, if he was to have a chance of nabbing him.

Drydon paced, his arms folded, one hand cupping his chin, as the medical examiner gave his report.

"Whoever that man was, Chief, his DNA isn't on file here." Drydon stopped pacing and turned to the ME.

"How can that be?" Drydon asked, dropping his arms to his sides. The ME spread his hands.

"The only explanation is, that he wasn't born on Earth, Chief. That's why his DNA isn't in our files."

"Then how the hell are we going to identify him?" the doctor shrugged.

"It will be impossible – unless we get a lucky break, like someone comes looking for him." Drydon frowned as his brow furrowed.

"Thank you, Doctor." The ME stood regarding Drydon with a questioning look.

"What are you going to do with this information, Chief?" Drydon clasped his hands behind him.

"That's something I'm going to have to think about." The ME nodded, turned, and walked from the office.

Garnet paced with an anxious expression. Ruby watched, helpless, and was becoming more worried about his state of mind. She reached out and put a hand on his arm, stopping him. He regarded her with a lost look.

"Why haven't they said Camden is dead?" he asked. "Why haven't they released any report about the body they found?" Ruby closed her grip on his arm.

"They often have trouble identifying a body by DNA if it isn't on file. Why does Camden bother you so much, Jovan?" He held up his right hand.

"I got this hand on Forten. Camden took my hand by doing something I never thought he would do. He used a pulsar rifle to take my hand off. That's why I have to know if he's dead or alive. I'm not making a move until I know one way or the other." Ruby had an idea.

"Maybe they want people to believe Camden is alive," she suggested. "After all, he used to be a marshal." Garnet raised an eyebrow as he considered her words.

"You could be right, Ruby. Maybe they don't want to admit losing the marshal that captured me. But I'm still going to wait and see if they release any information." Ruby embraced him, becoming ever more concerned at his mental state.

Susan and Les sat in front of Farrel's desk with Les holding a puzzled look.

"I wonder why Earth Authority hasn't released the identity of that body they found?"

Les asked. Farrel shrugged.

"Maybe they're trying to flush Garnet into the open," Farrel replied.
"That makes sense," Susan said, nodding. "They could be delaying it to keep Garnet guessing. It would keep him in an uncertain frame of mind." Les regarded her with a frown.

"Well I'm damn curious to know who that victim was," Les said. "They can't hold off telling the public for much longer."

"Maybe not," Farrel said, confidently. "But I think they know exactly what they're doing."

Angel stood beside Drydon, in his office, their eyes locked on a small TV screen.

They listened, and regarded the newscaster with serious expressions.

"Why have the authorities withheld the name of the murder victim?" the newscaster asked. "Is it because they don't want it known that it was a revenge murder from the prison planet Forten? Could the victim, in fact, be ex-marshal Les Camden, the man who dogged Jovan Garnet until he was taken into custody? It's time the authorities released the name of the victim, and let the truth be known." Drydon turned a troubled look to Angel.

"What can I do, Corey? If I tell them the victim can't be identified because he was an off worlder, with no DNA record here, the media will press on with this rumor that the victim was Camden." Angel got a slight smile as she had an idea.

"Chief, you should release just what you said," she replied. "That will create more confusion, and might force Garnet into exposing his whereabouts." Drydon's expression changed to one of satisfaction.

"I'll take your advice," he said, and pressed the comlink on the audvid unit on his desk. The face of his receptionist appeared on the screen.

"I want you to take down what I'm about to tell you," he said. "And I want it released to the media as soon as possible."

Ruby burst into the room with an excited look.

"The news from Earth just came through, Jovan. They're claiming that the victim was an off worlder who had no DNA record on Earth." Garnet brow furrowed as he regarded her with a confused look. Ruby's mouth dropped open.

"Don't you understand, Jovan? It's a coverup! Camden's dead and they don't want to admit it." Garnet blinked and shook his head.

"How can I be certain? I must be certain, Ruby." She put her hands on his cheeks and looked into his eyes.

"Jovan, Camden is dead. Your people on Earth killed him. They came through for you, like I thought they would." He regarded her with a confused look.

"I must have confirmation, Ruby," he said, emphatically. "I'll contact my people on Earth and have them get all the details they can. I must be certain!" Ruby shook her head and turned away from him with a pitiful look.

Les went to the door after hearing the chime. He was surprised to find Farrel standing on the other side with an odd look.

"Come in," Les said. "Want some coffee?" Farrel shook his head.

"Have a seat," Les said, wondering what this was about. Farrel sat down across from Les and regarded him with an unreadable expression.

"What's happened?" Les asked. "Is Susan –" Farrel raised a hand.

"Susan is fine, Les. But I don't know if you are." Les leaned forward and regarded him with a puzzled look.

"What do you mean?" Farrel leaned back and rested his arms on his legs.

"Earth Authority released a statement saying that the body they found was that of an off worlder with no DNA record on Earth." Les frowned and nodded.

"That sounds plausible," Les said. Farrel clasped his hands.

"The media isn't buying it, Les. They think you're dead, that the victim was you." This brought an astonished look to Les.

"This could work to your advantage," Farrel continued. "If Garnet is convinced you're dead, he'll feel he can move openly. This might draw him out." Les was considering his words and felt he was correct. But he didn't think Garnet would give himself away until he was certain, Les thought.

"We'll just have to wait and see what happens," Les said. "Can you have somebody keep an eye on Ruby's Place? If Garnet wants to leave, he'll have her lease him a ship."Farrel nodded. Les began to consider what he could do if Garnet was seen. But Les would have to move cautiously on this world. He had restrictions he had to abide by.

Angel came into Drydon's office with a slight smile. Drydon was at his desk and turned an expectant look to her. She stopped in front of the desk and rubbed her cheek.

"Well?" he asked. She got a smug look.

"It's working, Chief. The media's not buying it. They think there's a cover-up to keep the public from knowing it was a revenge murder against Les." An enlightened look came to Drydon.

"That's good, Corey. Let them believe what they want to. It might work to our advantage, and get Garnet out into the open." Angel was hoping for the same results.

"Let's hope we're right, Chief," she said. "We don't say anything more and let the media carry their rumor, and hope Garnet believes it." Drydon nodded.

"That's the way to let it proceed," he agreed. "And hope Camden's ready to move."

She smiled and nodded.

"I would bet he's been ready to move since this story broke," Angel said.

"Damnit, Jovan!" Ruby exclaimed, in a loud, frustrated tone. "Camden is dead. Get that idea and hold onto it." He stood staring at her with a blank look. She took hold of his hand. Pulled him to the sofa, and sat him down. Ruby sat down beside him and he turned his face to her.

"It's over, Jovan. You're in the clear to go wherever you want." His expression slowly became one of understanding as he regarded her for a long, silent moment.

"I want you to get me a ship, Ruby. I've got things to do, places to go, and people to see." She gave him a quick kiss and hurried from the room.

The audvid sounded and Les pressed the comlink. Farrel regarded him with a pleased look.

"You were right about Garnet being here, Les. A little over an hour ago, Ruby chartered a small ship. Looks like Garnet is planning on leaving." Les felt no elation at the news, only the thought that once again he was going to be in pursuit of a dangerous felon.

"Can you have the field get my ship ready?" Les asked. Farrel smiled.

"Already done," Farrel replied. "You can leave whenever you want." Les nodded.

"Thanks, Farrel. I've got to say goodby to Susan."

"She's on her way to your apartment," Farrel said. "She doesn't know what I just told you. I didn't learn about it until after she had left, and I didn't have the heart to tell her.

She cares a lot for you, Les." Les now had something to do he would have preferred to avoid.

"I'll tell her, Farrel. And thanks again for your help." He broke contact and turned to the door as the chime sounded.

Susan got a disappointed look when Les told her what Farrel had related to him.

"I'm going after Garnet as soon as I know he's left." She was suddenly embracing and kissing him. She stepped back with tears spilling from her eyes.

"It's dangerous going after Garnet, Les. But I know you have to do it. So all I can say is, good luck and be damn careful." He took her hand and patted it. What a difference between this woman and Eilene. He couldn't help but make the comparison, just as he haddone with Angel.

"I intend to do just that. I'm not going to let him get the better of me again." He took her hand and they left the apartment.

Les didn't care to admit it, but it felt good to be back on the ship with something to occupy his time. He had a gut feeling Garnet was headed for Varian Four, and Angel. He hoped Garnet didn't 'know she was on Earth and safe. For the present, Les had to concentrate on trying to out think him. He was in no mood for any of Garnet's 'surprises.Les hoped to pull off some surprises of his own. He knew he still had to proceed with caution, as Garnet might be even more dangerous than previously.

Garnet sat in the pilot's seat lost in thought with an uneasy feeling. He wasn't as certain as Ruby that Camden was dead. It was an odd feeling that kept him from believing the marshal was dead. He couldn't explain it, but felt it was correct. He was used to seeing the body of his victim. Was not seeing Camden's body his cause for unease? There had to be someway he could make certain that body was Camden. But how? He was working through scenarios that might verify his death that were undeniable. But Garnet could come up with no viable way to do so. Until he had indisputable evidence that Camden was dead, he was going to have to assume he was alive, for his own safety.

If he could only get Corey, Garnet felt that would draw Camden out – if he was alive.

"Damnit!" he exclaimed, angrily. "He is alive. I know he's alive." He felt that was the only sure way to be certain. He also knew she wasn't on Varian Four, had no idea where she was, but knew she would have to return. He would have to be careful in trying to find out where she was. Once he knew that, he would make his move to get her and find out if Camden was dead. He had to be certain! Garnet felt he had no other alternative.

"I'm worried about you, Corey," Drydon said. "Garnet must know you're not on Varian Four, and he'll do everything he can to find you." Angel regarded him with a perplexed look.

"Why would he do that?" she asked. Drydon spread his hands on the desk.

"He may not accept the fact that Camden is dead," he replied. "He probably believes that if he can get his hands on you, he can discover the truth. I'm going to have your apartment put under round the clock surveillance to be on the safe side. After all, he was able to get word to people here to kill Camden. He might do the same to find out if you're here, and take you." Angel shook her head.

"But everyone believes Les is dead," she said. "Why wouldn't Garnet?" Drydon got a pronounced frown.

"Garnet's a predator, Corey. And if he has any uncertainty, he'll go with his survival instinct until he's sure he's safe." She felt Drydon was over reacting.

"But there's no way he can show his face here," Angel said. "He would be arrested immediately, if he dared to come here." Drydon nodded.

"That may be so," he said. "But it doesn't rule out the possibility of him having some of his people kidnap and deliver you to him." Angel's shoulders slumped. She knew Drydon could be right.

"I don't think anything like that will happen, Chief. After all, very few people know I'm here. And none of his people know what I look like." Again, Drydon nodded.

"True, Corey. But I'm going to take the safe way rather than risk your abduction." She nodded, accepting his reason, even though she felt it was wrong.

After cautiously contacting some of his informants, Les felt certain Garnet was aware that Angel wasn't on Varian Four, and that he had no idea where she was. That was good news. But where was Garnet? He wasn't killing people, and that left Les more or less in the dark as to where he might be. But, he thought, I've got to think like Garnet if I want to figure out where he is.

"All right, start thinking like Garnet," he said, prodding himself. Les had a sudden hunch Garnet would go to Varian Four and wait for Angel to return. On the other hand, he would have a problem if he showed up in the city. How many people were there Garnet could count on to get her and take her to him?

"She's got to remain on Earth for her own safety," Les said, to himself. "How can I tell her without giving myself away?" He sat cupping his chin, thinking. Les concluded that the rangers would be the safest way to get a message to Drydon, and make certain Angel remained where she was. He turned the pilot's seat and worked out a course for the nearest ranger installation.

13

For a few days, Garnet just wandered through space trying to work out how he was so certain that Camden was still alive. It was uppermost in his mind. He couldn't understand how he could ignore the evidence for a vague feeling he couldn't pin down. He began to think that, just maybe, he was losing his grip on reality.

"No! It isn't anything like that," he said, aloud. "Then what the hell can it be?" He finally forced himself to start thinking about Varian Four and Angel.

Garnet was determined to get his hands on that woman and prove to himself, and everyone else, he was right about Camden not being dead. But, he realized, it was such a vague plan. Garnet had no idea of when she might return, or even if his people could successfully grab her. They're knowing he was on the loose, she could have very tight security around her. How long should he wait? He knew he couldn't very well stay there for long with nothing to do.

Then he began to wonder where Camden might be – if he was alive. It was apparent he wasn't on Earth as no one had seen him for sometime. Why hadn't he come to Casin Three? Surely, Garnet reasoned, he would have a strong suspicion that he would be with Ruby. But he hadn't showed up there either. He was at a loss; the evidence said that Camden had been murdered on Earth. He had made the request that he be murdered. It seemed his man had done the job. But Garnet just couldn't get rid of the indistinct feeling that Camden was alive. He knew it would plague his mind until he knew for certain one way or the other. Camden was dead or he wasn't.

"He isn't dead," Garnet said, in a cold tone.

Susan lay in a troubled sleep. She began rolling from side to side, her arms flaying wildly. She and Les was approaching a dark rundown house where they suspected Garnet was hiding out in. They saw no light coming from it. The wooden steps creaked and moaned as they went up on the porch. Les reached out and pressed the door release. It swung open with a rasping sound on rusty hinges. Cautiously, Les stepped inside, followed by her.

Both had taken their weapons from their holsters. Susan was sweating and tense as they moved further in. It was hard to see anything in the dark. They stopped when they heard a slight sound coming from a closed door. They moved to it silently. Les pressed the release, the door opened slowly, and there was a sudden flash that hit Les in the chest and he dropped to the floor. Susan up stifling a scream. She was sweating and her heart racing, but she quickly realized it had only been a dream.

As Les headed for the ranger outpost, his thoughts were evenly moved from Angel to Garnet. He wished he could quickly take Garnet into custody so he could be with Angel on Varian Four. But he was realistic enough to know that taking him quickly was only a pipe dream. He still felt Garnet was heading for Varian Four, but how long would he remain there? Les had no idea. Would he stay for awhile, contact his people in the city, then head back to Casin Three? Les wished he had better insight into Garnet's thinking. If he believed Les was dead, why was he trying to get Angel? He had more questions than answers.

Les glanced at the monitor and saw his destination. He turned the pilot's seat and began preparing to land.

"This is special agent Les Camden, Pi One Eight Delta, request permission to land." A sultry female voice replied.

"Pi One Eight Delta, permission granted. Use pad Beta Seven.

"Thanks." Les began taking the ship off automatic and turned it down into the atmosphere.

Ruby had hired a young man named Mitch as a personal assistant. He would handle everything relating to the bar and leave her free to keep the books up to date daily. She was worried about Jovan. He hadn't seemed himself since his escape, and it had become much more apparent after they heard that the marshal had been murdered on Earth. Ruby still felt he harbored the illusion that Camden was still alive, and this was distracting him from what he wanted to be doing. She knew there was no more she could do to get him to face reality.

She went to the keypad and punched in the code. A tray slid from the wall and she picked up the glass. Ruby began pacing, sipping at the drink, and wondering where Jovan had went. She hoped he hadn't gone to Varian Four to try and get that woman. Having her wouldn't bring Camden back from the grave, but might prove to be a lot of trouble for him. The way Jovan had been acting made her feel completely helpless in trying to help him.

"He's a stubborn son of a bitch!" she exclaimed, aloud. But Ruby knew she would do anything she could to help him.

Angel was passing a window in her apartment when she saw a vehicle park across the street. What got her curiosity up was that no one got out. She stepped past the window, leaned against the wall, and peeked out. She knew it wasn't from the security people, and it gave Angel a chill. Had Drydon been right after all? Could whoever was in that vehicle be watching her apartment for Garnet? On the other hand, it could be nothing. She couldn't decide which, but made up her mind to watch for it tomorrow afternoon.

The next morning, Angel told Drydon about the vehicle. He became alarmed.

"I'm going to put extra security around your apartment, Corey, just in case," he said.

"If it turns out to be nothing –" he shrugged. "Well, no harm done." Angel wasn't ready to believe that Garnet had somehow found out where she was and was having her watched.

"I don't see how Garnet could know I'm here, Chief," she said. "Besides, as I said, none of his people would know what I look like." Drydon rubbed his lip in a nervous manner.

"Nevertheless, Corey, I'm not willing to risk it being a real threat. Camden would probably do the same."

"And if that vehicle doesn't return today?" Drydon spread his hands.

"As I said, no harm done."

"Have you heard anything from Les?" Angel asked. Drydon shook his head.

"The last I heard was from Farrel informing me that Camden was finally on Garnet's tail. But I wish we would hear from him. I never believed that no news was good news."Angel agreed with that.

"We'll hear from him when he has something to report, I guess," she said.

Later that afternoon, Angel saw the same vehicle, from the previous day, park across the street. Knowing that Drydon had assigned extra security to the area, it made her feel a bit uncomfortable. She went ahead and began fixing dinner. The audvid unit sounded and Angel went and pressed the comlink. She saw Drydon with a pleased look.

"No need for you to worry about that vehicle, Corey. It's only a private investigator trying to spot a cheating husband." His words made her a little less anxious. It had turned out to be nothing, as she had earlier thought.

"I'm glad to hear that, Chief. It would be very unsettling if Garnet's people found out where I lived." He could tell from her tone that she was still on edge.

"Rest easy, Corey. We've got you covered." The screen went dark and she took her finger from the comlink.

Garnet sat in the plush booth across from a heavily muscled man with brown hair and blue eyes. He had stopped on this world because he felt the need to talk with someone.

"What's the matter, Jovan? I thought you would be overjoyed at the death of the marshal." Garnet took a drink from his glass and glanced around the bar. There were few people here, and none close enough to overhear their conversation. He looked back at the man.

"Weisler, I'm convinced Camden is still alive. Where he might be, or what he might be doing, I have no idea." Weisler got a surprised look.

"What about the evidence, Jovan?" Garnet narrowed his eyes and lowered his voice.

"It's all rigged. A cover story for Camden. I never know where I might run into him." Weisler shook his head.

"Christ, Jovan! How did you ever come to such a conclusion?" Garnet took a drink and decided to tell him.

"Did you ever have the feeling that something was true when everything pointed to it being not true?" Weisler got a confused look and shook his head.

"That's a bad way to explain it, I know," Garnet said, defensively. "But I can feel

Camden is alive." Weisler puckered his lips and tilted his head.

"Maybe you're right, Jovan. Thinking it over, the evidence does look a bit contrived.

But why wouldn't he be hot on your tail?" Garnet shrugged and took a drink.

"I wish I knew. All I can come up with is, that there's some sort of elaborate plan afoot to take me into custody." Weisler frowned and lifted his glass.

"Have any of your people come up with anything?" Garnet shook his head and finished his drink.

"Well what can you do?" Garnet thought for a moment before replying.

"Just keep moving. I'm not going to stay any place long enough to be recognized and give him a clue as to where I might be."

"In that case, let me buy you another drink before you leave, Jovan."

[143]

As soon as Les cut the ship's power, he loosened the straps, and headed for the hatch.

When it opened, he saw a ranger officer waiting for him. As he came down the ramp, the officer stepped forward.

"I'm to escort you to the office of Commander Beltram, sir." Les gave him a nod.

"Let's go," Les said.

The office was modern and occupied by a tall, solid built Afro-American with hair graying at the temples. He stood when Les was shown in. As he approached the desk, Beltram extended his hand and they shook.

"Mr. Camden," Beltram said, in a strong baritone voice. "I've been looking forward to meeting the man who took the notorious Garnet down." He waved Les to a chair. Les sat down and got right to business.

"I would like to use the rangers' communication to get a message to Chief Drydon and Angelena Corey. The message is for her to stay discrete, and remain on Earth, for her own safety." Beltram got a puzzled look.

"Corey was with me when I nailed Garnet," Les explained. "I believe he's looking for her so he can prove that I'm alive." Beltram got a confident look and nodded.

"I'll have your message sent at once. By the way, would you do me the honor of dinning with me?" Les smiled.

"After what I've been eating on the ship, I would be more than glad to join you."

Beltram laughed.

"You must tell me about Garnet," Beltram said. "I done a thesis on criminal minds to get my commission. But that was long before Garnet showed up in public."

"I'll tell you what I know," Les said. "But he seems to have undergone a radical psychological change. I can't be certain if the change is temporary or permanent."

"I understand," Beltram said. "But just learning something about him is of interest for me."

Les was glad to have a meal that wasn't a heated ration that passed for a meal on the ship. The food was delicious and enjoyable. As they ate, Les told Beltram everything he had learned, and heard, about Garnet.

"I've extensively studied his criminal record," Les said. "But I could find nothing that would have changed a first class chemist and teacher into a coldblooded killer. It's a blank I would certainly like to fill in."

"Perhaps you should look at his earlier record," Beltram suggested. "The clue might be there." Les nodded as he considered the suggestion.

"Next time I get the chance, I'll do that." Beltram smiled.

"If not, one could conjecture about his change and never arrive at a solution.

Ruby sat at a corner table holding her drink and listening to the din of conversations. As she lifted her glass, she saw an acquaintance of her's come through the door. Alvea looked around, saw her, and came toward her table.

"I need to speak with you , Ruby." She got a chill at her tone and waved her to a chair facing her. She sat down and regarded Ruby in silence for a moment.

"Has Jovan contacted you lately?" he asked. Ruby shook her head.

"Not a word in weeks, Alvea. Why?" She glanced around and saw they were isolated enough so that no one could hear what would be said.

"I've been hearing from people who know him, Ruby." She stiffened at her grim tone.

"What have they been telling you?" she asked, apprehensively.

"That he's a wanderer, going to different planets like he's lost, and not staying very long on at any one place." She got a frustrated look as she inhaled.

"Damn!" Ruby exclaimed, harshly. "Why can't he accept the fact that the marshal is dead?" Alvea's eyes widened as she got a surprised look.

"Is that what's wrong with him?" she asked. Ruby nodded.

"He contacted someone on Earth to take him out. I don't know why, but after it was done, Jovan wouldn't believe it." Alvea got a puzzled look.

"Some of those I've spoken to," she said. "Heard Jovan talking like he might run into the marshal at any time. They just listened, and kept their mouths shut." Ruby quickly made up her mind.

"If only there was some way to get a message to him. If so, I would ask him to come back to me." Alvea shook her head.

"Nobody ever knows where he's going," he said. "He just shows up where no one is expecting him." She gave Ruby an odd look.

"Ruby, you know I'm a friend of Jovan's. But I have to put it to you this way. Do you think his mind is functioning normally?" Ruby laughed.

"He hasn't acted normal since the news of the marshal's death came out," she replied.

"I've never known him to so stubbornly refuse to accept the facts, but that's exactly what he's doing." Alvea nodded.

"Anyway, Ruby, I'll try and get your message out quickly," Morton said. "Maybe we'll get lucky and will get to Jovan." She slowly shook her head.

"I doubt it will do any good," she said. Alvea stood, keeping her eyes on Ruby.

"It never hurts to try, Ruby." she turned and walked to the door. Ruby watched her back until he went out. Ruby got a bitter frown and took a drink.

"Nothing is going to change that stubborn son of a bitch's mind," she mumbled.

14

Garnet approached Varian Four cautiously, coming down on the night side of the planet then circling to the other side. He put his ship down close to where Camden had taken his hand off. He would wait for Corey to return, have a couple of men grab her and bring her to him. At least, he hoped for the opportunity to do that. He would then wait and see if Camden showed up to save her again. If he didn't show up within a week, Garnet could feel certain he was dead. Although he still strongly felt he was alive. His immediate task was to set up his base and make radio contact with his main man in the city. Garnet had sent word ahead that he would make contact by radio, as he didn't dare show up in the city. He wasn't aware of his now anomalous behavior, and thought, had become.

He set up his camp opposite the side Camden had fired from, just about where he had been surprised. As light began spreading across the sky, he took a radio from his pack and lifted it to his face.

"Stuart, this is Jovan." A burst of static and a voice came through clearly.

"I've been expecting to hear from you. Good to hear your voice again, Jovan." Garnet was impatient.

"Has she returned yet?" he snapped.

"No. I haven't been able to find out where she went either. What do you want me to do?"

"Wait until she returns. When you get the chance, grab her and bring her to me. You can find me by keeping your radio open on this frequency."

"Okay. Be seeing you, Jovan." He lowered the radio, stuck it in his pack, and took out a power bar. Garnet took a bite and sat down, wondering how long he would have to wait.

"What did you want to see me about, Chief?" Angel asked, coming into Drydon's office. He had called her after getting Les' message from the ranger commander.

"A message from Camden came to me through the rangers," he replied. "He wants you to remain here and out of sight. Garnet knows you're not on Varian Four, but he also doesn't yet know where you are." She regarded him with a surprised look.

"I have no plans to return to Varian Four any time soon," she said. "If you can get a message to Les, tell him not to worry." Drydon nodded.

"I'll see what I can do," Drydon said, and regarded her with a concerned look. "We both want you to be safe, Corey." She smiled and nodded.

"I don't think I could be safer anywhere else, Chief."

Les sat in the pilot's seat thinking about what the ranger commander had inquired about.

"Assuming Garnet is on Varian Four," Commander Beltram had asked. "How do you intend apprehending him?" Les was now considering that question. Easier said than done, he thought. He knew he would be governed by whatever circumstances he found. He would just have to improvise, use no set plan. It was going to be extremely dangerous, as he well knew. Garnet was thirsting for revenge against him. Les inhaled deeply.

"I only wish I had some idea of what to do," Les said, to himself, as he glanced over the instrument panel. He was only hours from Varian Four, and his first task would be to locate Garnet without giving himself away. The rangers had acquired, and given him, the frequency codes of Garnet's ship so he could use long range sensors to track it. Then Les would land, make his way to the ship, and observe what Garnet was up to. He knew hewould have to be very cautious, and alert to the fact that there might be others with Garnet. Going after him alone was dangerous enough, but Les knew that if three or more men were with him, he wouldn't stand a chance. One man, Les decided he would take the risk. He just didn't know for sure how he would go about it. Les also knew that he would have to take any opportunity that offered itself, if he was to succeed.

Garnet paced, uncertain and insecure, but he wouldn't admit the latter to himself. He hoped Camden was dead so he could have peace of mind. All he could do was wait until he was absolutely certain that the marshal was dead. But he still felt Camden was alive, and that he would never get real proof of his death until he stood over his body. In the meantime, he couldn't afford to let down his defense. Garnet decided to contact Stuart and see if there was any progress finding out where Corey was. She was, he felt, the only chance he had for solid proof that Camden was no longer around to dog him relentlessly.

He picked up the radio and lifted it to his face.

"Stuart? Stuart, are you there?"

"I'm here, Jovan."

"What have you found out about Corey?" The pause was a bit longer than Garnet felt comfortable with.

"No one seems to know where she went, or when she might return. If you want my opinion, Jovan, she followed Camden to Earth. That's the only thing that makes sense." Garnet's brow furrowed as he got a confused look.

"I never thought of that. I'll have to get word to my people on Earth and see what they can find out."

"I think that's your best chance, Jovan. You might get lucky there. Just keep me informed, so if someone does get her I can bring her to you after she's delivered."

Les brought the ship in low and slow, listening to the sensor beep more loudly. He watched the surface on the monitor and it suddenly dawned on him that Garnet had returned to the place where he had lost his hand. This certainly spiked Les' curiosity. He wondered what Garnet was trying to prove by returning to this place. He would be able to get close to him after dark. Right now, he had to find a concealed place to land.

As twilight fell, Les left the ship and headed for where he felt Garnet was. He was still puzzled as to why he had returned to where he had been taken down. It seemed to Les that maybe his time incarcerated had altered his thinking. He decided that maybe he should review Garnet's last psych file.

It was déjà vu for Les as he climbed the rock face he had scaled when he had saved Angel, and took Garnet out of circulation. In the deepening twilight, he peered over the edge and saw Garnet, standing beside an electric lantern, holding a radio to his face. He paced back and forth making a dark shadow on the ground that moved with his every step.

"Now listen, Stuart, get word to Frazier. I have no other way to get word to Earth. If anyone can find out if Corey's on Earth, he can. If she is there, I want her grabbed and brought here." It was now becoming clear to Les what Garnet was up to. He couldn't bring himself to believe Les was dead, and planned to get Angel here to draw him out. Garnet wanted his revenge in the same place he had suffered his humiliation.

"So that's what he's up to," Les mumbled. "Well he's put himself in his own prison this time." Les decided to watch and see what developed. He would contact the rangers and have them get word to Drydon and Angel that he had been right about where Garnet had gone. But he had to emphasize that Angel had to be guarded against any move to grab her.

As Les slipped away, he decided to watch Garnet over the next few days and see what he could find out about his mental state. He hurried back to the ship, powered up the communication system, switched to the secure ranger frequency, and began sending his warning to Angel and Drydon.

After shutting down the ship's main power, Les decided all he could do now was get some rest. He sat thinking about Garnet, wondering how he might have changed during his time on Forten. Les concluded he would have to watch him closely, if he wanted to know how Garnet's thinking had been altered – if it had. Now he would just get some sleep.

15

The following day, Les was able to determine that Garnet was in touch with more than one person in the city, but was telling no one where he was. Some of his actions began to puzzle Les, until he correctly deduced that Garnet wasn't accepting, as fact, his death. This was causing him a lot of mental stress. Until he knew for certain Les was dead, he wasn't taking any chance of letting his guard down. That's not the way to get revenge, Les thought. After watching for awhile, Les shook his head and went back to his ship to get something to eat.

As he ate, he considered how he might take Garnet quickly into custody. This time he wouldn't have to worry about someone else getting killed, and that helped him to concentrate on the job at hand. But Les couldn't help but see Garnet struggle with his mental turmoil, and that gave him some satisfaction. At least, he was now feeling what a lot of his victims probably experienced before he took their lives.

Returning to his spot on the ridge, Les found Garnet was nowhere to be seen, and all his gear was gone. He felt an empty feeling in his stomach as he wondered where Garnet had gone. He slid down, hurried back to his ship, and quickly powered up the sensor. It was silent. Garnet had taken off leaving Les in the dark as to where he might have gone. Les silently swore at his lack of action against Garnet. He should have taken him when he had the advantage, now it was too late. But where had he gone?

Once in space, Garnet was at a loss. He couldn't go back to Ruby's, as it would seem he was running from a ghost, and that wouldn't do his reputation any good. Where was he to go? As Garnet thought about it, he could decide on only one place. He turned the pilot's seat and set a return course to Varian Four. He was consumed by the obsession that Camden was still alive. He could feel it, and it wasn't something he could ignore.

Les sat frustrated, wondering what he could do, when the sensor began to pick up the signal from Garnet's' ship, and it was growing louder. Les leaned forward and listened with a slight smile.

"Nowhere to run, Garnet?" Les asked, as the signal increased in volume. Les felt he was returning because this was the only place he had a chance to draw him out, and find out if he was alive. But Les was wary enough, and knew what he needed to know, to keep the psychological pressure on Garnet. Les had to plan some sort of action against him; he couldn't put it off any longer. He couldn't just sit on his ass and do nothing. He decided that he would have to be certain of Garnet's state of mind before he could attempt to take him into custody.

Garnet was in a quandary. He could run, but had no place to run to, or he could just wait and hope someone would bring him the answer he needed. It was pressing on his mind that he had no freedom of action. It was a difficult idea to accept that he couldn't do as he pleased – and it might be caused by a ghost. Yet he felt he had to be certain that Camden was dead, even though his instinct told him he was alive. He sat on a rock trying to make up his mind as to what he could do. He knew he was the cause of his problem, at not believing the marshal was dead, but was reluctant to admit it to himself. He just couldn't take the chance that his old adversary was alive and looking for him. What he didn't know was that Les was watching him at that very moment.

Garnet could not shake the feeling that anyone who could take him down would die so easily as the corpse that had been found on Earth. It couldn't be Camden. It couldn't! He then began to think that maybe he just didn't want Camden dead – that he was wishfully thinking that because he wanted to kill Camden, not leave it to somebody else. His confusion grew as he let his mind slide into turmoil over a question he couldn't answer.

As Les secretly watched Garnet, he felt no satisfaction seeing him torn mentally, and this in turn, began showing up in his physical appearance. His uncertainty showed plainly on his face. But he felt a bit pleased to see him suffering through the anguish he had caused so many of his victims. Yet Les had to come up with a viable plan to take him into custody. The idea of just confronting him wasn't something Les felt he was prepared to do. It was apparent that Garnet was desperate, and there was no telling what he might do. So Les came down on the side of caution. Les was worried that if he confronted Garnet, in his present state of mind, he might think he was a ghost showing up where he had been bested and turn the weapon on himself. Les knew he had to be careful how he would go after him. He decided to get his observations to Drydon, through the rangers, and request an updated psych file on Garnet.

Angel had been working as Drydon's assistant, and enjoying the diversion. When she came into his office, he looked up from the paper he held.

"Got a report from Camden," Drydon said. "He sent it along with a request for an update on Garnet's psych file." She stepped beside him, read over the paper, glanced at him and shook her head.

"People like Garnet don't change their profile," Angel said. "He's just unwilling to believe what he wants to accept as the truth." Drydon raised an eyebrow.

"I believe you're right, Corey. But Camden seems to think Garnet's changed, and he's on the spot observing the suspect." She folded her arms and frowned.

"He should be told to take Garnet as his old self," she said. "That's the only way he'll be able to take him down." Drydon nodded and put the paper on the desk.

"I'll get the word to him as soon as possible," he said, standing, and walking from the office. Angel turned and watched him leave. She raised her hand and rubbed her cheek.

She got a worried look as she considered that Les was wrong in thinking Garnet had changed. That idea could prove fatal for him.

Les heard the shouting before he got to the top of the ridge. Peeking over, he saw a man and woman, with her hands tied behind her, facing an outraged Garnet.

"You dumb son of a bitch!" Garnet shouted. "This isn't Corey. Where the hell did you find her?" The man's face was red, his expression fearful, and Les could tell he was trying his best to keep his temper under control.

"In the city," the man replied, keeping his voice level. "She fit the description you gave me, and I thought she was the one you wanted." Garnet jerked an arm around in a frustrated gesture.

"What do you want me to do with her?" the man asked. Garnet turned a cold look on him.

"She can't be allowed to return to the city," Garnet said. "She can tell the authorities where I am."

"So what do you want me to do with her?" Garnet regarded him with narrowed eyes, nodded, pulled his weapon and killed them both. Les ducked and realized he didn't need an update on Garnet; he was still the same coldblooded killer he had taken down almost a year ago. Now his inaction had cost two more lives. He was going to have to make a move on Garnet before anyone else was murdered by him.

Les lay against the rock ridge wondering how he should move on Garnet. He knew his lack of action had cost two people their lives, and he was determined not to let anyone else die because of his inaction. He pushed himself away from the rock and slid down tothe base, got to his feet, and moved around the ridge. Les' wariness took time before he stopped at the side of the opening and took a quick peek in. He saw the bodies, but not Garnet. He drew his weapon and began a slow movement into the bowl-shaped interior.

Les was just about inside when he stopped and took a quick look around. Garnet was gone. He moved quickly to the bodies and checked to make sure they weren't still alive. As he stood, he silently cursed at taking so much time to get here. Finding both dead, Les now had to consider where Garnet had went. There was only one place he could have gone – his ship. Les holstered his weapon and hurried from the bodies heading for his ship.

Reaching the ship, Les activated the hatch, went on board, and powered up the sensor. He turned to the frequency of Garnet's ship. He heard the signal growing weaker. He hurried back to the hatch, closed it, went back to the flight deck and strapped himself in. Les hoped he had the time to get close enough to Garnet's ship to be able to follow him without being picked up. Garnet was still just as frustrating as before. He pressed the engine start switch and was pushed down in the seat as the ship rose from the surface

In space, Garnet still knew he had no place to go. He had to devise someway to get to Earth and find Corey. He felt doing it himself was the only way he could be certain he had who he wanted. But how could he do it? Garnet knew he was wanted, and that all law enforcement officers would be looking for him. He sat thinking until he recalled a doctor whom could alter one's looks. A change of face was just what he needed. Garnet quickly adjusted the ship's course. That would give him the advantage he needed to get Corey and prove that Camden was alive. He felt this was his only chance, and he was determined to take it. This was going to prove him right.

Garnet learned the doctor's home address and decided it would be safer to visit him after dark. He waited in his ship, planning what he would do once he was on Earth, until time to head for the doctor's residence. He cautiously made his way along dark streets, avoiding any street an officer might be patrolling.

Soon he stood before the doctor's house and carefully worked out how he would convince the doctor to do what he needed done. And Garnet knew there was only one way to convince him. He stepped to the door, hesitated, then pressed the door chime. The door opened and Garnet faced a short, thin man with gray hair and dull brown eyes covered with rimless glasses. Garnet smiled.

"I require your service, Doctor, and I can pay very well. I need to alter my looks. I've been told you can do this without much trouble." The doctor stepped to the door and looked around beyond Garnet, turned his face to him and nodded. Garnet stepped through the door and the doctor closed it.

"Follow me," the doctor said, and led off with Garnet walking behind him.

As they entered an office, Garnet came up with his reason for a face change.

"I have family on Earth and I want to surprise them when I return." The doctor glanced at him and nodded, with an expression that said he wasn't interested in his motive. He motioned Garnet to a chair and took a seat facing him.

"I'll explain the procedure," the doctor said. "Now the change will only last for about thirty days, then your face will gradually return." Garnet nodded.

"That will do just fine, Doctor." The doctor took a looseleaf notebook from his desk and opened it. Pointing to the page, he explained the operation.

"A metal mask will nano-mold your face into its shape. Your facial molecules will hold that shape for about twenty-three days, then your natural face will begin to return to its normal state." Garnet listened with interest.

"I have a number of masks you can choose from." Garnet nodded, feeling impatient.

"Then let's get on with it, Doctor."

He followed the doctor to a room that contained a glass case that held six masks.

Garnet looked at them, selected one, and knew this was Arthur Green. Using that name was another chance to draw Camden out. They went to another room where the doctor began prepping him for the face change. He had Garnet lay down on a surgical table, slipped the mask over his face, and connected the wires.

Through the rangers, Les sent word to Angel and Drydon that he had lost Garnet's trail. He couldn't be certain, but there was a chance Garnet might try to get to Earth and search for Angel. If anything came through, that even remotely related to Garnet, to let him know and he would return. Until then, Les would try to pick up Garnet's trail again.

"Well, Corey," Drydon said. "What do you think about this communication from Camden?" Angel cupped her chin and thought for a moment.

"If Les thinks Garnet might try to come to Earth," she replied. "I think we should take it seriously." Drydon frowned.

"But all law enforcement officers know him by sight. How could he possibly get by them without being recognized?" That had Angel baffled, but she felt it was imperative they follow Les' hunch.

"I don't think he would risk coming here in his own ship," she said. "So I suggest we have the names of all passengers coming in on transports, be listed, recorded, and brought to us." Drydon nodded.

"I'll contact the officials who can do that," he said. "But I'm still puzzled as to what we'll be looking for when Garnet is so familiar?" It quickly occurred to Angel what

Garnet might be trying.

"The name Arthur Green," she said. "It was the alias he used when he came to Varian Four. He's probably going to use it to try and draw Les out, if he can't get his hands on me." Drydon raised an eyebrow.

"You really think Garnet still believes Camden is alive?" Angel nodded.

"Apparently Garnet's a hard one to convince of anything he feels couldn't have happened. Until he's assured of Les' death, he'll continue to believe he's alive."

"We'll keep a sharp eye out for that name," Drydon said."But knowing what he looks like, we'll get him when he steps off the ship."

As the ship cruised on autopilot, Les sat in the pilot's seat looking lost. He hadn't gotten a clue as to where Garnet had been in the past two weeks. His frustration was evident in his expression. The only thing he was certain of was his gut feeling that Garnet had gone to Earth. It was the only logical place for him to go. It was the only probable place for Angel to be. But how could he do it without being taken into custody? That's what had Les stumped. But he felt certain that Garnet had found some way to get on Earth without being taken into custody.

16

Garnet had a surge of anxiety as he stood at the top of the transport ramp, but he kept a calm, neutral expression. He looked down and saw the immigration officer checking IDs as the passengers filed past. He knew every law enforcement officer would know his face, but that wasn't the face he was wearing, and it would keep for the next seventeen days. More than enough time, he hoped, to get what he came here for. He started down the ramp following the line of passengers and holding his forged identity card. When he came to the immigration officer, he handed over his card, watched as the officer examined it, and handed it back without comment. Garnet was on Earth, free, and determined to get his hands on Angel, or indisputable proof that Camden was dead.

He was wary of taking a chance of contacting anyone he knew. He decided to check into a trivial hotel in the rundown section of the city. But there was one person he knew he could count on, and felt he might need her help. He would have to do this mostly on his own, and felt confident he could accomplish what he had come here to do. Garnet smiled as he began planning how he was going to get Corey. He would have to keep a discrete watch on the Marshal HQ and see if she came out. He would then follow her to where she was living, wait until after dark, and grab her. He knew it wouldn't be easy to get her off the planet, but he had to take her to Varian Four and wait for Camden to show himself by coming after her. But what if he was dead? Garnet had to take that possibility into his plan, even if he didn't believe it. He wasn't certain what he would do if it turned out to be true. It gave him a disconcerting feeling.

Angel sat in the office viewing the security discs as passengers debarked from the transports. She was on the fifth disc when she saw a man that matched the name of Arthur Green. She quickly pressed the pause and studied his face. It wasn't Garnet, but Arthur Green was the name he had used on Varian Four. A coincidence? Angel reversed the disc and watched as he came down the ramp. She then felt certain this was Garnet. It wasn't his face, but the walk and his build certainly matched Garnet's. When she put it on pause again, she pressed for a printout of the face.

Drydon compared the printout Angel had brought him with a photo of Garnet. He glanced at her and shook his head.

"I see no resemblance to Garnet," Drydon said. Angel knew she had to put forth her belief and try to convince him to believe her.

"Sir, I was with Garnet for sometime. I know the face isn't his, but the build and walk definitely are. No two people walk alike. I don't know how his face was changed, but I'm certain that's Garnet." Drydon regarded her with a raised eyebrow at how emphatic she was.

"I respect your power of observation, Corey, but how in the hell could Garnet have altered his face?" That was what perplexed her the most.

"I'm not certain, sir. But with the new molecular altering units floating around, it's possible Garnet was able to find someone, a doctor, who would perform such an operation – for a price." Drydon nodded.

"Also, sir, as I told you, Arthur Green was the name he used on Varian Four."

"All right, Corey," Drydon said, nodding. "I'll have a tail put on this Arthur Green just to see where he goes."

"Thank you, sir. I appreciate the gesture." Angel turned to go when Drydon stood.

"You're really certain this person is Garnet?" he asked. She turned her face to him and nodded.

"Yes, sir, I am. And I don't want to become his hostage again. It's his unpredictability that frightens me. You can never tell when he just might kill you for the fun of it."

Drydon got a stunned look.

"Well rest easy, Corey. We've got you covered." She gave him a nod, turned, and left the office.

In the early afternoon, the receptionist came in and handed Drydon a PDA. As he read, he suddenly felt a bit more respect for Angel. He looked up from the PDA and regarded the receptionist.

"Are you certain this is correct?" he asked. She nodded.

"Yes, sir. After Arthur Green left the port authority building, he just vanished. He never showed up at the address on the transport's list. Of course, you must remember he landed two days ago and could be anywhere now." Drydon got a worried look as he handed the PDA back to her.

"Inform the men watching Corey to keep a very close eye on her apartment. It appears that Garnet has found a way to return to Earth without being identified."

"Yes, sir," she said, and hurried from the office. Drydon was now concerned about Angel's safety. But all he could do was alert the men on the scene. He rubbed his cheek nervously, feeling a bit helpless in this unanticipated situation.

Garnet had been careful to cover his tracks and not contact anyone he knew. This was, hopefully, to be a solo mission. He had been keeping a discrete watch on the Marshals HQ building, hoping to see Corey or Camden emerge. But in the week he had done do, he had seen neither of them. He was beginning to feel that maybe Camden was dead and Corey some place else.

The next day, Garnet was late getting to the building. But he was in time to see an unmarked vehicle pull up at the entrance and Corey come out and get in. He couldn't follow the vehicle on foot, and that meant he was going to have to contact the one person he trusted implicitly to discover where Corey was staying. He knew exactly where he had to go.

Garnet hadn't considered, when he pressed the buzzer beside the apartment door, that

he didn't look anything like himself.

"Who is it?" asked a muffled voice, from the far side of the door. He got a puzzled look.

"It's Jovan." There was a long minute of silence before he had a reply.

"Who are you trying to fool?" It quickly registered that he didn't have his own face.

"I had a molecular face shift so I could come here without being arrested. My own face will return in a week or so." Still the door didn't open.

"Adele, you've got to believe me. I need your help."

"I have no way of knowing you're who you say you are. So why should I trust you and open the door?" Garnet had a sudden inspiration and began telling her, in detail, of their last romantic interlude. It didn't take long for the door to open.

"Okay. So you are Jovan. What do you want from me?" He smiled.

"If I can come in, I'll tell you." She slowly moved aside and he went into the apartment. He was aware that she still wasn't certain about his identity. The apartment was just as he remembered, decorated elegantly but simply. Adele pushed the door shut and turned to him.

"Would you like a drink, Jovan?" He regarded her, smiled and nodded. He sat down in a soft chair as Adele went to a stand that had glasses and liquor bottles on it. She turned her face to him.

"The usual?" she asked.

"Of course." She poured the drink and took it to him. She handed it to him, folded her arms, and regarded him as he took a stiff drink. He lowered the glass with a pleased look.

"Just the way I like it," Garnet said. She dropped her arms to her sides and looked relieved.

"Now I can believe you're Jovan. Nobody else I know likes their drink that strong. So tell me why you're here." He quickly related what he wanted her to do, finished his drink, and turned his eyes back to her.

"I had to have this face put on so I could come here without being taken back into custody. But now I have only a week or so left to finish my work and get away from Earth before my face returns to normal." Adele nodded.

"All right, Jovan. I'll tail her and find out where she lives. Then what?"

"I want you to lease me a ship, Adele. I'll get Corey and be away from here before anyone realizes that anything is amiss."

It was late afternoon when Les landed at the isolated ranger base. It felt good to be back on Earth, but he had other things on his mind. He was escorted to the base commander's office where he quickly informed the man why he was there.

"You have my full cooperation, Mr. Camden," the man said. He was tall, muscular, with black hair and gray eyes. His voice carried confidence that Les felt was an indication of a strong personality.

"I appreciate that, Commander Adams," Les said. "Now I would like to contact Chief

Drydon and see if he's learned anything about Garnet."

"No problem. I'll get the chief on the line." Adams proceeded to link with Drydon's office. Les had an idea.

"Have the chief put his unit in scrambler mode," Les said. Adams nodded as Drydon appeared on the screen.

"Put your unit in S-mode, Chief," Adams said. He saw Drydon flip a switch.

"The line is secure," Drydon said. "Why is such a measure necessary?" Les stepped behind Adams and bent down.

"Because I don't want anyone to know I'm back, sir," Les said. "I haven't been able to get any idea as to where Garnet has gone." Drydon nodded.

"Maybe Corey has come up with something that might help, Camden. She watched the passengers coming off transports and saw one person she has a gut feeling about. I'll transmit what she saw." The screen changed to show a man walking down the ramp and checking through immigration. Les watched the man closely.

"It's the wrong face," Les said. "But everything else about him says Garnet."

"But how could he change his face?" Drydon asked. Les thought for a moment.

"I've heard rumors of a device that can restucture flesh on a molecular level," Les replied. "But it only lasts for about a month. If that is Garnet, he has a limited time to do what he's come to Earth for – get Angel." Drydon reappeared with a grim frown.

"Corey also mentioned such a device," Drydon said. "Should I warn her?" Les shook his head.

"No, sir. She already senses who he is, and will take what precautions are necessary. I don't want her knowing I'm here, as it might disrupt her daily pattern. If Garnet is watching her, I don't want to give anything away."

"Very well, Camden," Drydon said. "What are you going to do?"

Discrete surveillance, sir. I would like for you to see if you can get me an apartment across from Angel's. Maybe he'll make a move where I can get him."

"Be damn careful, Camden," Drydon said. "You know how unpredictable Garnet is.

There's no telling what he might do." Les nodded.

"My main problem will be avoiding people who know me," Les said. "I can't afford to allow any chance of Garnet discovering I'm on Earth, and alive." Drydon nodded and the screen went dark.

For the second day, Adele was parked across, and down from, the main entrance of the building. Her first attempt to follow Angel had failed because she had gotten blocked in traffic. Today she was determined not to let that happen again. At the same time as previous, she saw Angel come out and get into the unmarked vehicle. Adele hit the ignition switch , pulled into the street and followed.

The next day, Adele was parked in her usual spot when it suddenly occurred to her why Garnet had insisted that she use a different rental vehicle each day. If they noticed the same vehicle following each day, it could make them suspicious. She shook her head, wondering how he could be so smart.

She followed the vehicle to the same apartment house as on the previous day. Now she was certain where Angel lived. But in which apartment? Adele sat pondering that as she watched Angel get out of the vehicle and go into the building. The vehicle pulled away as she saw the door of the apartment house close. She decided she would have to leave it to Garnet to discover which apartment Angel occupied. Her part in his plan was almost at an end. Adele pulled away from the curb and headed back to tell Garnet what she knew.

Garnet kept glancing at her as he paced, lost in thought. He stopped and turned to her.

"Thank you, Adele. I'll have to take over now and end this chase." The tone of his voice sent a chill through her.

"Are you going to kill her?" Garnet regarded her for a moment and shook his head.

"No. I need her to draw Camden out so I can kill him." Adele said nothing, but as far as she was concerned, Camden's death had been proven beyond a doubt. She began to wonder about Garnet's mental state. After all he hadn't acted like himself since he had come to her for help. She also knew there was little more she could do.

Drydon had been able to get a ground floor apartment across from where Angel lived. After dark, Les was brought in and established in the apartment. Now he could do round the clock surveillance and the vehicle could be withdrawn. Drydon had no illusion that the surveillance vehicle stuck out like a sore thumb. Now it would be up to Les to make certain Angel was safe. And, Drydon felt, she couldn't be in better hands.

Les first noticed the very attractive woman who parked when the unmarked behicle dropped Angel off. He gave her no particular attention until the next day when he saw the same woman in a different vehicle follow the same pattern. This sparked his curiosity and he decided to watch for her the next day.

Les saw her appear in a different vehicle the next afternoon, following the same routine of watching Angel exit the unmarked vehicle, enter the building, and waiting until the unmarked vehicle was gone before she pulled away. By now, Les felt certain she was being the eyes of Garnet, and that meant he would have to make his move soon. Les knew he had to try and figure out what that move would be.

It was late afternoon, and Garnet stood staring at his reflection in the mirror. He could see his face was beginning to morph, and that meant he would have to move quickly. Adele had found out where Corey lived. He knew he had to get her, take her to the ship, and get away from Earth very soon now. All he had to do now was work out how to get into the building, discover which apartment she lived in, and carry out his plan. Now it was a question of time, and Garnet knew that time was now pressing in on him.

Les now faced a dilemma. He was certain Garnet would move to kidnap Angel soon, but what could he do to prevent it? Les couldn't get into her apartment. He would risk being recognized if he went out on the street. That would take away his only advantage over Garnet. What could he do? Les began thinking through alternate scenarios so he could take some action to protect Angel. The only scenario that seemed to be successful wasn't one to his liking, but it was the only one that left him with the advantage of choosing a course of action. And, like it or not, Les was determined to follow it through.

In the fading light of the day, as the streetlights were coming on, Adele pulled the vehicle to the curb and shut off the engine. She looked at Garnet and saw he was finally beginning to like his real self. He turned his face to her.

"This won't take long, Adele. When I bring her out, we'll go straight to the ship." She nodded with a serious look, not wanting to tell him she thought he was wrong about Camden. He hadn't been seen since before that body had been found. He opened the door and got out, stood looking around, then headed for the alley. Adele watched him as he went to the alley behind the apartment building and out of her sight.

In the alley, Garnet checked the hypo to make certain he had enough sedative to knock Corey out for at least ten hours. The last thing he wanted was having to deal with her awake. He got a slight smile as he returned the hypo to his pocket. Satisfied, he took the electronic code reader from his pocket and turned it on. He had had a difficult time obtaining this instrument, and it had cost him more than he liked, but now he had it, he was ready to do what had to be done to force Camden into the open. He still carried that odd feeling that he was right about the marshal being alive – somewhere.

He stepped to the rear door of the apartment building, took a small screwdriver from his pocket and began removing the screws from the top of the electronic lock, removed the cap and inserted the connectors into it. He read the screen as the door's code showed up. Garnet felt gratified, but knew he had one more problem – how to locate Corey's apartment. He was aware he had to get away from Earth soon, before his face was restored and he was identified.

He had the code on the screen and disconnected the unit and replaced the cap. Garnet pressed the code into the lock and the door opened. He pushed it open and stepped inside.

He closed the door behind him and listened. The only sound he heard was muted music coming from one of the apartments. Garnet moved up the stairs. On the second level, he was surprised, and pleased, to find the tenant's last name displayed beside the door.

Not finding her name beside the four doors, he went back to the stairs and down to the first level. Garnet moved quietly, carefully, reading the nameplates beside the doors. The last one, at the front of the building, was Corey's apartment. Now that he had found her, Garnet had to fight down the urge to move swiftly. That could prove dangerous. Steadiness was what he needed right now. He quickly tapped into the door's code and went through the same procedure as he did at the rear door, got the code, and prepared to collect his prize.

Les felt certain that Garnet would strike soon. He contacted Drydon and told him what he thought should be done to apprehend Garnet and make certain Angel was safe. Drydon listened and nodded as Les told him the plan he had come up with.

"I'll call Corey in," Drydon said. "Let's see what she has to say about it." Les nodded.

"I can't ask anymore than that, sir. But emphasize to her that Garnet wants her to draw me out. I don't think she'll be in any danger." Les got a frustrated look.

"I can't believe he still thinks I'm alive – unless he learned how to read minds." That set Les to thinking about the success he had had of figuring out what Garnet would do. There had to be an answer, but that was for another time.

When Angel entered Drydon's office, she immediately noted the odd expression he regarded her with. She stopped in front of the desk and regarded him with a questioning look.

"You wanted to see me, Chief?" Drydon nodded.

"Please, sit down, Corey. I've been contacted by Camden." Angel couldn't conceal her surprise as she sat down.

"Has he located Garnet?" she asked. Drydon gave her a slow nod.

"I had a copy of that disc you said was Garnet transmitted to him," he replied. "He agreed with you." This puzzled Angel.

"If he agreed, then why isn't he here?" Drydon got a hard frown.

"He's been in an apartment across from yours for about a week now," Drydon said.

"He's been watching, and feels Garnet is going to try and attempt to get you soon." Angel looked at him with a perplexed look.

"What does he want me to do?" Drydon felt unsettled as he sat up straight and folded his hands on the desk. He quickly outlined Les' plan to her.

"He wants you to have a transponder implant," Drydon said. "He would like for you to allow yourself to be taken by Garnet."

"He what?" Angel blurted out. Drydon spread his hands.

"He believes you will be in no danger. He asked me to tell you to remember what he said at the time he saved you from Garnet. He said you would understand." She thought about that day, and recalled what Les had said, and what she had said. She turned a confident look to Drydon.

"Let's get the transponder implant put in, sir."

Garnet pressed the keys and the door clicked open. He pushed it wider and stepped into Angel's apartment. He was surprised at how elegant it was with such simple furnishings. He quietly pushed the door shut and moved toward the dining room, where he saw Angel at the table eating. He stood watching her for a moment before making his presence known.

He quickly stepped in beside the table and felt he would soon be vindicated by this woman. Angel froze when she saw him, and that his features were almost normal. Her eyes widened in fear as she stared at him.

"Who are you?" she asked, in an alarmed tone. "What are you doing in here? What do you want?" He regarded her with a slight smile at her not recognizing him.

"I want Camden," he replied. "Nothing else need concern you." He moved quickly to pull the hypo from his pocket and plunge it into her shoulder. Angel dropped her fork, started to stand, but was hit with dizziness and sat back down.

In a moment she was unconscious. Garnet slipped the hypo back in his pocket, stepped to the chair and pulled it away from the table. He took her from the chair and lifted her up and over his shoulder. He went to the door, peeked out, saw no one, and quickly moved to the stairs and down to the rear door. He opened it, looked around, stepped out and headed down the alley.

Garnet hurried to the mouth of the alley, stopped, and looked out on the street. He saw the sidewalk was devoid of any strollers. He went quickly to the vehicle, opened the side door, and put Angel on the backseat. He climbed in and turned his face to Adele.

"Get us to the ship, Adele. I now have the one thing that will bring Camden to me."

She regarded him with a cynical look.

"What are you going to do with her if it turns out that Camden is dead?" Garnet got a cold look. He hadn't thought she would doubt him. He kept his eyes on her as he replied in a hard tone.

"I'm not wrong, Adele. I'll be the one who kills Camden – no one else can." She engaged the engine and pulled away from the curb. She was beginning to think his mind had become unhinged by his obsession that Camden was still alive.

Unknown to Garnet, Les had just watched his assault on Angel, and used all his self-restraint to keep from rushing to her defense. As Garnet lifted her to his shoulder, Les lowered the binoculars. He turned and activated the audvid unit, pressed in the code, and

Drydon's image appeared.

"He has her, sir." Drydon got a sad look and nodded.

"What are you going to do now, Camden?" Les already had his plan laid out, and knew Angel was in on the basics of it.

"I'll be heading for the landing park, sir. I think I know where he'll go, and I'll be following. It may take a few days before I know for certain where he's going, where I believe he is, but I'm not losing his trail again."
"Be careful, Camden, and good luck."

"Thank you, sir. I'll do my best." He released the comlink, turned, and hurried from the apartment.

Les was surprised that he made it to the landing park before Garnet. He went to the security office, presented his identification, and told the officer what he needed to know.

The officer looked up from the monitor.

"A two crew ship was leased to a Miss Adele Blythe yesterday." Les nodded.

"Get a photo?" Les asked. The officer swung the monitor around and Les now knew the name of the woman who had been watching Angel.

"Can you give me that ship's frequency?" The officer worked the monitor and quickly wrote down the frequency and handed the paper to Les. He glanced at it and put it in his pocket.

"Thanks. I'm going to my ship," Les said. "I'll be leaving about half an hour after that ship. When I'm gone, would you please contact Chief Drydon and tell him I'm on the fugitive's tail?" The officer nodded.

"Be glad to."

"Thanks again," Les said, turned, and headed for his ship.

As he got to the hatch, Les saw a vehicle pull up beside the other ship. Les recognized Garnet immediately. His face was normal again.

"No wonder he's in such a hurry to leave," Les mumbled. He watched Garnet open the side door of the vehicle, lift Angel out, say something to the woman driver, and hurry to the ship's hatch. After he went on board, the woman turned the vehicle around and sped away. Les activated the hatch and boarded his ship.

Exactly thirty minutes after Garnet lifted off, Les followed suite. He wasn't certain, but he was betting that Garnet was on his way to Varian Four. If Les was right, then he would soon have the means to shatter Garnet's nerve. Now that he had Angel, the advantage was clearly in Les' hands.

17

It took a few days of careful shadowing before Les fairly certain that Garnet was heading for Varian Four. He exhaled as he knew that, at least, this time he had a plan. He knew Angel would play her part, and that should really shake Garnet. Now Les would have to get his ship down without Garnet being aware of it. Les leaned back and clasped his hands behind his head. It seemed the days of Garnet surprising him was over. He could now initiate his own surprises. Les felt certain his surprises would be ones Garnet would never consider using. For the first time, since his original encounter with Garnet, Les felt confident that he would soon have him in custody.

Angel sucked in a deep breath and opened her eyes. She immediately found her hands were tied and she was strapped in a bunk. She looked around and saw Garnet sitting in the pilot's seat.

"What do you want with me?" Angel asked. He swung the seat around and she saw his face was normal.

"You!" she exclaimed, feigning surprise. "Who was that man who kidnapped me? What did he want with me?" He smiled.

"He was a friend of mine who owed me a favor. You were that favor. Now where's Camden?" Angel shook her head and regarded him with a pitying look.

"Didn't you hear he was murdered?" Garnet got a hard frown.

"I don't believe that. I've never believed it. All the evidence was fabricated to give him a cover story. Now tell me where he is." Angel regarded him with a hard look, but was surprised at how right he was.

"The last time I saw Les was the day before his body was found." Garnet narrowed his eyes on her as he felt she was telling the truth. But just because she hadn't seen him didn't mean Camden was dead. He could be hiding, waiting for the opportunity to pounce on him. And now that he had Angel, the truth would be finally revealed.

"Where are you taking me?" He turned the seat so that his back was to her.

"The one place Camden will know where to look for you." Angel felt she knew where that was, but decided to act dumb.

"And just where is that?" He glanced over his shoulder at her.

"You'll find that out when we get there," he replied, in a cold tone. She decided she had pushed her luck far enough with Garnet and decided to remain quiet. And he didn't seem interested in any further conversation.

Time passed slowly as Les followed Garnet's ship at extreme range. But there was no longer any doubt that he was headed for Varian Four. Les was now considering how to get his ship down without alerting Garnet, and the only way that could be accomplished was a landing farther from where he wanted to be. It would mean a longer walk and take more time, but Les was determined it would have to be that way if he was to surprise Garnet. And he was looking forward with relish at turning the tables on Garnet.

Les brought his ship in almost the opposite side of the planet from where he was going. Keeping it low, he sat down about two miles from his destination. It was almost dark, and he decided to wait for morning before going after Angel and Garnet. He knew there was nothing he could do in darkness – except maybe get Angel killed.

As they walked at a steady pace, Angel saw where Garnet was taking her, and she turned a puzzled look to him.

"Why are you bringing me here?" she asked. He gave her a hard look.

"It's where Camden took my hand. It's where I'm going to take his life." Angel got a dubious look.

"Lots of luck," she said, scornfully. "If you accomplish that, you'll be the first person to kill a dead man." He gave her a savage look.

[174]

"Camden is not dead! He can't be. Nobody could take him down but me." She noticed that he used the past tense in his last sentence, but said nothing. But she had been startled at how strong his belief was that Les was alive filled him.

Going into the bowl-shaped formation, Garnet slipped his pack from his shoulders and pointed to the same rock he had her sit on her first time here.

"Make yourself comfortable," he said. Angel went to the rock and sat down. Garnet opened his pack and took out two power bars, went over and handed her one.

"After you eat," he said. "Try and get some sleep. I want you looking fit when Camden shows up." Angel, still had her hands tied, tore open the wrapper with her teeth and slowly began to eat. As she ate, she wondered about what Garnet had in mind for Les. She knew he wanted more than anything to kill him, but exactly how he might carry that out, she had no idea. But the situation was definitely not to her liking.

When she awoke, in the gray light of dawn, Angel sat up, stretched and yawned. She quickly realized that Garnet was nowhere to be seen. She started to lower her hands to the rock when she realized she was no longer under any restraint. Putting her hands on the rock, she felt several power bars behind her. This puzzled Angel, and led her to conclude that Garnet was hiding, waiting for Les to show up and ambush him. But she had a week's supply of power bars; did that mean Garnet was going to stay out of sight that long? Angel was perplexed and didn't know what to think. Garnet had left her food, but what was she going to do about water? And how could she warn Les? If she tried to leave, she had no doubt, that Garnet wouldn't hesitate to kill her.

Les came out of the ship and activated the indicator. Its beeps would lead him to familiar territory, if that was where he had taken Angel. But Les had no doubt about where he would find her. He began walking, and the beeps remained steady. After an hour, Les had his bearings and turned the unit off. He moved quickly now to the gully where he expected to find them.

He quietly made his way up the steep slope and cautiously looked over the crest. He saw Angel below, her hands weren't tied, and there was not a trace of Garnet he could see. Les concluded the same as Angel had – that Garnet was hiding, waiting for him. Les settled in to wait for him to show himself.

As the sun began to set, Les began to believe that Garnet wasn't anywhere around. Could it be he just brought Angel here and deserted her? There was only one way to be certain. Les would have to return to the ship and check the sensor on Garnet's ship. If he was gone, Les could make his way back and get Angel.

He hurried back to the ship, activated the hatch, and went inside. Les powered up the sensor and got nothing but blasts of static. Garnet had left the planet, and was probably long gone. Les was confused by his erratic behavior, unless he thought that Les was dead and was punishing Angel for her part in his downfall. That was the only thing that made sense. But Garnet was no longer making sense. Les was frustrated when he realized that Garnet had, once again, surprised him. Les would now have to go back for Angel, all the while wondering where Garnet might have gone.

Climbing down behind Angel, Les held the flashlight on her.

"You shouldn't have come, Les. Garnet's waiting to kill you."

"He's not here, Angel. He's gone." She turned a surprised look to him as he helped her to her feet.

"Gone?" Les nodded.

"I can't explain his action," Les said. "But it sure as hell came as a surprise me." Angel smiled.

"So he can still surprise you." Les glanced at her with a raised eyebrow.

"Don't feel so smug," he said. "Come on, let's get to the ship. Now neither of us dare show our face. It's the only way to really convince him we're dead.

As Les led the way back to the ship, he pondered over Garnet's action. He wished now he had gotten the latest psych file and studied it, because he was now up against a man he didn't know at all. But where would he have gone? Back to Ruby? His brow furrowed as he tried to figure out what to do next.

Angel saw his expression, noted his silence, and knew what was on his mind.

"I can easily guess what you're thinking about," she said. Les glanced at her.

"Garnet kills his victims," he said, regarding her with a perplexed look. "Yet he left you alive with a week's supply of food. That's not the Garnet I know, Angel. Why did he do this in such a way? Why did he just dump you here? I've got more questions now than ever about him." Angel was quick to understand what he meant.

"I see what you mean, Les," she said. "But I still believe that people like Garnet don't change their profile." He looked at her with a puzzled frown.

"Then how would you explain his action? Why didn't he just kill you?" That was something she had been considering since he had told her Garnet had left the planet. It was something she felt hadn't any logical explanation, so she used the only argument she could think of.

"You can't predict what a psycho will do." Les looked at her in astonishment.

"Maybe so," he said. "But psycho killers like him don't leave their victims alive with a week's supply of food. That isn't in the package, Angel. I've got no idea of what he was thinking. Why did he just dump you here? I'm now looking for a stranger that I don't know anything about." She nodded and took hold of his arm. He stopped and turned his face to her.

"Some things are inexplicable, Les. Garnet is one of them. That's all we have to go on now." He considered her words and nodded.

[177]

"We're back to square one," she added. "That's where we have to start, and hope, we get some kind of break." Les felt she was right, and frustrated at having to begin over, and remaining out of sight while doing so.

"We still can't let it slip that we're alive," Les said. "We'll have to play this advantage as far as we can."

"I agree. It's the only thing that might get Garnet into the open. So where do we go, Les?"

"I'm not sure," he replied. "If we return to Earth…" He couldn't think beyond the present situation, and that only increased his frustration.

"You're right, Les. Returning to Earth is the best place for information to be funneled to us. It might be our only chance to get a lead on him." He felt relieved that he hadn't made the decision. Returning to Earth was a dangerous proposition, but it was the only thing they could do.

"Let's get to the ship," Les said, and they hurried on.

Garnet rubbed his forehead.

"Why didn't I kill her?" He asked himself, and answered. "You did! You untied her hands and left her unarmed. There was no way she can get to the city except through the jungle. And she won't make it through there alive. Well what about Camden?" Garnet got a puzzled look at having a conversation with himself.

"He must be dead. If he isn't, well he'll never know what happened to his ladylove. That should give him a lot of torment. Just like I felt when he took off my hand." He paused, raised an eyebrow, and got a pleased look.

"This worked out pretty well. And I didn't even plan it this way." Garnet lapsed into silence as he became lost in his thoughts. But one thought remained uppermost in his mind; that Camden was alive, and he still wanted to kill him.

When Drydon came into the office, Angel, Les, and Commander Adams stood. Drydon went to Angel, smiled, and took her hand.

"I'm glad to see you're safe, Corey." She smiled.

"Thank you, Chief. But we now have an even more serious situation to consider." Drydon turned his eyes to Les with a perplexed look.

"Let's be seated," Commander Adams said. They all sat down and Angel kept her gaze on Drydon.

"What sort of problem, Corey?" Drydon asked. Les glanced at Angel with an uneasy look.

"I believe Garnet has become mentally unstable, sir. It could prove a very serious problem. It also means Les can't anticipate what he might do, and that makes him far more dangerous." Drydon held a stoic expression.

"Would you care to explain? You can start by telling me what happened to you," Drydon said.

Angel quickly related what happened on Varian Four. Drydon looked surprised when she told him how Garnet had left her, alone and unmolested.

"I must admit," Drydon said. "That doesn't sound like the Garnet of the record." He glanced at Les and rubbed his chin.

"I can see why you wanted an update on his psych file, Camden," Drydon said. "How do you intend to proceed with your assignment?"

"I'm only guessing now, sir, but I believe he would have went back to Ruby. It would seem the only place he could feel safe. And he's in dire need to feel secure." Drydon nodded.

"Whatever you need, ask for it. I'll see that you get all available help. You're going to have to be very cautious,

Camden. There's no telling how Garnet might react when he sees you." Les got a hard frown.

"He'll react exactly as I believe he will, sir. He'll try his damnedest to kill me."

"Of that I have no doubt," Drydon agreed.

As Angel and Les were having dinner, she put her fork down and ran a finger over the short pink scar on her left wrist. She glanced at Les.

"I thought it would be a bit more painful having the transponder removed," she said. Les took a bite and regarded her with a neutral expression.

"It was only minor surgery," he said. "And you're a strong person." Angel turned an odd look to him.

"What can you do about Garnet now?" Les shrugged.

"All I can do is guess from his past actions. Whether I'm right or wrong, I can only find out when I confront him." Angel didn't like what she was hearing.

"You're taking an awful chance doing it that way, Les. His condition makes him much more likely to kill quicker than he did before." He smiled and waved his fork at her.

"He didn't kill you," Les said, and got a puzzled look. "And that's what baffles me the most. You were there when I took him down. Instead, he gave you a week's supply of food and left you unharmed. That is contrary to what he's done before."

"Maybe he just accepted that you were dead, and decided to walk away from it,"

Angel suggested. Les shook his head.

"Maybe so," Les said. "But there's something else about Garnet. He's not killing people like he used to. I'm very curious to discover why." Angel took a bite and had an uneasy feeling.

"He must be feeling awfully insecure," she said. "What would an insecure killer do if faced with arrest?" Les scratched his head.

"Become careless," he replied. "If Garnet's lost confidence in himself, he's going to screw up. And I hope to hell I can be where he screws up and take him down again."

Garnet had been staying with Ruby since he had abandoned Angel. He hadn't told Ruby what he had done for fear of looking soft in her eyes. He felt certain Angel was dead, and he almost believed Camden, too, was dead. It had been over three months, and no one had seen the marshal. Garnet knew that had he been seen, it wouldn't have taken long before he would have heard about it.

Yet he still had some doubt he couldn't wipe from his mind. Garnet felt lost. He didn't know where to go or what he could do. He had also noticed the odd looks he sometimes got from Ruby. He didn't know what she was thinking, and as long as she didn't press him for an answer, things would remain fine.

Ruby stood at the bar nursing her favorite drink. She was trying to figure out what was bothering Garnet. Since his return he hadn't acted like his old self, moreso than before. She felt, instinctively, that something was deeply troubling him. She hoped he still didn't believe that marshal was still alive. That was the last thing he needed; a persecution complex from a dead man. But until he decided to tell her, Ruby wasn't going to press him. Just leave him alone, she thought, and sooner or later Jovan would tell her what was bothering him.

Garnet felt he had to do something, and it suddenly occurred to him what it was. He had to return to Varian Four and confront his ghost. It could prove to be the one thing that would free him from his uncertainty. He must go – now! Garnet finished his drink, put the glass down, and started for the door. He stopped halfway across the room. What the hell was he doing? He had no reason to tell Ruby he was leaving. It wasn't any of her concern. He turned and headed for the rear door.

Ruby came in and was mildly surprised to find Garnet gone. She wondered where he might have gone, but decided not to try even to guess. She thought that, just maybe, he had decided it was time he got back into action. Ruby hoped so, and knew she would see him when he had finished what he had gone to do. After all, it was about time he began being decisive again. He would tell her about it when he got back. At least, she hoped he would.

When Garnet walked into the bowl-shaped gully, he looked for Angel's body. Not seeing it didn't surprise him as he felt she would have drawn the attention of one of those jungle beasts. He walked slowly to the spot where he had lost his hand, raised his artificial hand and looked at it. Garnet recalled how he had wounded Camden twice because he had done just what he had expected him to do. How he had maneuvered him into Ruby's hands, and she had knocked him on his ass, because he did exactly what he felt Camden would do. Garnet's eyes went back to his hand.

"But I didn't expect him to do this," he muttered. It came to Garnet that he missed the challenge Camden had offered. It made him feel alive. He wasn't about to admit that he missed the marshal being in pursuit, but it was at the back of his mind.

He went to the rock where he had left Angel, pushed the power bars aside, and sat down. He looked around and felt he needed an adversary to keep him alert and planning. What could he do now to get back that frame of mind? He sat lost in thought as a cloud drifted over putting him in the shade for a moment.

When Les came into Drydon's office, he held a serious expression. He stopped in front of Drydon's desk.

"I've just gotten confirmation, sir. Garnet has been seen where I thought he would be, with Ruby. He was seen boarding a small ship at the landing park." Drydon got a surprised look.

"Where could he have been going?" Drydon asked. Les regarded him with a confident look.

"Since I was right about where he was," Les replied. "I'm going to guess he's going back to prison." Angel turned a startled look to Les.

"What are you talking about?" she asked, in a dubious tone. Les looked at her with a grim frown.

"I'm not referring to the prison we put him in," Les replied. "He's going to his own prison – Varian Four, where he left you. He's trying to work out how we brought him down, and how I took his hand. He hasn't yet come to terms with what happened."

"Since you were correct about where he was," Drydon said. "I have to assume you know what you're talking about, Camden. The question is, what do we do about it?" Les had been considering that question since he had heard from Susan.

"Garnet is in a delicate mental state, sir," Les replied. "Whatever we decide to do, it will have to be done carefully." Angel came to the desk with a hard look.

"Why the hell should we worry about his mental condition?" she asked, in a hard tone.

"He never cared about the people he killed." Les knew how she felt, and knew there were a lot of people who shared her feelings.

"Angel, none of us are like Garnet," Les said. "We're law enforcement personnel and therefore have a code we work by. That's the difference between Garnet and us. So we have to consider his mental condition."

"I agree," Drydon said. "But just how do we handle him without pushing him over the edge?" Les rubbed his ear as he considered the question.

"That's a touchy subject," Les replied. "I'm going to confer with couple of top psych doctors and see what they advise." Drydon nodded.

"After you talk with them," Drydon said. "Come back and let us know what their opinions are." Les nodded.

"I will, sir." Les glanced at Angel and saw she had a dubious look.

[183]

"I have to do it this way, Angel," Les explained. "I won't lower myself to Garnet's level." He turned and walked from the office.

Les was very careful not to be seen as he went to see two immanent doctors. He sat in the backseat of an official vehicle with darkened windows and accompanied by a police captain, who went in and asked the doctor to come with him. Les felt he had to get some idea of Garnet's mental state. He had to understand how to approach taking him into custody.

The captain opened the door and a muscular man with blue-gray eyes stepped onto the sidewalk. He followed the officer to the vehicle as the officer opened the rear door.

"Please get in, Doctor." The man climbed in and took the seat indicated. He relaxed and glanced at the man sitting across from him. The doctor's eyes widened in surprise and his mouth fell open.

"Hello, Dr. Samms," Les said, with an amused smile.

"I thought you were dead, Marshal," Samms said, in a strained voice. Les nodded.

"I'm using the death of an unknown man to keep Garnet thinking I am," Les explained. "But I've had a chance to observe his behavior for some time. I need a professional opinion as to his mental condition before I go after him again." Samms gave him a nod.

"I'll tell you what I can," Samms said. Les told him what he had seen, leaving out no action of Garnet's. Samms listened with an astonished expression.

"That's about it, Doctor." Samms got a studious look as he thought for a moment.

"I'm only guessing, you understand," Samms said. Les nodded.

"From his actions, it seems to me that Garnet is suffering from paranoia. I feel that was brought about by his not wanting

[184]

to believe you're dead. He has a complex about killing that has led him to the belief that only he could kill you, and it's difficult for him to accept that someone else killed you." It made sense to Les because he had come to almost the same conclusion.

"Thank you, Doctor. I feel the same as you. Now I have an idea about how to move against him with little trouble." Samms looked alarmed.

"Garnet's still a killer, Marshal. Don't take anything about him for granted." Samms opened the door and got out of the vehicle.

"I hope I don't need remind you, Doctor, that this meeting must be kept confidential," Les said. Samms nodded.

"I understand, Marshal. You can count on me to keep my mouth shut." Samms turned and went back to the main entrance of the building and went inside.

Les sent the captain to make certain he could see Dr. Richard Arlen without anyone seeing him enter the building. He watched the rear door from the vehicle until the captain opened it and motioned for Les to come in. He climbed from the vehicle, glancing up and down the alley, to make certain no one was there who could see him. He hurried to the door, stepped into the firewell, and the captain closed the door. Les hurried up the stairs to an unmarked door and knocked.

"Come in," a baritone voice said. Les opened the door and stepped into the plush office. He saw a tall, thin man with graying hair and sharp blue eyes. He stood and extended his hand over the desk.

"Marshal Camden," he said. "I'm glad to see you're alive. How can I help you?" Les shook his hand

"Garnet refuses to believe I'm dead." The doctor got a surprised look.

"Why would he still think you're alive?" Les frowned.

"Dr. Samms believes he's now paranoid." Dr. Arlen motioned Les to a chair.

"Tell me about Garnet," Arlen said. "He's a fascinating personality. From teaching at a university to a coldblooded killer." Les sat down and began telling him about his observations of Garnet. Arlen listened with a look of anticipation.

Les told him what he had told Samms, and finished with his idea of what Garnet was suffering from. Arlen leaned back with a pleased look.

"Amazing," Arlen said. "I agree with your idea that he's put himself in his own prison. The place where he lost his hand would be an almost irresistible draw for him. I also agree with what Dr. Samms told you. It seems clear that he has become paranoid because he can't accept your death."

"How would you suggest I approach him, Doctor?" Les asked. "I don't want him freaking out and killing himself." Arlen rubbed his eye as he thought for a moment.

"I don't think Garnet's suicidal," Arlen replied. "It would probably be more of a relief for him to know for certain you were still alive." Les nodded and stood.

"Thank you, Doctor. That's all I wanted to know."

18

As Les made his way along the corridor, he knew he had some hard thinking to do. He wanted a clear plan as to how he was going after Garnet, and he didn't want any unexpected results. His eyes widened.

"Everything about Garnet has been unexpected," he muttered. "So how do I come up with something that, at least, gives me a chance to succeed?" He kept thinking as he exited the building and climbed into the vehicle. He then recalled what Beltram had said about going back to the early records. Les decided that just might give him something to go on.

Garnet sat on the flat rock, in the gully, rocking back and forth, trying to make up his mind. Was Camden dead? There had been no sighting of him in months, but did that mean he was dead? Maybe he was hiding, making people think he was dead.

"That is very possible," Garnet mumbled, nodding. "On the other hand, if he is alive, where is he? Why hasn't he been coming after me?" He shook his head. All the evidence pointed to his being dead, and only his feeling was keeping Camden alive.

Garnet got to his feet and began pacing. What was he to do? Everything he knew seemed to say Camden was dead. But... He couldn't rid himself of the feeling that he was alive.

"How can I find out for certain?" He continued to pace, struggling with his divided mind. Garnet couldn't decide to accept the evidence as it stood, or go with a strong feeling of unease. To ignore evidence went against logic. Yet he couldn't accept that Camden was dead either. He just knew better!

Ruby paced with a worried expression, taking quick sips from the glass she held. She hadn't heard from Garnet in over a month. That, in itself, wasn't unusual, but it was his state of mind that concerned her the most. Ruby felt he had never accepted Camden's death, and kept on believing he was still alive. But what could she do? She turned and went to the door and opened it.

"Mitch," she called. The young man came quickly into the room. He had on a stylish shirt and light gray slacks. His intense green eyes locked on her as he brushed his dark brown hair back.

"Yeah, Ruby?" She regarded him with an unsettling look.

"I want you to ask around and see if anyone has heard from Jovan." He nodded.

"I'll get on it now," he said, turned, and left the room pulling the door shut behind him. Ruby resumed her pacing, worrying about Garnet, and knowing she was helpless.

Farrel looked up when Susan came in and stopped before his desk. He noted she had a pleased look.

"I haven't seen a look like that on you for a long time," Farrel said. "What brought it on?" Susan bent down and put her hands on the desk and smiled.

"One of my informants told me that Ruby has a man out trying to find out if anyone has heard from Garnet." Farrel leaned back with a slight smile.

"Well," he said, shrugging. "Of course that doesn't mean something has happened to him. And it doesn't give us a clue as to where Les is." Susan's smile got broader.

"Maybe not. But I think it tells us a lot about Garnet's state of mind." Farrel leaned forward and rested his arms on the desk.

"What do you mean, Susan?" She quickly sat down and leaned forward.

"I think Garnet still refuses to believe Les is dead. But since no one, we know of, has seen either him or Corey in some time, Garnet must be in a quandary as to what to believe. This is making him vulnerable." Farrel nodded.

"I see what you mean," he said. "But it still doesn't tell us if Les is close on his trail.

So don't get your hopes up, Susan."

[188]

"I'm not, Sergeant. But I can certainly imagine what might be going on out there somewhere." Farrel smiled and nodded.

"I can't fault you for that," he said. "Just keep your ears open and see what turns up." She nodded, stood, and hurried back out of the building. He watched until she passed out of sight. Farrel reached for the audvid unit. This was something Drydon would be very interested in hearing about.

Drydon regarded Angel and Les as they sat in front of his desk. Les noted his expression was unreadable.

"I had a communication from Sergeant Farrel," Drydon said. "It seems that Officer Burns discovered, through an informant, that that woman Ruby has a man out trying to find out if anyone has heard from Garnet. What do you make of that, Camden?" Angel and Les exchanged surprised looks.

"I wonder why she's so concerned about him?" Angel asked.

"His state of mind," Les replied. "Ruby probably has the idea that Garnet may be going off his rocker." Drydon raised an eyebrow.

"Why would she think that?" Drydon asked. Les shrugged.

"As long as I've been out of sight," Les said. "Garnet can't accept the fact that I'm dead. Why I don't know. But I feel he's on Varian Four, waiting at the place I took him down."

"Waiting for his revenge?" Angel asked. Les nodded.

"This can work to our advantage," Drydon said. "Would you like to go and see if you're right, Camden?" Les puckered his lips as he recalled what the shrinks had told him.

"Yes, sir," Les replied. "It will be interesting to see how far along his destabilization has become. But I'm still not certain it's a wise move for me to just walk in and face him. He could just be unstable enough to pull the trigger on himself." Drydon nodded.

"You could be right," Drydon said. "So be careful how you handle him."

"I'll be very careful, sir." Angel and Les stood and Drydon looked up at them.

"Sir, I think it might be expedient to take along a holographic projector," Les said.

Drydon got a perplexed look.

"Why?" Drydon asked. Angel was looking at him with the same sort of expression.

"It would be the safest way for me to approach him," Les replied. "Without putting myself in danger." Drydon rubbed his chin and nodded.

"I'll call and have a ship readied for you," Drydon said. Les nodded. They turned and left the office.

In the corridor, Angel stopped and put a hand on Les' arm. He turned his face to her.

"You know, Les, it's possible you face a Garnet much more dangerous than he was before. If his mind is unstable, there's no telling what he might do." Les tilted his head.

"Which means nothing has changed much, Angel. He was always a hard one to anticipate." She got an uneasy look.

"I've got a bad feeling about this, Les." He leaned forward and kissed her. When he pulled away he had a slight smile.

"Don't worry," he said. "I've got to be cautious no matter how I approach him."

As Les packed, the audvid unit sounded. Angel went and pressed the comlink. She was surprised to see Drydon looking back at her.

"Yes, Chief?" She saw him inhale deeply as he clasped his hands on the desk.

"I must speak to Camden." Angel nodded.

"I'll get him." She hurried into the bedroom and patted Les on the shoulder. He turned and saw her odd expression.

"The chief wants to talk to you," she said. Les' brow furrowed and he followed her out to the audvid unit.

"Yes, sir," Les said. Drydon got an agitated look.

"Camden, you have to take Corey with you. She can be a second ghost. The reason for this is, she could be in danger if she remains here on Earth. If anyone who knows Garnet happens to see her, he could ask one of his people here to kill her." Les nodded. Angel's eyebrows rose.

"Yes, sir," Les said. "I'll see that we get to the ship without us being seen." Drydon nodded.

"Good, Camden. I'll be waiting for your first report." The screen went dark. Les turned his face to her.

"You heard the man," Les said. "Better get packed." Angel smiled and kissed him.

"This time you won't have to alone or bored," she said, and walked toward the bedroom.

Garnet sat on the flat rock in the drizzling rain, like a king on a throne. He kept. Looking around like he was expecting someone. He heard someone coming, stood, and waited. He saw Les come into the gully with his weapon drawn. Garnet smiled.

"I knew you weren't dead, you son of a bitch." Garnet drew his weapon and fired. The pulse passed through Les and impacted the rock wall. Garnet stared in confusion, then began laughing.

"A ghost! I killed a goddamn ghost!" He laughed until he collapsed on the rock racked with sobs. He became silent for a moment, sat up, and got a savage look.

"I know you're alive, Marshal. And I'm going to hunt you down, you bastard, and kill you." He got to his feet and walked with a determined stride from the gully. Garnet had a cold determination to prove that Les was alive, and it was he who would kill him.

Ruby paced as the man stood regarding her. She turned her face to him.

"Are you certain, Mitch?" she asked. He nodded.

"No doubt, Ruby. No one has seen or heard from Garnet in over a month." She continued pacing, rubbing a finger over her lips. She was now very worried about him.

"Put out the word," Ruby said. "That if anyone hears from Jovan to get word to me right away." He gave her a nod, turned and went out pulling the door quietly shut.

Angel and Les had been away from Earth for a few days when she noticed that an encrypted message began coming through. With a surprised look, Angel glanced at Les who was checking the instruments.

"We have en encrypt coming in," she said, Les turned the seat and regarded her with a puzzled look.

"Why would we be getting an encrypted message? And from whom?" he asked. Angel glanced at him and smiled.

"I'll tell you that after I decrypt it." She took the message from the slot, reversed it, and entered it in a lower slot. The message moved back through the unit and came out the other side. Angel pulled it out and read it. With wide eyes, she turned to Les.

"It's from the chief. Garnet's been seen on three worlds, almost in a direct line from Varian Four," she said. "He's made no effort to keep himself out of sight, and he's been asking only one question." Les looked at her with a dubious expression.

"What's his question?" he asked. Angel regarded him with a grim look.

"Has anyone seen Marshal Camden?" Les leaned back and thought for a moment.

"Has the sightings been confirmed?" he asked. Angel nodded.
"Everyone of them." Les knew he would now have to confront Garnet as soon as possible, before he started killing again.

"What planet is next in line for him to land on?" Les asked. Angel turned on the star chart monitor and moved a finger along it.

"Trukon Three," Angel replied, glancing over her shoulder at him. He gave her a nod.

"Then that's where we're heading," Les said. "Let's hope we get there before him." He turned the seat and began moving his hand over the control panel.

As Susan stopped before Farrel's desk, she noted his grim expression.

"Has something happened?" she asked. He slowly nodded.

"There have been three confirmed sightings of Garnet on as many planets," Farrel replied. "He's asking only one question; where is Marshal Camden? Susan, he's hunting for Les."

"How can he still believe Les is alive?" she asked. "Everyone else believes he's dead.

It just isn't rational. Where is Les?" Farrel shrugged.

"No one knows," he replied. "I talked with Chief Drydon less than half an hour ago, and even he doesn't know where Les is." Susan frowned and pulled her shoulders back.

"The chief had an encrypted message sent, Susan. But I'll bet Les already knows about those sightings, and is working out how to deal with Garnet." She slumped into a chair and regarded him with a lost look.

"And if he hasn't heard?" she asked. "He could walk straight into a trap." Farrel leaned back and began playing with a pen.

Like it or not," he said. "Les is on his own, and I'll bet on him coming out on top."

Ruby was startled when the door quickly opened and Mitch stood regarding her with an odd expression.

"What is it?" she asked with a shudder. He nervously rubbed his ear.

"There's been three definite sightings of Garnet, Ruby. On three different worlds."

"So he's alive," she said, in a relieved tone. Mitch slightly shook his head.

"Alive yes, Ruby. But he was asking only one question on each planet. Where is Marshal Camden? He's chasing a ghost." She got a frown and turned her head.

"Shit!" she exclaimed, sharply. "Why can't he accept the fact that the marshal is dead?" Mitch shrugged.

"I don't know, Ruby. But you can imagine what people are thinking about him."

"What can we do to help him?" she asked. Mitch shook his head.

"Nothing. We don't know where he is, or where he'll go in his search for a ghost." Ruby folded her arms and turned to the window.

"Have someone try to follow him after the next sighting," she said. "We've got to get him back and out of sight." Mitch spread his hands.

"I'm afraid he's on his own, Ruby. Besides, how can you stop a man from looking for a dead man?" She looked over her shoulder at him with a frown.

"You're right, of course, Mitch. Just keep listening, and tell me where he's going."

Ruby sat at a corner table nursing her drink and listening to the buzz of a dozen conversations. As she lifted her glass, she saw an acquaintance of Jovan's come through the door. He looked around, saw her, and came toward the table.

"Mind if I sit down, Ruby?" She got a chill at his tone and waved him to the chair facing her. He sat down and regarded her for a silent moment.

"Have you heard from Jovan lately?" he asked. She shook her head.

"Not a word in weeks, Morton. Why?" He glanced around and saw they were isolated enough so that no one could hear what he was about to tell her.

"I've been hearing from a few people who know him, Ruby." She stiffened at his grim tone.

"What have they been telling you?" she asked, apprehensive. He leaned forward and rested his arms on the table.

"That he's moving from planet to planet, talks like a man who is lost, and never staying very long on any planet." Ruby got a frustrated look as she inhaled.

"Damn!" she exclaimed, harshly. "Why can't he accept the fact that the marshal is dead?" Morton got a surprised look.

"Is that what's wrong with him?" Morton asked. She nodded.

"He just can't bring himself to believe that the man who brought him down is no longer around to do it again." Morton got a puzzled look.

"Some of those I've talked to," he said. "Have heard Jovan talking like he might run into him any time. They knew better than to contradict him." Ruby quickly made up her mind.

"If there's some way to know where Jovan's going, maybe you can get a message to him. If so, ask him to come back to me." Morton shook his head.

"There's no way to know that," he said. "He just randomly shows up on a world where no one is expecting him." He gave her an odd look.

"Ruby, you know I'm Jovan's friend. But I've got to ask you, do you think his mind is functioning normally?" Ruby laughed.

"He hasn't been himself since the news of the marshal's death broke," she replied.

"I've never known him to so stubbornly refuse to accept the facts, but that's exactly what he's doing." Morton nodded.

"Anyway, Ruby, I'll get your message in the pipeline," Morton said. "Maybe it will get to Jovan." She slowly shook her head.

"I doubt it will do any good," she said. Morton stood keeping his eyes on her.

"It never hurts to try, Ruby." He turned and headed for the door. Ruby watched him until he went out. She looked down at her glass.

"That bullheaded bastard won't change his mind for anything," she mumbled.

The place was crude, and permeated by a slight odor of many unwashed bodies over a long period of time. In a shadowed corner, Garnet sat with a drink regarding the man who sat across from him.

"What are you looking for, Jovan?" Garnet took a sip from the glass and returned it to the table.

"I want to know where Camden is." The man regarded him with no change of expression.

"He's dead, Jovan. If he wasn't, don't you think he would be hot on your tail?" Garnet shook his head and got a hard frown.

"He's alive, Kern. I know it. He's in hiding so I'll believe he's dead." Kern took a drink and looked down at the glass.

"I don't like to bring things up from the past Jovan, but that man took you down. Why would he want to hide now, instead of coming after you?" Garnet had to concede his point, but he still wasn't buying the idea that Camden was dead.

"I still believe he's alive," Garnet said, emphatically. "Why he would be in hiding, I don't know." Kern put his glass down and rested his arms on the table as he kept a steady gaze on Garnet.

"All right, Jovan. I'll put out the word and see if anyone can come up with anything. But I think you're chasing a ghost, and it's going to be damn hard to catch it." Garnet leaned forward with a defiant look.

"The marshal's alive, Kern. I can feel it! I may not know what Camden's doing, but he's alive."

As Garnet journeyed on to his next meeting, he had to decide how to face the real possibility that Camden was dead. If Kern, whom he had just left, couldn't learn anything, then he might learn something through Maya and Dealth, that proved beyond a doubt , that the marshal was still alive, or... It was a reality Garnet knew he would have to accept whether he liked it or not. He moved his fingers over the controls adjusting the speed of the ship. All he was interested in now was just finding peace of mind. If Camden was dead, he could get on with his life. But if was alive, as he firmly believed, he would have to track him down and kill him. Either way, Garnet would find the peace he so desperately needed.

Maya was a cute woman with light gray eyes and dark blonde hair, but her expression was hard. She lifted her drink as she regarded Garnet with a dubious look. She took a drink and lowered the glass.

"Jovan, Camden is dead. He hasn't been seen for months," she said. Garnet got a hard determined look.

"I don't believe that. He's hiding somewhere." Maya got a sad look and shook her head.

"Then why hasn't he showed up anywhere you've been? He's dead, Jovan. Get hold of that and hold onto it." He emphatically shook his head.

"He's alive!" he exclaimed, sharply. "I know it. Call it a gut feeling, an intuition, Maya. Why he hasn't been seen, I don't have any idea, unless it's to make me feel secure. I then get careless and he gets me again. And I have no intension of going to Forten for the rest of my life." Maya finished her drink and put the glass on a stand beside her chair.

"All right, Jovan, you win. I'll get people working to see if you're right. But you have to promise me that if my people can't find any proof that Camden is alive, you'll accept the fact that he's dead." He nodded.

"You got a deal, Maya. But I know Camden is alive somewhere." He finished his drink and stood.

"Let Kern know what you find out," Garnet said. "Now I've seen him and you, I've got one more person to see." Maya stood and stepped close to him.

"And who is that?" He put his arms around her and pulled her against him.

"Kral Dealth," he replied. "Between the three of you, it should be easy to prove if

Camden is dead or alive." She leaned forward and kissed him. When she pulled away, Maya put her hands on his cheeks and gave him a longing look.

"When you get this settled in your mind, Jovan, come back to me." He pulled her tight against him and kissed her.

Kral Dealth had been born into wealth and power. He was tall with a solid, muscular build, sharp hazel eyes, and graying hair. He had high cheekbones that gave his face the impression of being sculpted. He had known Garnet when he had taught at the university, and had closely followed his career of criminal activity. He had, on occasion, used Garnet's talent to get dirt on people who opposed programs he wanted to set in motion. They had never been close, but they respected each other, and was always willing to do favors for one another.

He was mildly surprised when Garnet showed up at his door, and astounded at his request. They sat in the library with drinks as Kral considered how to answer Garnet. He concluded that he could only relate what he had heard.

"Jovan, all I've heard from people in high positions is, what a shame to have lost a marshal like Camden. I know that's not what you want to hear, but it is what I've heard." Garnet's expression showed his disappointment.

"I'm afraid you just have to accept his death," Kral continued. "And get on with your life." Garnet shook his head.

"Then why do I have such a strong feeling that Camden is alive?" Kral shrugged.

"It could be because you have such a lust for revenge, on the man who took your hand, it won't let you rest." Garnet considered what Kral had told him, but couldn't bring himself to believe it. The feeling he had was too strong. He couldn't be wrong. He finished his drink and stood.

"Thank you, Kral. I appreciate what you've told me. But until I have conclusive proof that Camden is dead, I've got to assume he's alive. I must be certain. I have to be certain!" Kral stood and extended his hand to Garnet.

"I understand, Jovan. You must do what you have to."

Angel and Les sat regarding each other in silence. They had just received a communication informing them that Garnet had left the planet they were heading for. That wasn't what caused their silence, but that Garnet was actually hunting for Les was stunning news.

"What now?" Angel asked, breaking the silence. Les didn't answer immediately as he

was contemplating what course of action he would now have to follow.

"Well there's no sense of my playing dead any longer. I'll have to find a way to get it out that I've been on some highly classified security mission, After that, we'll just have to see what Garnet does." Angel became alarmed at that aspect.

"You'll be giving him the initiative, Les." He nodded.

"I know. But I can't think of anything else I can do." Angel shook her head.

"There must be another way," she said, feeling this would put him in an awkward and dangerous position. But Angel couldn't think of anything different either.

"I think we should put this before the chief, Les. Maybe he can think of a different course of action." Les got a puzzled look and shook his head.

"How the hell does Garnet know I'm alive?" She reached over and put her hand over his.

"Maybe it's a wish," she replied. "If you were dead, he would have no chance for revenge." Les considered her words and gave her a nod.

"So his wish comes true," he said. "But he's in the open now and hunting for me. The only way to put an end to it is to face him. But on my terms, and the place I choose."

"What about talking to the chief first?" Angel asked. Les bit his lip as he thought about that.

"I guess it wouldn't hurt," he replied. "But I doubt he'll be able to come up with something different." She gave his hand a squeeze and got a pleased look.

"Maybe," Angel said. "But we won't know that until we get to talk with him. Besides, we have that holographic projector we can use, if the need should arise." Les got a hard frown.

"Once he finds out he's been right all along, he'll want to get at me as quickly as he can. And, Angel, I intend to use that against him."

"I wouldn't be so sure of that, Les. As you told me, Garnet's not stupid."He hesitated for a moment then turned the pilot's seat to the console and began plotting a return to Earth.

19

Ruby stood looking out a window at the gray, overcast sky. She turned at the knock on the door. She went to the door, opened it, and saw a sad faced Mitch. She stepped aside, allowing him to enter. She closed the door and turned to him.

"You have some news about Jovan?" Ruby asked. Mitch nodded.

"I'm afraid so, Ruby. He's going from planet to planet asking if anyone has heard about Camden."

"And what have people been telling him?"

"That Camden is dead. But he stubbornly refuses to believe it. He insists that he's alive." She quickly turned around leaving him her back to stare at.

"Why the hell can't he just accept that the marshal is dead?" she asked. "I've never known Jovan to act like this."

"I don't know, Ruby. I wish there was someway to help him." She looked over her shoulder, then turned back to him.

"There just might be a way," she said. "Mitch, I want you to get with Nick Colter, go over all the planets Jovan has been to, and try to work out where he'll go next. Maybe he can be intercepted, and talked into coming back here." Mitch nodded.

"I'll get on it, Ruby." He turned and walked from the room.

Susan came into Farrel's office and stopped before his desk. He looked up and saw she had a look of anticipation.

"What is it?" he asked, unprepared for what he was about to hear. Susan sat down and clasped her hands on her lap.

"I heard from an informant that Ruby is sending a couple of guys after Garnet," she said. "They're going to try and convince him to come back here." Farrel regarded her with a stunned look. He couldn't understand how such information had been allowed to get out.

"Well, Farrel, what are we going to do? Call Drydon and have him inform Les, or prepare to take Garnet down ourselves?" He began rubbing his chin as he thought about it. He turned his eyes back to her.

"We're going to do both," Farrel replied. "Les might not make it here before Garnet does. I want to set up an indiscrete surveillance at the landing park, with instant communications so we can move with all speed when Garnet sets foot here." Susan smiled, stood, and let her arms fall to her sides.

"I'll see to the details immediately," she said, and hurried off.

Les stood behind, and to the side, of Drydon as he faced the media.

"When I informed the media that Marshal Camden was missing, it was a cover story because he had been assigned to a deep security operation. I also told you that body was an off worlder with no DNA sample here," Drydon said. "You took it for a cover up and ran with the rumor. Now who is embarrassed? Certainly not me." Les got a slight smile as he looked over the reporters' faces and could tell that Drydon's words had hit home.

"I hope the next time I release anything newsworthy, please recall that I don't intentionally mislead the media. Under certain circumstances – for security purposes – I have to put cover stories to protect our agents. Anything further will be released by my receptionist," Drydon concluded, and turned away from the reporters.

When he turned to Les, he saw his receptionist coming toward them with an unsettled look. Drydon patted Les' arm and nodded toward her. When Les saw her expression, he knew something was up. She stopped before the men and spoke in a low voice, in case a reporter was within earshot.

"We just got a communication from Sergeant Farrel," she said. "Ruby has two men looking for Garnet. She wants them to bring him to her so she can care for him." Les and

Drydon exchanged glances.

"What do you think of their success, Camden?" Drydon asked. Les was thinking about

something else. He blinked and shrugged.

"They should have a better chance of finding him than anyone else, sir. I'm going to have to get out to Farrel and help set up a plan to take Garnet into custody." Drydon nodded.

"Good. Let Corey remain here. This could prove to be a bloodbath when Garnet feels he's trapped."

"I'll keep you informed as to how things are proceeding, sir."

After leaving Drydon, Les headed for the record center. He had a suspicion, but couldn't prove it until he had as full a bio of Garnet as he could obtain. He would start with his time as a university teacher and work back from there. Les already had full knowledge of his criminal record. He felt he had put this off for too long.

He stopped at the counter and was faced by a short, cute clerk. He told her what he wanted to see and she assigned him a privacy booth where he could use the computer to scan records without anyone seeing what he was reading. She also informed him how he could pull up related records he might want to see. Les thanked her and stepped into the booth and slid the door closed. He sat down before a keyboard and monitor and began his search for Garnet's secret.

Les became so engrossed in what he was reading that he lost track of time. He traced Garnet's life patterns through his teaching years, his college years, and even through his teens. When he finally got to the copy of Garnet's birth certificate, the date almost seemed to leap from the monitor into Les' consciousness. He leaned back and stared at it, rubbing his chin, and contemplating what he should do with his new found knowledge. One item he decided not to share now with anyone else until it was the right time to reveal it.

Les was completely absorbed by what he had learned. At the apartment, Angel noted his distraction but didn't press him about it. Most of the afternoon, he sat quiet, as if his body were there and his mind somewhere else. At dinner, he ate automatically until Angel gripped his arm and seemed to break his trance. He looked at her and blinked as if he had no idea where he was.

"Les, what's wrong with you? You've been in some sort of trance since you returned." He noted the concern in her voice and felt her warm, soft hand on his. Les couldn't tell her everything – not yet. But he could tell her some of the things he had discovered about Garnet.

"I went to the record center and went through Garnet's life. I know him better now than I know anyone else." He lapsed into silence and regarded her with a wandering look. She gave him a nod.

"Go on, Les," she urged. He thought quickly about what he would tell her.

"He went through school and college as an honor student," Les began. "He never caused any trouble, and went out of his way to help tutor poor students. It wasn't until after he got out of prison that he became a coldblooded killer. I even went over the prison records and found he was a model prisoner. But the one thing I didn't find out was what caused him to change so radically." Angel listened with interest until his last sentence, and this brought a puzzled look to her.

"That's astounding," she said. "The only thing I can think of that might cause such a change is a deliberate decision to do so." Les shrugged.

"That's as good as any reason I've come up with, Angel. It's so hard to believe someone could just change like that." She nodded.

"I know. We need to check with those shrinks. Maybe they can give us a better insight into such a character change."

The place was filled with loud conversation and laugher amid the tinkle of glasses. Two men sat in a shadowed corner, silent and sullen. The tall, lanky one suddenly slammed his hand on the table.

"Goddamnit, Randall! What the hell does Ruby expect us to do?" The stocky man shrugged.

"Find Garnet and get him to go back to her, I guess. At least, that's what she said she was paying us for." The lanky man's lips drew into a tight line.

"And just how the hell do you suggest we do that? Every time we get to where we had been told he was, he's gone. We've been chasing his ass for over a month, and haven't come within two days of him." The stocky man lifted his glass and took a drink.

"As long as Ruby's paying us," he said, lowering his glass. "We have to keep after Garnet. Who knows, we could get lucky and get some place ahead of him." The lanky man shook his head.

"You're ever the optimist, Randall. Let's eat and get back to the ship."

Ruby sat at her desk balancing her accounts when there came a rapid knocking on the door before it was pushed open. In stepped Mitch with an expression that shocked her.

"What's wrong, Mitch?" Ruby asked. He came to the desk and stopped with a look she couldn't describe.

"It's Camden, Ruby. He's alive! Drydon has given the media hell for supporting the rumor that Camden was dead when, in fact, he had been working under deep security." Ruby was quickly on her feet, her mouth open.

"How could Jovan have known? We all believed Camden was dead." Mitch nodded.

"And we were wrong, Ruby. I don't know how, but Garnet somehow knew about Camden while we just accepted what was spoon-fed to us by the media. We have to find a way to let Garnet know we're behind him." Ruby rubbed her cheek as she thought about that. She glanced at Mitch.

"I'll see what I can come up with, Mitch."

[206]

"Well hell, Randall, what do you think we ought to do now?" Randall shrugged.

"I don't know. Contact Ruby, I suppose." The lanky man shook his head.

"Now that it's out that Camden is alive, and on Earth, neither Ruby, nor anybody else, is going to keep Garnet from going after him." Randall nodded.

"I think you're right about that. So why don't we just go back and see what Ruby wants us to do now? Facing her is better than contacting her from out here." The lanky man nodded.

"Strap in, Randall. We're heading home."

Angel sat on the sofa, in the apartment, as she watched the rerun on TV. She had to smile when she heard Drydon berate the media. Les had insisted that she stay out of sight, and not become a target for Garnet again. But a troubling thought had been in her mind since Les had told her what he had found in the records of Garnet. She felt certain he had kept something from her, and it bothered her. All she could do was wait for him to disclose it, and wonder why he hadn't told her before. She saw Les standing beside Drydon, leaned forward, and studied his face. Angel couldn't read any specific mood he was displaying. But what had he not told her? She wished he would tell her what he was keeping to himself.

Farrel's finger lifted from the comlink and the screen went dark. He turned to face Susan, who sat in front of his desk. They had just watched a delayed broadcast of Drydon facing the media.

"I think the chief handled that rather adroitly," Farrel said. "But what can Les be planning now that everyone knows he's alive and where he is?" Susan shrugged.

"Probably figuring out how he's going to go about getting Garnet, I guess," Susan replied. Farrel raised an eyebrow.

"That shouldn't be hard," he said. "Not with Garnet looking everywhere for him." Susan stood and regarded him with a confident look.

"I believe Les will have a good plan, and do what has to be done to take Garnet into custody." Farrel shook his head.

"I wish I had your confidence, Susan. But from what we know about Garnet, Les isn't going to have an easy time taking him." She smiled.

"Maybe not. But I know he'll do it. Now I have to get out on patrol." Farrel watched her back as she walked to the door. He had a strong sense of pity for her, knowing she stood no chance with Les.

Les regarded Drydon across the desk trying to fathom what he was thinking. He had just been told what Les had learned from garnet's record, all that is, except the one item of information he had also kept from Angel. It troubled Les somewhat, but it was something he would have to learn to deal with.

"What are you going to do, Camden?" Les frowned.

"I want Angel to remain out of sight. I don't want Garnet finding out she's alive , too. Then I'll just have to wait until I hear from him." Drydon got a shocked look.

"You expect him to contact you?" Les nodded.

"Garnet will let me know where he is, and when he wants to settle the bile between us. Of that I have no doubt." Drydon gave him an alarmed look.

"Won't that be dangerous, Camden? I mean going after him when you have no idea what he might try." Les shook his head.

"I already know where he'll want to settle our score – Varian Four. He feels he has to bring me down at the same place I took him down. It's become an obsession with him, and I'll accommodate him when he wants, sir." Drydon shook his head.

"It still sounds dangerous to me, Camden."

Garnet pressed the switch that locked the ship on the automatic landing frequency. He sat with a gloating look. He had been right while everyone else had been wrong. Camden was alive! He had known that. But how? He shook his head. He would just have to keep wondering about that. A green light came on and he prepared for landing.

He unstrapped himself, went to the hatch and activated it. Garnet stepped out into the warm sunshine and began walking to Ruby's. He got a smile as he wondered what she would think now that he had been proven right. Garnet moved along lost in his thoughts. He didn't care if any law enforcement person saw him because he knew they wouldn't bother him, they would leave him for Camden, and that suited him.

Susan brought the hover car to an abrupt halt and stared at Garnet walking along like he had nothing to worry about. She had sense enough not to try to stop him, but decided Farrel needed to know about this so he could contact Les. Susan quickly turned the car around and headed back to HQ.

Ruby was about to take a drink when she heard the rear door open. She turned, and her eyes widened and her mouth fell open.

"Jovan! What are you doing here so openly?" He got a confident smile.

"I'm letting Camden know where I am. No other person in law enforcement will dare make a move on me now. They will leave me to Camden. So there's no need to worry."Ruby regarded a man who had been vindicated beyond any doubt. She knew what he was planning and didn't need to ask.

"You must tell me, Jovan, how the hell you knew Camden was alive when everyone else thought he was dead?" This brought a troubled look to him.

"I'm not sure, Ruby. Call it a gut feeling. But I knew he wasn't dead. I just knew!" She put her glass down, went to him, and kissed him. When she pulled away from him she smiled.

"Welcome back, Jovan."

When Les came into the apartment, Angel went to him and they embraced and kissed. When they parted, he kept his hands on her waist and regarded her with a confident look.

"I would like for you to remain completely out of sight, Angel," Les said. "I don't want Garnet finding out you survived his abandonment on Varian Four." She got a frown as she looked at him.

"Mind telling me why?" He took his hands from her waist, went to a table, poured drinks, returned and handed her one.

"He'll be counting on me coming after him for having killed you," he replied. "I want him to think that so he won't consider doing anything else." Angel took a drink and regarded him for a moment.

"You're holding something back, Les. What is it?" He shook his head.

"I'm not holding anything back. I just want him focused on what I told you. Garnet's going to believe that my motive for revenge will make me act carelessly. Then I can take him without much trouble." Angel nodded.

"All right, Les, I'll go along with your scenario. But I still think you're not telling me everything." He took a drink and flashed an innocent look to her.

"What makes you think that?" Her eyes narrowed and she tilted her head.

"I'm not certain," she replied. "But I have a strong feeling that you know more than you've told the chief and me." He smiled.

"All I'm interested in is putting Garnet back on Forten where he belongs. Then we can get back to our quiet life together." She got a dubious look but nodded.

"All right. I'll take you at your word. But if I find out –"

"There's nothing to find out," Les said, quickly. A bit too quickly for her.

As the day paled into twilight, Ruby's curiosity got the better of her as she and Garnet had dinner.

"I'm really curious, Jovan. Could you tell me how you felt Camden was alive?" He put his fork down, pyramided his fingers, and got an odd look.

"It was almost like I could touch his mind. It was a feeling so strong I couldn't ignore it. But I knew I was right about his being alive." She regarded him with wide eyes.

"That sounds really spooky, Jovan." He nodded.

"That it was, Ruby. That it was." He resumed eating.

Susan came into the office, stopped before the desk, and regarded Farrel with a glum look.

"Garnet's not doing anything to conceal his presence at Ruby's," she said. "Were you able to contact Les?" Farrel looked at her with a calm expression and nodded.

"He already guessed where Garnet would be, Susan. Les is waiting to get some hint at what Garnet's going to do, then come after him." She got an uneasy look.

"I think it's a mistake for Les to go after Garnet alone. We know how unpredictable he is." Farrel got a slight smile.

"Care to suggest somebody better able to do the job?" Susan quickly shook her head.

"That's not what I meant. I just don't like the idea of Les doing it alone." Farrel stood, came around the desk, and put a hand on her shoulder.

"Susan, there's no one better suited to go after Garnet alone than Les. Don't trouble yourself with negative thoughts. Les can, and will, do the job." She agreed with his last sentence, but still had misgivings.

Garnet suddenly stopped lifting his fork and gave Ruby a sidewise glance.

"I must devise a way to let Camden know where I'll be waiting without it seeming to be a set up. It must be foolproof so his anger, at having lost his lady, blinds him into coming after me. His wanting to destroy me will make him careless – and I'll be the one who has his revenge." Ruby got a dubious look.

"I think that's a mistake, Jovan. You can't assume that revenge will drive him. Camden's always seemed to be very self-controlled." Garnet jabbed the fork in her direction as a flash of anger crossed his face.

"You know nothing, Ruby! I knew he was alive while you were convinced otherwise. I have a sense about Camden that you don't. So I know I'm right. I just have to convince him where I am and he'll come after me." Ruby kept quiet and lifted the glass to her lips. She knew better than to say anymore, even though she strongly felt that he was wrong.

When the door chime sounded, Angel went to the door, took a quick look through the peephole, and opened the door. Drydon stepped in and turned to her.

"I'm glad you could make it for dinner, Chief," Angel said. Drydon almost smiled.

"I don't get many chances for a home cooked meal," he said. "But I'm also curious as to what Camden has in mind for Garnet." Angel closed the door and took Drydon's arm as they walked toward the dining room.

"Let's not discuss business over dinner," she said. "Let's just relax and enjoy ourselves." Drydon nodded, glad to get away from the pressure he had been under since Garnet had appeared openly.

During dinner, the conversation was kept to small talk. Although Drydon felt certain that Les dropped a few hints to his thinking about what had to be done. After dinner, they went into the living room and Angel poured them all a brandy.

She handed Drydon and Les each a glass and picked up hers and took a seat facing the two men. Drydon took a drink and turned his gaze to Les.

"Well, Camden, want to tell me what you have on your mind?" Les took a drink and put his glass on the coffee table in front of them.

"I can't work from a set plan, sir. I've asked Angel to stay out of sight and not risk Garnet learning that she's alive, and change his mind about how I'll react. I would like it discretely leaked that I've left Earth. Then it will be a cat and mouse game as Garnet believes he's leading me to Varian Four." Drydon raised an eyebrow and got a bewildered look.

"Leading you to Varian Four!" Drydon exclaimed. "Why there?" Angel leaned forward with a confident look.

"It's where Les took him down," she said. Les nodded.

"He wants his revenge where he had his greatest humiliation," Les said. "So you see, sir, I know where I'll be going and what will be waiting for me." Drydon got a satisfied look and nodded.

"That sounds like a definite plan to me," Drydon said. Les smiled.

"From beginning to end, sir, it's all going to be a cat and mouse game," Les said.

Drydon rubbed his eyebrow.

"Good thinking, Camden," he said, as Les got a pleased look.

Ruby was both alarmed and puzzled. Garnet seemed almost happy as he paced, rubbing his hands together. She couldn't contain herself and put a hand on his arm.

[213]

"What is it, Jovan?" He turned an excited look to her.

"Camden knows I'm here, and he's left Earth. Now it's just a game to lead him to Varian Four." Ruby's brow furrowed.

"Varian Four?" she asked, not comprehending why he wanted to face the marshal in the same place he had been brought down. Garnet nodded vigorously.

"Of course, Ruby. I must seek my revenge where I faced humiliation. There's no other way I can do it. I have no second choice." She couldn't grasp his reasoning, or why he was going out of his way to lure Camden to Varian Four. She turned from him and glanced over her shoulder.

"Want a drink, Jovan?" He turned to her with a slight smile.

"Why not, Ruby. We'll drink to Camden's demise, in the near future."

As they had breakfast, Angel decided to express her concern. She put her fork down, clasped her hands, and rested her elbows on the table.

"Les, I feel uneasy about you going after Garnet. I can't explain this feeling, but it's quite strong." He regarded her and swallowed.

"There's no reason for you to feel that way. I'm confident that I'll be able to put him back where he belongs." Her expression clearly showed that she didn't share his confidence. Les put his fork down and rested his hands on the table.

"Look, Angel, I know Garnet better than I did before. His disadvantage is that he doesn't know me. That gives me the edge." She unclasped her hands but continued to leave her arms on the table.

"I understand that," she said. "But Garnet is unpredictable. You can't be certain he'll react in the way you might anticipate. Maybe that's what makes me feel uneasy. I just don't know." He reached across the table and put his hand over her's and smiled.

"I appreciate your concern, Angel. But consider the fact that I'm always uneasy when I have to face Garnet. I can't afford to let that uneasiness control me. I have to let my knowledge and experience guide me." She seemed to relax and got a slight smile.

"You're right, of course," she said. "Maybe I'm just being silly." Les gave her hand a gentle squeeze and shook his head.

"You're not being silly. You've had your encounters with Garnet and have some sense of what he's like. Your unease is a natural reaction. I don't want you worrying about me. Remember, I took him down once, and I'll do it again." Les smiled and took his hand from hers.

"Let's finish our breakfast." Angel nodded and they resumed eating.

Later that morning, Les met with Drydon.

"Have a seat, Camden. It's been verified that Garnet is with that woman Ruby. I sent a warning to Farrel not to let any of his people try to take him into custody. We don't want anyone killed uselessly." Les nodded.

"That warning was a wise move, sir. Garnet will remain on Casin Three waiting for me. I don't intend to disappoint him." Drydon's eyes narrowed as he regarded Les. He didn't like Les' sense of confidence.

"Don't underestimate what he might do, Camden. Being confident is necessary, I know. But don't let it lead you into acting recklessly." Les got a slight smile.

"With Garnet, I never intend to be reckless, sir. But I do intend to put him back on Forten." Drydon's expression softened as he nodded.

"Very well, Camden. Your ship is ready and you can leave anytime." Les stood.

"After I tell Angel goodbye, I'll leave, sir." Drydon stood and extended his hand. Les took it.

"Just be careful, Camden. Good luck." He watched Les leave the office with an unsettled look.

20

Ruby came into the apartment, closed the door, and turned a satisfied look to Garnet. He was almost his old self again, and she was grateful to be relieved from how she had thought he was losing his mind.

"How long do you think it might take Camden to get here?" she asked, concerned and curious. He turned his face to her with a confident look.

"I expect him in the next few days," Garnet replied. "After that, we'll just have to see how things develop. I intend to see that circumstances work to my advantage." Ruby wasn't sure just how much he could control events, or even if he should try.

"I'm working out a plan, Ruby. One that I feel sure will give me the edge over Camden. There are a few details I have yet to clarify, but I'm confident it will work." She went to the wall panel and glanced over her shoulder.

"Want a drink, Jovan?" He detected doubt in her tone, but didn't mention it.

"Thank you, Ruby. We can toast to my victory over Camden." Why did he keep harping on that? She wondered. The tray slid out and she picked up the drinks, turned, and handed him one.

Susan was in a dilemma. She was in love with Les, but knew he had a relationship with Corey. She tossed and turned in bed trying to decide what to do. Keep her mouth shut and be miserable. Or tell Les how she felt? What sort of position would that put him in? Anyway Susan looked at it it was a no win situation for her. How could she have gotten herself into such a position? Right, she thought, as if I consciously made myself fall in love with him. She sat up on the bed, put her feet on the floor, and went to the bathroom. She got a drink of water and came back and lay down, and her thoughts began a rerun in her mind.

Exiting the ship, Les saw Susan coming toward him. They met at the bottom of the ramp.

"It's good to see you, Les," she said, extending her hand. Les took it and gave her a nod.

"I wish it was under different circumstances." They walked to the car.

"Is he still with Ruby?" Susan glanced at him and nodded.

"When he comes out, he parades around unfearful of any law enforcement person bothering him. That makes me feel humiliated." They got in the car and fastened their seatbelts. Les turned his face to her.

"Drydon put out a warning for all law enforcement personnel to stay away from him." She turned a surprised look to him.

"Why?" Les tilted his head.

"He didn't want anyone getting killed needlessly." Susan regarded him for a moment in silence.

"That makes sense, I guess," she said, and started the car.

"What does Farrel think about it?" Les asked. Susan shrugged.

"He put out the order that none of us was to interfere with Garnet in anyway." Les nodded.

"He showed good judgment. I've got to try and think about what Garnet will try now that he knows I'm here." This brought another surprised look from her.

"How can he know that, Les? You just arrived." Les got a slight smile.

"He probably knew when I would arrive. He has informants all over. Nothing regarding him fails to reach him."

"I wish we had such an efficient intelligence net." Les laughed and Susan got a bright smile.

After shaking hands with Farrel, Les took the chair beside Susan. Farrel sat down and clasped his hands on the desk.

"Well, Les, any idea about how to get Garnet out of Ruby's place?" Farrel asked. Les rubbed his ear as he considered the question. He lowered his arm and regarded Farrel with a grim look.

"Wait for him to come after me." That wasn't the answer Farrel had expected.

"What makes you think he will?" Farrel asked. Les straightened up in the chair.

"That's why he escaped from Forten. He wants to get back at me more than anything else. He must know that I can't make a move against him here. So I believe he'll make a move on me sooner rather than later." Susan put her hand on Les' arm and he looked at her.

"He could ambush you, Les. He might kill you before you even know he's around." Les patted her hand.

"Don't worry about that, Susan. Garnet wants to make certain I know who is doing the killing."

"Do you want some protection?" Farrel asked. Les glanced at Susan.

"I've got Susan with me. What more would I need?"

As they had dinner, Les noticed a nervousness about Susan. But it seemed she was in no hurry to get off her mind what was bothering her. After a few moments of awkward silence, Les broke it.

"What's bothering you, Susan? If you're worried about what Garnet may try, don't."She raised her eyes to him.

"It's not Garnet. It's you." Les' brow furrowed as he got a puzzled look.

"Me! How?" Susan put her fork down and rested her arms on the table.

"I'm in love with you, Les." He opened his mouth and she raised a hand.

"Let me finish. I know you have a relationship with Corey, and there's no chance for anything between us. But the least you can do is make love to me. That will be something I can remember and cherish." He had no way, no thought, of how to answer her. He regarded her in silence. Susan stood, came around the table, and took hold of his hand.

"Let's go the bedroom," she said, and pulled him to his feet.

"I can't make a move against Camden here, Ruby," Garnet said. "But with Corey dead, he's become very chummy with that woman officer." Ruby lowered her glass and regarded him with a look of curiosity.

"What are you planning, Jovan?" He began to pace, clasping his hands behind him. He stopped and turned to her with a secretive look.

"I need that woman," he said. "Then I need to let Camden know where I've taken her. He'll come after us, and that will give me the choice of where to face him."

"Varian Four?" she asked. He nodded. Ruby put her glass down and went to him.

"Your second idea will be easier done than the first," she said. "Getting your hands on that woman won't be so easy. How do you intend to accomplish that?" Garnet rubbed his chin as he thought for a moment.

"I'll have a couple of men grab her while she's on patrol," he replied. "It will have to be a quick grab, before she can communicate what's happening to her." Ruby got a dubious look.

"That may not be as simple as you think, Jovan. She's a trained law enforcement person, and quite capable of taking care of herself." He got a smile that sent a chill up her spine.

"That's true, Ruby. But she can resist only if she's conscious. I'll have one of the men carry a hypo that will quickly render her unconscious. So you see, it won't be that difficult." She smiled and slipped her arms around his neck.

"You think of everything, Jovan."

"Well, Les, you've been here a week and Garnet hasn't made a move against you,"

Farrel said. Les nodded as he paced, puzzled over Garnet's action, or lack of action.

"He's not stupid, Farrel," Les said. "Making a move against me here would be too dangerous for him. He's not willing to take such a risk, especially if he can lure me to a place where there's just the two of us. My guess is he's going to leave abruptly, knowing

I'll follow him." Susan stood.

"I've got to get out on patrol," she said, glancing at Les.

"Let us know if you hear anything," Farrel said, noting her sad look.

"Be careful out there," Les said. Susan nodded, turned, and left. Les turned to Farrel.

"Make certain all frequencies of Garnet's ship are in my ship's computer." Farrel smiled.

"Already taken care of, Les." Les smiled.

"You always have everything done before I ask," Les said. Farrel laughed.

As Susan began her patrol, she was unaware that she was being followed. The man tailing her had been told by Garnet to follow her, learn her pattern, but not to bother her. He would follow that last order – for a time. But he had his own ideas about how to treat women. He would wait for his chance, then act on his own, and for his own satisfaction.

Garnet wasn't aware that the man he was paying to follow Susan was also moving to his own plan. Ruby regarded Garnet with a worried look.

"I wish you had gotten someone else to follow that woman, Jovan. There's something about Giles that gives me the creeps. I know he has a record of violence against woman. He might act in a manner that could disrupt your plan." He put his hands on her arms and smiled.

"Don't worry, Ruby. He knows better than to cross me." She got a hard frown.

"What good will it do to kill him if he's already screwed up your plan?" He lost his smile as he regarded her with a concerned look.

"You're right, Ruby. I'll pay Giles off and get someone else to follow her." She quickly embraced him.

Angel looked at the audvid image of Drydon with her brow furrowed in puzzlement.

"It's been over a week, sir, and nothing has happened between Les and Garnet." He nodded.

"It has me baffled too, Corey. Unfortunately Camden can't openly go after Garnet on that world. He's under restrictions, but Garnet isn't. Why he's remaining inactive is anybody's guess." Angel cupped her chin.

"So there's nothing we can do to help Les?" Drydon nodded.

"Nothing, Corey. If I learn anything new I'll inform you." His image faded, leaving her to ponder what Garnet was planning.

"I don't understand what Garnet is up to," Les said, glancing from Susan to Farrel.

"It's just not like him to remain so quiet." Farrel rubbed the back of his neck.

"It seems to me that he's planning something that will be a surprise for us." Farrel said.

"I agree," Susan said. Les glanced at her and gave a nod.

"We have to anticipate what he might attempt," Les said. "It will give us something to work with so we can be ready for anything he might try." Farrel and Susan agreed, but remained silent.

Ruby was perplexed as she sipped her drink.

"Why hasn't Camden tried something, Jovan?" He looked at her with a raised eyebrow.

"He can't. Not here anyway," Garnet replied. "Which gives me an idea. If I leave, he'll follow. I should be able to lure him to a planet where I can, at least, wound him again." Ruby got a concerned look and went to him.

"You're safe here, Jovan. Why risk an encounter with him?" He patted her arm.

"I'll use a holographic projector to hold his attention while I take him from behind. Instruct the landing park to ready my ship to leave, Ruby. I'm damn tired of waiting." She nodded and went to the audvid unit.

As Les paced, the audvid unit on Farrel's desk sounded.

"Yes?" Farrel asked, pressing the comlink.

"This is Slosky at the landing park." Those words stopped Les in his tracks.

"We just got instructions to prepare Garnet's ship for departure." Farrel glanced at Les, who nodded.

[223]

"Do you know when the departure is scheduled?" Farrel asked.

"As soon as the ship's ready," Slosky replied. Farrel frowned as he thought for a moment.

"Prepare Mr. Camden's ship," Farrel said. "He'll be leaving shortly after Garnet. And thanks for the onfo, Slosky."

"Okay, Farrel," Slosky said. "I'll see to it immediately." Farrel broke the connection and turned his gaze to a puzzled Les.

"What the hell is he up to?" Les asked, more to himself than Farrel.

"Whatever it is," Farrel said. "It can't be anything good." Les glanced at him as he ran his hand over his chin.

"I agree," Les said. "I was sure he would try something. But why is he leaving at this time and so abruptly?" Farrel's eyebrows lifted.

"Could be because neither of you dare make a move against the other here, Les." Still rubbing his chin, Les thought about what he said and concluded he must be right.

"That makes sense," Les said. "He' going to try and lure me into an ambush. What he doesn't know is that I have the advantage in tracking his ship. I'll know where he's going, where he's landed, and that he's waiting for me." Farrel spread his hands on the desk.

"That's true, Les. But you won't know when, or how, Garnet plans to act." Les nodded.

"When it comes to Garnet, there's always risk," Les said. "Now I'm going to the landing park and wait for him to leave." Farrel stood and extended his hand.

"Good luck, Les." He smiled and took the offered hand.

"Thanks, Farrel. I'll need all the luck I can get."

Garnet watched the instrument console intently. He got a slight smile as his sensors detected the ship following him.

"You're doing good, Camden," he mumbled. "Just stay with me and I'll give you a nice present." He noted the ship was holding its distance, that meant the bait had been taken. Garnet was anxious, but patient, for the showdown, but he wanted it on his terms.

He made up his mind not to rule out anything Camden might try. He had learned from his adversary. Now he would put his learning to the test and see how well it worked. He was hoping for positive results – the killing of Camden. He expected no less. But maybe he wouldn't kill Camden just yet. He was looking forward to an exciting chase to get his mind back in shape. Yes, Garnet thought, a stimulating chase was just what he needed. And Camden was just the man to provide it.

Thirty minutes after Garnet left, Les lifted off and kept his ship at a safe distance from Garnet's ship. He felt it was too early to guess where Garnet was heading. Les would have to wait for a more clear idea of his destination. He was confident that Garnet had no idea he was being followed. This gave Les confidence that he had the edge when it came to facing Garnet. Not knowing where he was going gave Les some unease, but he pushed it from his mind as he thought of putting Garnet back on Forten. He was looking forward to a quiet life again, without any interference from Garnet. Now that, he thought, was really worth considering. Having once escaped from Forten, the authorities there would be doubly sure it didn't happen again. Les felt it was only a matter of time till he accomplished his goal.

Angel was lifting the coffee cup when the audvid sounded. She put the cup down, went to it, and pressed the comlink. She saw Drydon regarding her with a pleased look.

"I've had a communication from Farrel, Corey. Garnet is out of his lair and Camden is on his tail." She couldn't stifle the shiver that ran through her.

"I hope Les knows what he's doing. And I pray that he'll be cautious." Drydon chuckled.

[225]

"I wouldn't worry about that," he said. "He knows how to take care of himself, and in all probability, Garnet too." Angel couldn't shake the uneasy feeling overtaking her.

"With Garnet, Chief, I always worry." Drydon quickly lost his slight smile.

"I'll let you know if I hear anything more, Corey." The screen went dark. She took her finger from the comlink and turned with a worried look. Angel knew Garnet was cunning, and had something definite in mind. She was concerned that he could pull off some kind of trap and kill Les. But all she could do was wait and hope. She had confidence that Les would do his job without hesitation, but so would Garnet.

When Mitch came in, he found Ruby pacing, her right elbow resting on her left hand, her right hand cupping her chin. She had a worried expression and didn't notice him standing by the door.

"What's the matter, Ruby?" She started and dropped her arms to her sides as she turned to him.

"I'm worried about Jovan. I only hope he knows what he's doing drawing Camden after him." Mitch shrugged and spread his hands.

"He's been able to get out of a lot tougher scrapes than facing the marshal," Mitch said. Ruby nodded.

"I know. But Camden has become an obsession with him. My concern is that it will make him reckless in seeking revenge."

"Come on, Ruby. Garnet is too smart for that. I'll bet he has a plan all worked out that will entail the least risk to himself." She regarded Mitch and seemed to relax.

"You're probably right, Mitch," she admitted. "Yet I can't help but worry about him.

He's been so changed since he escaped from Forten." Mitch nodded.

[226]

"Being incarcerated there is likely to change anyone." Ruby got a slight smile.

"Thank you, Mitch."

After three days, Les was perplexed. He still had no idea of where Garnet was headed. It seemed he was just wandering through space. Les felt he was working to some kind of plan, and he just hadn't figured it out yet. He strained his mind trying to understand what Garnet was up to. Just when he needed his special insight into Garnet's mind, it seemed to have failed him. Maybe, Les thought, it's not me, but that Garnet had learned a way to block his mind. If that was the case, he was going to have to be extremely cautious. All he could do was follow and see where he was going. But, he admitted to himself, this seemingly wandering of Garnet made him uneasy.

Garnet sat watching his monitor and glancing at his sensors with a slight, wicked smile. His lips moved in a low mumble.

"Confused, Camden? Well things will clear up in a couple of days. Then the final game will begin, and only one of us will be alive at the end." He suddenly broke out in laugher, and pointed to the monitor.

"You'll be even more confused after we arrive at out destination," Garnet said, in a loud, threatening tone. He was more than confident he would be able to handle Camden like a puppet.

Ruby turned when the door opened. She saw Mitch standing there with a frown. He spread his hands and shook his head.

"Nothing, Ruby. No one has heard from either Jovan or Camden. They just seem to have vanished." She rubbed her eye and began pacing.

"Where the hell could they have gone? And why hasn't anyone heard from them?" Mitch shrugged.

"It's hard telling, Ruby. They're both working to their own plan. How it works out, we won't know until one of them shows up." She glanced at him and nodded.

"All right, Mitch. Keep our ears open for anything. They can't remain out of touch for much longer." He nodded and turned to the door. Ruby turned to the window and looked out, unable to shake her feeling of disquiet.

Angel was in a stunned silence regarding Drydon's image on the audvid unit.

"Vanished?" she asked, in a tense voice. He nodded.

"I'm afraid so, Corey. The rangers have been monitoring the frequencies of both ships. There hasn't been any sort of communication from either." She nervously rubbed her cheek as she considered what might have occurred.

"Is it possible the ships collided, Chief?" Drydon shook his head, holding his neutral expression.

"No. If there had been a collision, both ships had emergency transponders that would have automatically activated." Angel lowered her hand to her leg.

"What do you think has happened, sir?" Drydon spread his hands on the desk.

"Just what Camden said. They're playing a game of cat and mouse with each other. Neither wanting to give away their position by communicating with anyone." She felt slight relief at his answer since it seemed logical.

"The only trouble is," Angel said. "Both consider themselves the cat and not the mouse." Drydon frowned.

"If I hear anything more, Corey, I'll let you know right away." The screen went dark, and she stood staring at it for some minutes. Waiting, for her, was becoming an almost unbearable burden.

After five days, Les was still perplexed. He had followed Garnet into unknown space.

But, Les thought, Garnet seemed to know where he was going. It was now certain he was heading for the second planet from the star. Les made a quick sensor sweep of the planet and found it had an oxygen-nitrogen atmosphere, and its gravity was slightly less than Earth. Les shook his head as his brow furrowed. It seemed clear that Garnet had been to this planet before because he had come to it with no deviation. But what was down there that Garnet wanted? Les saw his ship begin to glide into the atmosphere.

Les made a couple of orbits to be certain of the location of Garnet's ship. He took the ship off automatic and turned it down into the atmosphere. He made certain he landed far enough from Garnet's ship so his landing wouldn't be observed. Once down, Les loosened the straps and headed for the hatch, strapping his sidearm around his waist. Stepping outside, Les was looking at a pristine world unsoiled by civilization. He took a deep breath and headed in the direction of Garnet's ship.

Garnet was very careful as he loaded the disc into the holographic projector. He didn't want Les catching on too quickly to what he was seeing. He chuckled slightly when he thought of the expression on Les' face when he found out what he was really facing. When he left this planet, Garnet knew the final act of their duel would begin, and he was determined to be the one who would walk away. Camden would be dead and he would be free to take his life back.

Les moved quickly, but cautiously, until he saw Garnet's ship. He kept out of sight until he saw Garnet leave the ship. Bewildered, Les wondered why Garnet had come to this world. It didn't make any sense. But he could no longer expect that from him. He carefully followed him, making certain he remained unseen. It was weird, but Garnet was headed for a rocky depression similar to the one on Varian Four. Les began moving slowly up the side to where he could look down into the place.

At first, nothing was in view, then he saw Garnet come through the opening and stand looking around. Then he began to pace, as though waiting for someone. Les didn't want to take the chance of someone else getting killed this time. He drew his weapon and stood up.

"Garnet!" He looked around, but didn't seem to notice Les standing on the crest. Les frowned.

"Up here," Les said. Garnet just stood staring off into space. Les began moving down the inside slope believing he was trying to lure him closer before making a move. Still Garnet paid him no attention. Les got an uneasy feeling and made certain his weapon was aimed at Garnet, should he try anything. At the bottom, Les moved toward Garnet, his weapon set on full stun, ready to fire. But he still got no attention from him. Then it suddenly dawned on Les that he was facing a holographic image.

"Shit!" he exclaimed sharply, holstered his weapon, and began quickly climbing back up the slope. Over the top, down to the ground, and Les broke into a furious run for his ship.

It took him a quarter of an hour to reach his ship. He activated the hatch, hurried inside, and began powering up the systems. He moved his finger over the control panel and got a cold frown and slammed his hand against the top of the console.

"Son of a bitch!" Garnet was gone, and he had changed all the frequencies of his ship. Les sat feeling disgusted, knowing that Garnet had known he was being followed. He had let Garnet surprise him yet again, and now he would have to find some other way to hunt him down. But where would he begin? Back on Casin Three? It was a possibility, but Les was hoping for a break that could shorten this chase.

21

It was almost eight in the evening and Angel was listening to classical music when the door chime sounded and made her start. She stood, went to the door and looked through the peephole. She was surprised to see two security men she knew from Drydon's office. She opened the door and faced them.

"Yes?" she asked. The ranking officer spoke.

"Chief Drydon sent us to bring you to his office."

"What's this about?" Angel asked, puzzled. The officer shook his head.

"We don't know, Ms. Corey. We were just told to come and bring you to the chief's office." Angel nodded.

"I'll get my jacket." She turned off the music, grabbed her jacket, and turned off the lights.

The ride to Drydon's office was in silence. Angel was wondering what could be so important as to have her come to his office this late in the evening. She had an uneasy feeling that it might be about Les. But, on considering that, she knew Drydon would have called her, not have her come to see him. She watched the streetlights drift past as she decided not to jump to any conclusion until she heard what Drydon had to say.

When Angel was shown into Drydon's office, she saw him sitting behind his desk with a look that was a cross between worry and disgust. He stood and motioned her to a chair.

"Please have a seat, Corey. I called you here at this time so there was little risk of your being seen." She sat down and he did the same and folded his hands on the desk.

"I'm afraid I have gotten some disturbing news from Camden. He's lost Garnet's trail." Angel leaned forward with an alarmed look.

"How was he able to do that?" Drydon got a hard frown.

"Garnet kept him occupied by the use of a holographic projector. While Camden was doing this, Garnet changed all the frequencies of his ship and left the planet." Angel shivered.

"That's very odd, Chief," she said. "Les had planned to use a holographic projector in the same way. Remember?" Drydon's brow furrowed.

"It seems those two know each other much better than we've been led to believe. But how?" Angel shook her head.

"I don't know – yet. But I intend to get to the bottom of why they think so much alike. It's intriguing, and a little frightening, too."

"I hope you can find out something, Corey. Camden is trying to relocate Garnet and resume the chase. What the outcome of this will be is something we're just going to have to wait and see." She stood and regarded him with a determined look.

"I'll need a security clearance to get into the main computer, sir." He nodded.

"You have it, Corey. I hope you're successful in your search." He watched her back as she walked from the office. He hoped she would find what she was looking for. Camden and Garnet thought so much alike it was uncanny. But there had to be a rational answer, he thought.

Les was crusing along trying to think of where to look for Garnet when the ship's communicator showed an incoming message. He pressed the comlink down and listened.

"This is Ranger Base Delta Blue Six, calling Special Officer Camden. Come in."

"This is Camden. Go ahead, Ranger." A loud burst of static came through the speaker.

"I have some information that may be of interest to you, sir. An unknown ship was tracked to the planet D4A. It could be the fugitive you're after."

"Thank you. I'll investigate and see what it's about." Les released the comlink, quickly put in a course for the planet, and leaned back hoping this was the break he needed. Les knew an unknown ship was one the rangers didn't have the frequencies to, and Garnet had changed his. So it was a good bet that was Garnet's ship down there. Les felt Garnet didn't know he had been spotted by the rangers, and had sent Les his location.

He made four orbits to make certain he knew the location of the ship, but Les began to wonder what would bring Garnet to a planet of ruins. There had to be something valuable enough to bring him here. It suddenly dawned on him that he was what Garnet felt was valuable on this planet. Les took the ship off automatic and turned it down into the atmosphere. But how could he have known Les would follow him here? A question for another time.

Taking a calculated risk, Les brought his ship down close to the unknown ship, and kept it as low and slow as safety would permit, allowing him to land less than a mile from it. He put his ship down where it was shielded by thick woodland. He unstrapped, stood, and turned to the bulkhead locker. He took out his sidearm and strapped it on. He went to the hatch and activated it.

He moved among the dark brown trees with bright green leaves, listening to the sounds of animals unseen in the underbrush. Les stopped when he came in view of the ship and took a hard look around. He saw no one outside the ship, but it was Garnet's ship. He knew that by the registration number on the side. But was Garnet in the ship, or out and about looking for him, and waiting to begin his killing again. Les decided he was out, and slowly proceeded away from the ship and in the direction of the ruins.

The ruins held a definite alien shape with heaping piles of rubble lying on the ground with odd shapes that gave Les a shudder. He moved deeper into the city wondering why Garnet had selected this planet for their face off instead of Varian Four. Then Les recalled that Garnet would have no idea he was here, and made it a false premise that he had come here for a face off. He knew there was no use in trying to out guess Garnet, but to stay alert and concentrate on why he was here. He moved cautiously, constantly turning his eyes around and looking for any movement.

Well into the ruins, Les heard only the wind whispering among what partial structures still stood. No animals lived here, and that made him curious. He drew his weapon and started taking more pain to keep under cover. A pulsar charge exploded against the ruins just above his head. Les quickly moved behind a large pile of rubble.

"How the hell did you find me?" Garnet shouted. Les had to smile.

"That's my job, Garnet, remember." Les knew Garnet was moving, changing his position to keep him guessing. Les decided to tell Garnet what he had learned as he moved.

"I know something about you, Garnet, even you don't know." Les waited, but got no response. He decided to move too, so Garnet wouldn't be able to have a place to concentrate on.

"We're brothers, Garnet. My mother gave birth to unidentical twins. She was acting as a surrogate mother. When we were born, the woman you called mother had a contract for one child, and she took you." Les waited for a response, but for some minutes all he heard was the slight breeze. He knew Garnet was considering what he had just heard.

"There's no way I'm buying that, Camden. I have to give you credit though. You're a much more imaginative liar than I thought." He had reacted just as Les thought he would.

"You can look up the record on Forten, Garnet." Silence. Les moved again, trying to get close to where he had last heard Garnet. It took time because he had to move slowly, cautiously, and carefully among the ruins. One misstep and he could bring loose rubble down on him.

When Les got to where he thought Garnet had been, he heard a ship powering up and lifting off. He leaned against a pile of rubble and felt disgusted that he had let Garnet get another one over on him.

"Goddamnit! I've got to be more conscientious about what he might do."

In space, Garnet poured on the speed. But Camden had given him something to think about he would rather not consider. He recalled that when he had taught at the university, they had been conducting tests on twins, identical and unidentical, to try an verify if they possessed some sort of telepathic bond. They hadn't found a clear-cut answer, but their results were very impressive. Garnet began to wonder if that was how he knew Camden wasn't dead? Then a flow of memories of his encounters with him and how he had seemed to know what Camden would do, with the exception of Varian Four.

Garnet knew he had to learn the truth – a truth he felt he should reveal to no one. He thought for some minutes and decided the only place he could search for the truth was on Casin Three. He considered how he would react if Camden was his brother. Here he faced a grim choice of killing Camden or being sent to Forten for life. It was a decision he could defer – for awhile. He quickly worked out a course and set the ship on automatic.

Les walked slowly to his ship as he knew Garnet would get out of the area as fast as he could, not affording Les any chance to follow him. If Garnet hadn't believed him – and that seemed pretty certain – he wouldn't try to access any records. But he knew Garnet couldn't afford not to, if he wanted to know the truth. Les was now betting he would head back to Casin Three and access all the records he could find.

Les activated the hatch and went on board. He powered up the ship's systems and lifted off. All he could do was hope for another chance sighting of Garnet's ship; and that seemed rather improbable of happening twice. It seemed all he was getting from Garnet was more frustration.

Angel pulled up Les' records, it took most of the day to go through them. When she came on his birth record, she froze. Les had never mentioned a twin brother. Angel assumed his mother had never told him she had been a surrogate. But what about this unknown brother? A sharp shiver ran her spine as she made another assumption.

"Garnet!" she exclaimed, sharply. That was what Les knew, and had been holding back. He had come to Garnet's records and had found a truth he had never known about. She began to wonder how he had taken it that Garnet was his brother. How would that have changed him? Angel was certain someone learning they had a brother they had never known would surely cause some sort of change.

"If Les knows Garnet is his brother, how will it affect his job?" she asked, aloud. But there was no one in the room to give her an answer. Now she would have to go through Garnet's records for confirmation, but would do that later. She shut down the computer, stood, and knew she had to tell Drydon what she now believed.

Drydon leaped to his feet, bent over his desk, and pressed his hands hard against the top, his knuckles and fingertips whitening. It wasn't the sort of reaction Angel had expected.

"Camden and Garnet are brothers! How is it that neither knew about this?" Angel inhaled deeply.

"I believe neither mother told them, sir. After Les found out about it was when he started acting odd. Like we believed, he was holding something back. I'll know for certain after I look at Garnet's birth record. But I don't think I'm wrong. Should we let Les know that we know, Chief?" Drydon regarded her for a moment then shook his head.

"No. If he didn't tell us, there's no reason to let him know we've been snooping in his records." Angel nodded, agreeing. Drydon shook his head as he sank back down in his chair.

"Brothers! Unidentical twins! Damn, I never thought to see such a situation."

Farrel looked up when Susan came rushing in. He could tell from her expression that she was alarmed as she stopped before his desk. He gave her a moment to catch her breath.

"What's wrong, Susan?" She made a wild gesture with her arm.

"Garnet's back. You better contact Drydon so he can alert Les." Farrel got a hard frown at the news.

"You're sure about this?" Farrel asked. Susan nodded.

"One of my informants saw him going towards Ruby's place. There's no mistake. He's here and he don't seem to give a damn who knows it." Farrel rubbed his ear.

"I'll contact Drydon immediately. And, Susan, warn our people not to interfere with him." She slumped down in a chair with a worried look.

"I wonder what happened to Les?" she asked. "He had all the frequencies of Garnet's ship. How the hell was he able to get away from him?" Farrel raised an eyebrow.

"The only way he could have done that was by changing the frequencies of his ship. Not impossible, if he had enough time to carry it out."

"I hope that's the case," she said. "I don't want to think that Les came to any harm."

Farrel leaned forward.

"I wouldn't worry about that, Susan. Les is probably cussing up a storm because he let Garnet fool him again."

Giles pulled his vehicle to the curb and got a slight smile as he saw Susan get out of the hover car and hurry into the building. He knew what she was going to blabber about – that Garnet had returned. He was going to enjoy working her over. It was about time to take her out, he thought. He was ready, everything was in place, and he just had to wait for the opportunity.

Ruby regarded Garnet with wide eyes and an open mouth.

"I hadn't expected you back so soon, Jovan." He held his expressionless look.

"I have something very important to do here," he said. "When Camden shows up here, I want you to tell him I lured him here to gain time. And make no mistake, Ruby, he will come here." She got a dubious look.

"What makes you think he'll come here?" she asked. He clasped his hands and regarded her with that unchanging expression.

"Damnit, Ruby! He wants to take me into custody. I have a man at the landing park who will contact you when Camden arrives. I'm not going to tell you where I'm going so you won't be lying to him when you tell him you don't know." She got a determined look and decided to press him for an answer.

"What is it you have to do, Jovan? I've never seen you in this sort of mood before." He stood silent for a moment before replying.

"I have to learn the truth about something."

"The truth about what?" she asked. Garnet decided to tell her.

"Camden told me we were brothers – nonidentical twins. I have to learn if he was telling the truth. And the only way I can do that is by accessing the records." Ruby couldn't bring herself to believe what he had just told her.

"How can that be possible, Jovan?" she asked, trying hard to understand this idea.

"That is what I have to find out, Ruby. I believe its true, and that's how I knew he was alive when everyone else thought he was dead. I'll have a drink, then go."

At the record center, Garnet was looking at the same records Les and Angel had seen. It was true that Camden had been one of a set of nonidentical twins, but there was no evidence that he could see that made them brothers. Yet there was no other explanation for him knowing, without doubt, that Camden wasn't dead. He needed verifiable proof, not a transient idea. He delved into his birth record, and the transient idea became an indisputable fact. He decided not to go back to Ruby's. He would wait until after dark, then go to the landing park, stay in his ship until late, then leave.

When Les came down the ramp, he saw Farrel with a grim expression waiting for him.

This caused a wave of unease to sweep over him. He stopped before Farrel and waited for a moment. When he didn't speak, Les did.

"What's wrong?" Farrel shook his head as his lips drew into a tight line.

"Susan is missing. Her hover car was found abandonded, but there wasn't a trace of her." Les nodded as he quickly made up his mind.

"Take me to Ruby's, Farrel. I'm going to get some info that will help us find Susan." Farrel got a surprised look.

"You sure you want to do this, Les?" Les straightened his shoulders and took a deep breath.

"It's the only way I can think of to get a lead on Susan. And this time, Ruby is going to talk straight with me." Farrel nodded.

"All right, Les. Let's go to the car."

When Les walked into the bar, he saw Ruby sitting at a table facing the door. It didn't surprise him that she was waiting for him. He went to her table, pulled out a chair and sat down. He regarded her for a moment and leaned forward.

"Have you seen Garnet?" Les asked. Ruby nodded.

"He left a message for you," she said. "He lured you here to give himself more time. What for he didn't say." Les nodded, suspecting why Garnet had come here.

"Officer Susan Burns is missing. Did he have anything to do with it?" Ruby got a look that was a cross between surprise and disgust.

"Giles!" she exclaimed, in a disgusted tone. Les leaned across the table.

"Who is that?" Ruby got a cold look and hard frown.

"He's a cold, woman-hating bastard. He probably took her because Jovan had him watching her – until I convinced him to have someone else do it. Apparently Giles was working for his own ends, just as I told Jovan he would be." Les leaned back knowing she was telling him the truth.

"Can you tell me where I can find this Giles?" Les asked. Ruby nodded.

"I'll do better than that," she replied, in a cold tone. "I'll draw you a map to that son of a bitch."

Farrel pulled the car to the curb and they looked around. It was a rundown neighborhood littered with trash. Les glanced at the mouth of the alley that led to Giles basement apartment. Les gave the scene a quick lookover.

"Okay, Farrel, it's your territory and your personnel that's in trouble. How do you want to handle this?" Farrel rubbed an eyebrow as he thought it over.

"I'll go check out the front of the place," Farrel replied. "If there's a chance of taking him with no trouble, I'll give you a wave." Les gave a nod as Farrel got out of the car.

Farrel bent down and moved along the concrete fascade toward a small window. He raised up and peered through the window. He saw Susan tied in a chair; her arms tied to the armrests and her legs to the chair legs. Her head was slumped on her chest. He carefully looked around the room, but saw no one else. He moved back to the car where he stood, thinking and glancing at Les.

"Susan's in there, but I didn't see anyone else. I think Giles is gone." Les was quick to come up with an idea.

"Let's see if we can get inside and wait on him," Les said. Farrel nodded and they went to the door, tried it, and were surprised to find it unlocked. They moved inside and made a quick examination of the bruised and bloodied, unconscious Susan.

"We need to get her to a hospital," Les said, in a low voice. Farrel glanced at him with an agreeable look. They quickly turned when they heard footsteps coming down the alley and quickly took places on opposite sides of the door. Giles opened the door and walked in without suspecting anything. When he turned, Les and Farrel moved on him. Surprised, he meekly submitted to arrest.

"How did you find me so fast?" Giles asked, in a timerous tone. Farrel turned a hard look to him.

"It wasn't hard," Farrel replied, in a tight tone.

After putting wrist restraints on Giles, Farrel turned to Les.

"Use the car and take Susan to the hospital. I've called in another car to take this piece of shit to headquarters." Les quickly freed Susan from the chair, slipped her arm around his neck and lifted her up in his arms. He took her out, following Farrel, who kept pushing Giles in front of him.

Les opened the door and put Susan on the front seat and turned to Farrel.

"Will you be all right?" Les asked, nodding at Giles. Farrel regarded him with a grim frown.

"He won't be any trouble," Farrel replied. "A car is on the way and should be here any moment." Les nodded, hurried around to the driver's side, opened the door, and got in.

He pressed the ignition switch and pulled away from the curb.

Les paced in the waiting room, concerned about Susan, but thankful for Ruby's help in locating her so quickly. Farrel came in and stopped facing Les.

"How is she?" Farrel asked. Les shrugged.

"The doctor hasn't told me anything yet. But from what I saw, I think she will be allright. It appeared he just liked smacking her around." Farrel got a hard frown.

"Perverted son of a bitch!" Les clasped his hands in front of him.

"That's why Ruby sent us after him," Les said. "She wanted this guy off the streets, too, and I can't say I blame her." The doctor came in and stopped looking at them.

"She's going to be fine," the doctor said. "Sore and bruised for awhile, but okay." Farrel got a look of relief and Les exhaled loudly.

"I'm glad to hear that, Doctor," Farrel said. Les nodded in agreement.

"You two might as well leave. She won't be able to see anyone until tomorrow."

Outside the hospital, Farrel and Les stopped and regarded each other.

"What's your plan, Les?" He rubbed his ear as he considered the question.

"I'm going to stick around for a few days. Give Susan a morale boost, and hope some clue as to Garnet's location comes in." Farrel patted his shoulder.
"Let's go have a drink," Farrel said. "We'll take my car. I'll have someone come by and pick up the other one."

As they sat drinking beer, Les became curious.

"What about this Giles? What's his problem?" Les asked. Farrel shrugged.

"He's a small time punk, who has a record of assaulting women. I guess he goes after women because he knows he can overpower them. Just an egotistical bully." Les nodded.

"You mean he follows a natural law," Les said. Farrel's brow furrowed as he got a questioning look.

"What natural law?" Les regarded him with a frown.

"One I came up with. The powerful pick on the powerless only because they can without fear of being hurt in return." Farrel nodded.

"That sounds about right," Farrel said. "But how Giles was able to take Susan…" He shook his head.

"People like him have all sorts of tricks," Les said. "He probably set up a situation in which she suspected nothing, and then took the advantage."

"And that must be why he offered no resistance," Farrel said. "He wasn't in a position of control." Les nodded.

"Exactly. Giles knows when he can exercise power and when he has to give in to it." Farrel got a grim look.

"That was smart of him," Farrel said. "Because I certainly wanted to do some harm to that bastard."

22

The following morning, Les visited Susan. When he came in the room, she turned her face away, not wanting him to see her in such a condition. He stepped beside the bed and took hold of her hand. This made her turn her face back to him and he patted her hand.

"How are you feeling, Susan?" He turned his eyes down to her and spoke in a soft tone.

"Not very good. I feel I let myself down by falling for such a dumb trick." Les gave her hand a squeeze.

"Giles was prosecuted before for assaults on women. And Ruby told me Garnet hired him to watch you, until she talked him into getting someone else. It was Ruby who also told us where we could find you." Susan turned a surprised look to Les.

"Ruby did?" Les nodded.

"It seems she doesn't like Giles because he enjoys beating up on women."

Farrel came in and stopped beside Les and regarded her.

"Felling better, Susan?" Farrrel asked. She slowly shook her head.

"I feel humiliated." Farrel reached over and patted her shoulder.

"What happened to you could have happened to anyone," Farrel said. "We can't know what's coming until we face it." Farrel turned his face to Les.

"A message came in from the rangers, Les. One of their scouts spotted a ship and got the registration number. They checked and found it matched Garnet's ship." Les got a relieved look.

"Where was it heading?" Les asked, already guessing the answer.

"They couldn't be certain, but it appeared it was headed for Varian Four," Farrel replied. Les shook his head.

"He keeps going back to where I took him down. I wish I could figure out why he returns there. It just doesn't make sense." Farrel shrugged.

"Could be his mind has become somewhat unstable," Farrel suggested. Les looked back at Susan.

"I have to be going, Susan," Les said. "I'll see you next time I stop here." She looked at him and nodded.

"I understand, Les. Be careful." He turned and went to the door.

"Good luck, Les," Farrel said. Les glanced over his shoulder.

"Thanks, Farrel, for all of your help." He watched Les' back as he walked down the corridor. He turned back to Susan and she noticed his odd expression.

"What is it?" she asked. Farrel hesitated for a moment.

"Les didn't say not to tell anyone." She got an impatient look.

"What, Farrel? What did he tell you?" His shoulders slumped and he averted his eyes.

"Garnet is his unidentical twin. Les is going after his brother." Susan's eyes widened and she shook her head.

"My God! How can he do such a thing?" Farrel got a stern look.

"Because he's a law enforcement officer in pursuit of a felon." She regarded him in silence, and nodded.

When Angel came into Drydon's office, she was surprised to find him with what was a real smile, and made her wonder what could have brought this on.

"I have some news, Corey. Please sit down."

"News from Les?" she asked, taking a chair in front of his desk. Drydon shook his head.

"No. From the rangers. They spotted Garnet's ship heading for Varian Four." Angel frowned and she was puzzled that there had been nothing from Les.

"I wonder why Garnet keeps going there?" Drydon spread his hands on the desk.

"Maybe to remind himself of his humiliation and reinforce his desire for revenge. But the rangers informed Camden. I contacted Farrel and he said Camden's already in space trying for an interception." Angel held her frown as she leaned forward.

"If Garnet had a chance to get to a data bank and check the information Les, and we have, I wonder how he's taking it that his brother is after him?" she asked. Drydon shook his head.

"The real question is, how will it affect both when they face off?" Drydon countered.

"I doubt either of them have any idea about that." Angel rubbed the back of her neck.

"I just hope it doesn't affect Les' judgment."

"I wouldn't worry about that, Corey. Camden is too much of a law enforcement man to let that happen." She thought Drydon was taking too lightly the emotional effect such information would have on them both.

"I hope you're right, Chief."

"By the way, Corey, I'm sending you to the ranger base. That way there's no chance of anyone spotting you. Commander Adams said he has something interesting for you to do."

Garnet smiled as he thoughtfully patted himself on the back. He had made certain the ranger ship had identified his ship, and made it easy for it to shadow him. He was about to change course for Varian Five where there was ruins of an ancient city, and there he would wait for Camden – his brother – to come after him.

"My brother," he said, aloud, and shook his head. "I never would have thought such a thing possible, but facts are facts and have to be faced." It wasn't something he wanted to think about, but it seemed to remain in his conscious mind no matter what else he tried to think about. Garnet now knew he was in a much more complicated situation than he had ever been before.

Les had no way that Garnet had changed course and proceeded to Varian Four. He landed close to where he thought Garnet had come. He made his way to the gully and climbed to the crest. He peered down and saw no one. Puzzled, Les sat down and tried to think of where Garnet could have gone. He was certain that Garnet hadn't planned on giving him the slip. He moved down to the ground and began walking back to his ship. Les was both puzzled and confused at Garnet's action, and could only attribute it to his mental state.

On Varian Five, Garnet wandered amid the ruins, considering them to be like his life. He knew there would have to be a confrontation with Camden, one he could use to lead the marshal – his brother – back to Varian Four. He would send Camden a personal message and tell him where and when the end game would begin. But for some reason Garnet couldn't fathom, he couldn't think beyond facing Camden on Varian Four. It bothered him, and he decided he didn't have the time to ponder his mind's little peculiarities.

Les sat in the pilot's seat and concluded Garnet had been to Casin Three to go over the records. Whether he believed what he had learned, Les wasn't able to guess at. But this time, he hadn't told Ruby where he was going. So where to begin a search? Les was thoughtfully pondering that when a message came through recalling him to Earth. This really puzzled him.

"What the hell is this about?" he wondered, aloud. He tried to consider why he was being recalled, but the message had been plain. He turned back to the control panel and began setting a course for Earth.

When Angel came into Drydon's office, she had a glowing smile. Drydon looked up and got a pleased expression.

"Well, Chief, I'm now a qualified stealth ship pilot. Commander Adams was surprised, and pleased, that I learned to master the ship so quickly," she said, in a happy tone. "Being out at the ranger base for three weeks was really the best way for me to keep out of sight."

"I'm glad for you, Corey. You can pilot one of those ships back to Varian Four when you return. It should make your orbital space much safer." She got a serious look as she sat down.

"Any news from Les?" Angel asked. Drydon got a dry frown.

"Only that he hasn't been able to get firm trace on Garnet." She got a disappointed look.

"I wonder..?" Drydon raised an eyebrow.

"Wonder what, Corey?" She got a hesitant look.

"If twins do have some sort of telepathic bond, I wonder if one could block it from the other?" Drydon began rubbing his chin.

"That's a possibility, I suppose," he replied. "But there's no viable proof that such a bond exists."

The door opened and the receptionist came in carrying an envelope. She stopped and handed it to Drydon.

"This came by special messenger. It's addressed to you, sir, but it has no return address on it." Drydon got a puzzled look as he opened it. He took out a video disc, glanced at the receptionist and Angel, and back to it.

"I wonder who sent this?" he asked, absently.

"The only way to find out is to play it," Angel said. He got up and went to the small

TV, turned it on, and slid the disc into the slot.

Drydon was stunned, and Angel was quickly on her feet staring at the screen. The image of Garnet stared back out at them.

"I want this message to get to Camden," Garnet said. "In two weeks I'll be on Dracon Two. There's where the end game really begins. It will end on Varian Four, for obvious reasons. I don't want you to disappoint me, Camden – brother. I'll be waiting for you so we can finish our business." The screen went blank.

"I'll be damned!" Drydon exclaimed. "I've never seen such arrogance." Angel was now alarmed.

"Garnet's aware they're brothers. It's not in Les' favor to face Garnet when and where he chooses," she said. "What can we do, Chief?" Drydon turned to the receptionist.

"Put out a recall order to Camden," he said. "Have him return to Earth immediately. Give no reason. Just a plain recall order." She nodded and hurried from the office.

Susan had been out of the hospital for a week. She had had a difficult time convincing Farrel to let her return to duty. He felt she needed more time to rest and recuperate. But she had finally convinced him that work would be the best therapy for her. Now she could do what she had been planning since Les had told her about Ruby's help in locating her.

She pulled the car to a stop in front of the bar, turned off the engine, got out, and slowly pushed the door shut. Susan looked at the place, pulled her shoulders back, and headed for the entrance. Stepping inside, she noted that the few patrons paid no attention to her. She went toward the woman working behind the bar.

"What would you like?" the woman asked. Susan quickly plucked up her courage.

"I would like to see Ruby, please." The woman nodded, went to the far end of the bar, and pressed the comlink on an audvid unit. Susan saw her speaking, but couldn't hear what she said. The woman came back to her.

"She will be down in a minute." Susan nodded.

"Thanks."

Ruby appeared at the top of the stairs and came down with no particular expression showing. At the bottom, she turned and their eyes met. They held eye contact as Ruby came to her.

"You wanted to see me?" Ruby asked. Susan nodded.

"My name is Susan Burns. And I want to thank you for telling Les where to find me."

Ruby smiled and took on a relaxed pose.

"I would have done the same for any woman," Ruby said. "I despise Giles, or any man who beats on women. But I'm glad I could help." Susan extended her hand to Ruby who took it. Susan turned and walked quickly out. Ruby looked after her with an expression of pride.

Back at HQ, Susan told Farrel what she had done. He nodded with an agreeable expression.

"That was very courteous, Susan. Hell, who knows but that you put Ruby on a different life path." She laughed.

"I doubt that," Susan said. "When I was face to face with her, I got the impression that

Ruby will always be Ruby." Farrel's expression turned serious.

"I got a call from Drydon," he said, and noted her immediate attention. "He's recalled Les to Earth. He apologized that he couldn't tell me why, but my guess is it has something to do with Garnet." She got a concerned look.

"Do you think Les will be all right?" Farrel stood, came to the front of the desk, and put a hand on her shoulder.

"Brother or not, Les knows how to handle Garnet. I wouldn't worry about it." Susan nodded but held her concerned look.

Just after coming into orbit, Les was instructed to set down at the ranger base. He was becoming annoyed at these seemingly idle instructions with no reason given for them. Dutifully, he did as instructed.

As he came down the ramp, he saw a ranger waiting for him.

"A vehicle is waiting for you, sir," the ranger said. "Please follow me." Les followed him to a very impressive, and official looking vehicle. The ranger opened the door and Les gave him a nod and climbed in. He was really surprised when he found himself sitting next to Angel.

"What's this all about?" Les asked. She leaned over and kissed him. When she pulled away, she didn't smile. And that seemed to annoy him even more.

"I can't tell you a thing, Les. The chief asked me to bring you to his office and let you see for yourself." There was a grim undertone in her voice that made him uneasy. The vehicle started, was quickly away from the ranger base, and headed for the city.

When they entered the office, Drydon got to his feet and came to Les and shook his hand.

"I'm glad you're here, Camden. Something has happened that required your immediate attention," Drydon said, in a rapid fire voice that confused Les. He looked from Drydon to Angel and back.

"What's going on here?" Les asked. Drydon motioned for him to come with him, and Angel trailed along.

Drydon stopped by the TV, turned it on, and stepped back. Over the next few minutes, Les was enlightened about what was going on. When the disc ended, Les could think of nothing to say as he glanced at Angel. Garnet's words echoed in his mind.

"What did he mean by brother, Les?" she asked. He thought quickly and shrugged.

"Just an expression, I guess," he replied. Angel and Drydon exchanged glances. Les turned to Drydon.

"Have my ship readied, sir. If I'm going to keep this rendezvous with Garnet, I'll have to leave in the morning." Drydon nodded.

"I'll see that it's taken care of." Angel locked her arm with Les' and smiled.

"At least, you can have a home cooked meal before you leave," she said. Les turned his eyes to her and smiled.

"Sounds good," he said.

The next morning, after Les had left for the ranger base, Angel went to Drydon's office.

"Chief, I want to ask a favor." Drydon regarded her solemnly.

"What is it Corey?" She took a deep breath before speaking.

"I would like to follow Les in a stealth ship. I don't like the way he just brushed off that brother remark." Drydon raised an eyebrow and nodded.

"I think you're right, Corey. I'll call and have a ship readied for you. Just be careful Camden doesn't spot you." She got a smug look.

"He couldn't, even if he knew I was there, Chief."

Once Les was out of orbit, he decided to do a little bit of homework. He was curious as to why Garnet had chosen Dracon Two to begin their face off. He didn't really understand what Garnet was up to but hoped to get a clearer picture with some data. If either of them got wounded or killed on Dracon Two, that would be the end of it. Les began to believe that Garnet was becoming hung up on the game itself; that he must show that he was the better man. This ran through Les' mind as he requested the data of conditions on Dracon Two. What showed up on the monitor perplexed him. He read:

'Dracon Two is a world of the utmost turbulent weather on any known inhabitable planet. Parts of it are suddenly overpowered by violent thunderstorms, while other parts are having huge dust storms, or in the north, blizzards. It is definitely not a world a colony would thrive on. Although ancient ruins were discovered there, the conditions have prevented any archeological studies from being carried out.'

Les leaned back and locked his hands behind his head. He had no doubt that those ruins would be where he would find Garnet waiting. Ruins like that would provide adequate cover for an encounter. He wondered why Garnet seemed to have a thing about ruins. Very curious, Les thought. Well there's nothing else to do except to go there, and see how things worked out.

Forty-five minutes after Les lifted off, Angel was cleared, and began her watching of Les' back. She had gotten a bad feeling at the way he had so lightly brushed off Garnet's use of brother. She couldn't quite pin it down, but had gotten a fleeting impression that he didn't feel quite the same about Garnet as he used to, and that might prove dangerous, even fatal.

Angel closed the distance with Les' ship until she had a firm lock on it. This was three days out from Earth, and she was beginning to see what Les had meant about being bored and alone. But it was something she determined to put up with, as it had been her idea to follow, and if necessary, give him help.

She couldn't help worrying about how Les would handle Garnet when they finally face to face, figuratively speaking, she thought. All Angel could do was sit and listen as the lock on the ship ahead of her stayed at the same volume.

Garnet sat in the pilot's seat lost in thought, and nervously rubbing a finger over his lips and chin. He was working out how to handle Camden –

"My unidentical twin brother," he said, aloud. Then he went back to his planning. I'll pin him down in the ancient ruins, make him think I'm just waiting for a quick view of him, to finish him off. But, he kept thinking, I'll be making for my ship. Once he realizes I'm gone, Camden will have enough time to get to his ship and follow me to Varian Five.

[253]

On Varian Five, he'll have to hunt for me. He'll know where my ship landed and that will be his starting place. I'll be in my ship waiting for him to become engrossed in the hunt. Then I'll surprise him by lifting off and heading for Varian Four. Once there, I'll get serious about killing him.

"Kill my brother? Hell, I've never known him as anything except as a pesty lawman. Screwing up my plans." He lifted his right hand and stared at it.

"How could a brother take a brother's hand?"

Ruby had pondered, and fretted, over a decision she was fearful of taking. But for her edification, she had decided to take what action had to be done. A week ago, she had hired a man to go through all the records he could access of Jovan and Camden. Ruby had to know the truth, whatever it might be.

There was a knock on the door and Ruby went and opened it to face Mitch with the man she had hired. Mitch regarded her with an odd expression.

"This man says he has private business with you, Ruby." She stepped aside and waved them in. She closed the door and turned to the man with an anxious look.

"What have you learned?" she asked. The man had a neutral expression as he took papers from his pocket.

"I'm afraid it's true, Ruby," he said, in a mild voice. Mitch glanced from him to Ruby.

"What's true, Ruby?" Mitch asked, looking puzzled. She turned her face to him, nervously licked her lips, and began toying with her necklace.

"Jovan and Camden are brothers, Mitch. Nonidentical twins." There, she had said it. She had spoken the words she had hoped she wouldn't have had to say.

"What!" Mitch exclaimed. "How can that be?" She reached for the papers and the man handed them to her. She held them out to Mitch.

"Here's the records, Mitch. Read them here, because they are not leaving this room." The man cleared his throat and got her attention.

"Do you need me anymore, Ruby?" he asked. She shook her head and turned to a stand. She picked up an envelope and turned back to him.

"You've earned this, Christolph," she said. "And don't mention this to anyone else." He nodded as he took the envelope, pocketed it, and left.

Mitch's eyes widened as he read then turned his eyes to Ruby.

"I never would have believed it," he said. Ruby frowned.

"I wish I didn't have to. Brothers trying to kill each other is something that's very wrong."

"Maybe they'll come to some sort of agreement," Mitch suggested. Ruby shook her head.

"I doubt that. They've been in conflict too long, and neither will be able to get past it."

After a week, Angel was becoming impatient. She decided, after thinking it over, to go ahead of Les to Dracon Two. She knew he wouldn't even be aware of her passing him. She turned to the control panel, put the ship in high stealth mode, and cut in the main thrusters. The sudden acceleration pushed her into the seat.

The next day, she took the ship into orbit around Dracon Two and began scanning the surface. Certain areas of the planet had freakish weather that blocked her sensors. She kept orbiting and scanning, until the weather temporarily cleared. She felt that Garnet hadn't yet arrived. Angel reversed the sensors and began scanning the space around the planet.

After a few hours, she picked up Les' ship at extreme range, but so far not a trace of Garnet. Angel began to wonder if somehow she had missed his ship on the surface. That weather could provide good cover for a ship down there. He certainly wouldn't want Les getting here before him. Again, she reversed the sensors and watched closely as they tracked over the surface. But another area of extreme weather interfered. Feeling a bit frustrated, Angel decided to persevere with her search.

On her seventh orbit, she got a trace of what might be a ship on the surface, but she couldn't be sure until she got a clear reading. After two more orbits, she saw a clear indication of a ship on the surface near some ruins. Angel smiled as she imagined the expression on Garnet's face if he knew she was in orbit above him.

Garnet walked among the ancient stone ruins. He was feeling in a melancholy mood. The weather contributed to his mood as a misty rain was falling from a slate gray sky. His mind wandered to the ruins, wondering how they had come to be built, and what had become of the builders. He also wondered how he had reached this point in his life.

When Garnet was teaching, his future seemed set. He suddenly remembered Kathryn and how she had jilted him after the false charge had been made against him; she had even refused to speak to him. They were to have been married. He would have had a family now, instead of being on this foresaken planet. He absently brushed rain from his face.

Garnet began to wonder who had made that charge against him. He remembered his colleagues in the chemistry department. Abruptly, a name stuck in his mind: Brock Deavers. Garnet had been aware that he had been envious of his relationship with Kathryn. On closely recalling his memories, he came to the conclusion that Deavers was the only one who could have copied those pages, and planted them in his lab. He sat down on what appeared to be the steps of a temple and began to ponder his past. He now wondered why he had never suspected Deavers until now. Too bad Deavers was on Earth, he thought. If he were somewhere else I would hunt that bastard down and kill him.

Garnet shook his head and wiped rain from his face. He had to get out of this mood before Camden – his brother – arrived. He would need all his wits for dealing with him on Varian Four, and...

"And what?" he asked, aloud. He would kill Camden – kill his unidentical twin. But he was having qualms about that. He suddenly realized he was regretting the life he had chosen.

"Shit! Get a grip on yourself," he said, angrily. He got to his feet, wiped rain from his face, and absently walked off as the rain became a steady downpour.

Les brought his ship into orbit around Dracon Two and fired up his sensors only to find them blind over certain weather patterns. It was going to take longer than he expected to locate Garnet's ship. Les had hoped for a quick location, set down, and meeting with his brother. His brother! This fact lingered in his mind as he began an intensive search for the ship. But it popped into his mind that there were ruins on the planet, and Garnet seemed to have a penchant for ruins. Les quickly reset the sensors for the large ruins and quickly located them.

He now had to decide if he wanted to risk setting the ship down without knowing where Garnet's ship was. He took only a minute to decide that he had to risk it. Les took manual control and turned the ship into the atmosphere. He saw a clearing about a mile from the ruins and glided the ship there and landed. Les remained in the pilot's seat for a few minutes before unstrapping himself. He went to the bulkhead locker, opened it, and took out his weapon. He strapped it on and went to the hatch. He activated it, and it opened to reveal a sky filled with scudding, dark clouds. Les frowned, but left the ship and headed for the ruins.

Angel saw Les' ship go into the atmosphere, land, and was almost immediately covered by thick clouds filled with lightning at their tops.

"Damn! There go my sensors," she muttered, with a hard frown. She knew the only thing she could do was orbit until the storm had passed. But what would she find then?

Angel felt impatient to know what was going on down there. Brothers facing off against each other, it seemed incredible that such a situation could be happening. She was concerned about how Les would react under these circumstances. But all she could do was wait. And waiting seemed to become all the more intolerable as time passed.

The rain was pouring, lightning lit the landscape in bright flashes, and the thunder was deafening. Les was moving cautiously among the ruins wiping rain from his face and washoping to spot Garnet. Just as thunder roared again, a pulsar charge impacted above his head. He dove for cover and wondered where it had come from. He knew he had made contact with Garnet, but was his shot meant to miss?

Recalling what had been on the video disc, Les concluded that this was the beginning of the game Garnet wanted. He raised his head and another pulsar charge flashed above him and impacted the ancient stone ruin. But this time Les had seen where it had come from. Stooping, he moved cautiously around, hoping to get behind Garnet.

Les moved past jungle vines climbing the ruins until he felt he was in the right position. He stood as rain pelted his face and started toward where he hoped the game would come to an end. Just as Les stepped into the clearing, he started when he heard the sound of a ship lifting off. He looked up and saw the ship vanish into the thick clouds. Les holstered his pulsar and wiped rain from his face. Garnet was getting good at pulling this little trick on him. Les decided he wouldn't do it again. Although Les didn't know it, his next stop would be Varian Five.

23

Angel had only seconds to react when the collision alarm sounded. She quickly cut in the main thrusters and took the ship out of orbit. She glanced at the monitor and saw Garnet's ship speeding away from the planet. A few minutes later, Les' ship came out of the clouds in pursuit. Angel wondered what had occurred on the planet below as she followed Les away into space.

There must have been an encounter, and it seemed to her, had ended in a draw. But where they were now headed, she hadn't a clue. She thought it might be Varian Four, but with Garnet you never knew. All she could do was follow and see where it led.

Garnet began considering his plan for Varian Five. Twice now he had fooled Garnet – his brother – into believing he was where he wasn't.

"Hell! I didn't fool him. He was just too damn slow." Be that as it may, he couldn't count on it happening again. He felt Camden would stay within sight of the ship to prevent him from getting back on board. Garnet decided he would have to start at his ship and draw Camden away. But what was wrong with his original idea? Just stay in the ship and let the marshal search for him. But if he stayed too close to the ship, he would be killed when I lift off, and I don't want him dying that way. I want his death to be personal – face to face.

Les was thinking along similar lines. He knew he couldn't cover Garnet's ship, and that meant he would have the chance to get back on board without Les seeing him.

"Why would he want to do that?" he asked himself. That didn't make any sense. Varian Four was to be their arena of combat. Garnet had chosen it. Les was so concentrated in thought he almost missed Garnet's course change to Varian Five. Les got a puzzled look as he adjusted the ship's course.

"What the hell is he up to now?" Les quickly checked his course and found he was headed for Varian Five. He began to wonder if Garnet had made a mistake. Les shook his head knowing Garnet wasn't prone to mistakes. All he could do was follow and see what he had in mind.

Angel got a puzzled look when she noted that Les had changed course, and was headed for Varian Five. She could only guess, but had to assume that was where Garnet was headed, too. She tried to reason why, but could only believe he had some nasty surprise up his sleeve. At least on Varian Five, her special camera would allow her to see what was happening. And, if necessary, intervene.

Garnet took his ship down to Varian Five. But he still had no idea what he would do when Camden – his brother – landed. He felt Camden wouldn't fall for being drawn away into the ruins. So what could he do? Garnet felt that the marshal wouldn't come after him without some idea of where he was, and that he wouldn't enter the ruins where he wouldn't be able to move quickly. Garnet was stymied. The only thing he could think of was to face him. But this wasn't the planet he wanted him to die on. What sort of chance was there of facing him, without killing him, and getting away? He got a slight smile as an idea occurred to him.

Les took his ship down and landed as close as he could to Garnet's ship, wanting to make certain he got the message that Les wasn't going to be drawn off and give him time to get back to his ship. The communicator crackled and Les pressed the comlink.

"Yeah?"

"I'll meet you halfway between our ships," Garnet said. "Out in the open, in plain sight of each other." This surprised Les, but he couldn't refuse.

"All right, Garnet. I'll leave my ship now, and expect you to do the same."

"I'm on my way out – Brother." Les quickly strapped on his sidearm and went to the hatch. He activated it and it opened on a wide clearing with sparse vegetation.

Les went out and started across the clearing. He quickly saw Garnet coming toward him. They stopped about six feet apart. Both had their weapons holstered as they faced each other.

"You're an intelligent man, Garnet. You had to know the consequence of your action." Garnet got a hard frown.

"If I hadn't been framed, I would still be teaching, and have a family. Instead I'm facing a brother I never knew I had wanting to have me incarcerated for the rest of my life." His words sparked sympathy in Les, but that didn't excuse Garnet's crimes; ones that he had willingly committed.

"You can always enter rehabilitation," Les said. "If you're successful, you won't have to remain on Forten for the rest of your life." Garnet regarded Les for a moment in silence. Les knew he was considering the offer. Garnet suddenly drew his weapon and fired, hitting Les with a stun charge. Garnet walked over and looked down at him.

"I got my second back, Marshal – Brother." He turned and headed back to his ship.

Angel watched as the two men approached each other. She could see they were speaking but couldn't hear what was being said. She started when Garnet drew his weapon and fired. Angel knew it had been a stun charge because there had been no flash. She watched as Garnet looked down at Les, then turned and walked back toward his ship.

She felt certain it had been a light stun charge to give Garnet time to get to Varian Four and prepare for Les' lethal reception. Angel decided to wait and follow Les when he came around. Her sensor showed Garnet's ship leaving the planet and heading in the direction she had anticipated. After seeing what he had done to Les, she held nothing but contempt for Garnet. Nothing, she felt, would ever provoke sympathy for him in her.

Les pushed himself up, rolled over, and rose to a sitting position. He moaned slightly as he rubbed his head. After sitting for a few minutes, he slowly got to his feet and headed for the ship. As Les walked, he realized Garnet had surprised him again. Not once, but twice. First by coming here to Varian Five. That was something Les didn't try to understand his reasoning for that action. Then, without any warning, drawing his weapon and firing. Les now felt foolish for having trusted Garnet. But maybe his words had gotten through to Garnet. From his tone when he talked about teaching, and having a family, had come across to Les as sincere.

When he stopped at the hatch, Les silently vowed that this was going to end on Varian Four one way or the other. He activated the hatch and went on board. As he powered up the ship, he knew he was going to have to be careful because he didn't want to kill his brother.

Angel watched Les' ship rise through the atmosphere and set course for Varian Four. She quickly set course to follow. Garnet had said Varian Four would be his last stop. She was now concerned about how Les would react in this sort of situation that was nearing it's climax. Angel decided she would have to land and get to the bowl-shaped gully before Les. She cut in the main thrusters and sped away, leaving Les to follow. She felt she had to be in place, just in case the family tie had some unforeseen consequence.

Garnet had landed his ship in a spot where it couldn't be easily seen, and went off on foot toward the fateful gully. As he walked, he kept thinking about what Camden – his brother – had said about rehabilitation. He struggled not to think about what that could mean for his life. He now knew who had framed him, and felt he could prove it. He might not be able to get Kathryn back, but he had Ruby.

Yet his mind stubbornly fought against such a course of action. He tried hard to turn his thoughts to facing his nemesis, and having his revenge. Revenge? It now seemed such a hollow word, almost meaningless. He kept walking toward his destination, maybe his fate. But Garnet had to go through with what he had told them he would do. He couldn't back down now.

Angel didn't have to worry about where she landed because she could leave the ship in stealth mode and be practically invisible from the air. She made her way to the gully and climbed the slope Les had and peered down. She felt a surge of relief when she saw that Garnet hadn't yet arrived. Now she would have to wait until the faceoff between the brothers occurred before she would intervene. If Les done what he was supposed to, she wouldn't have to intervene. But if she detected any hesitancy on his part, she would take immediate action.

Les struggled mentally with the question about how to face Garnet. He didn't want to kill him because he believed he could be rehabilitated and put back in society as a progressive person and teacher. He believed him that he had been framed, but he had still wantonly committed crimes. And after what he pulled on Varian Five, Les was unsure he could avoid killing him. But he had to avoid that. Both had the same mother! And that meant something special to Les. He would just have to wait until he faced Garnet and see how he reacted before he made his decision.

Garnet sat eating a power bar and contemplating his future. Once Camden – his brother – was out of the way, he would have his life back. But, he thought, what sort of life? He hadn't much cared for being a badass. It just hadn't fit his temperment, and he would like to go back to teaching and research.

"Stop it! Goddamnit, you can never go back. Never!" He threw the half-eaten power bar down, stood, and continued walking to his destination – and his future.

Angel was also eating. But her meal was emergency rations the rangers had provided her with. She had selected a location where she could observe unseen, and she could clearly see the gully. But Angel was wondering where Garnet was. He had to have landed by now. But, she concluded, he must have landed a distance away from the gully to make it harder for Les to spot his ship. That meant he had to be walking to the gully, and she had no idea how long it might take him to get there. She was certain he would show up before Les, and be waiting to carry out his threat to kill Les. But would Les somehow prevent that from happening? She could only wait and wonder at the outcome.

Les was coming up on Varian Four, and for the first time in his law enforcement career, he was feeling anxiety. But he knew he had to put that aside and do what he had come here to do. Put an end to Garnet's criminal career, and hopefully, get him rehabilitated and back into society. He knew that wasn't going to be easy with him, and he had to be alert for anything he might try. This time, he couldn't afford to let Garnet surprise him.

He took manual control of the ship and turned it down into the atmosphere. He made no effort to try to conceal his landing. Les knew Garnet would be waiting for him, and he was eager to get this unpalatable situation over with. He suddenly had an insight that seemed to make sense to him. Maybe Garnet had been returning to the sight of his downfall because he wanted it to happen again. Les couldn't be certain of that, but it could prove to be the truth, especially after what he had told Les.

Les cut the power to the ship, went to the bulkhead locker and took out his sidearm and strapped it on as he went to the hatch. He activated it and watched it open. This, he felt, might prove to be the toughest day of his life. He hesitated for a second, then went down the ramp and began walking toward the gully.

As Garnet walked into the gully, he drew his weapon and checked its setting. Satisfied, he reholstered it and sat down on the flat rock to wait for his brother to arrive. His thoughts kept going back to the idea of rehabilitation, and that he might be able to teach again. Garnet felt being able to do that meant more than anything to him. But he wasn't here to talk to Camden about how he could apply for rehabilitation; he was here to kill him. But that thought held little appeal for him now. But he couldn't back down now. He had to go through with what he had threatened, he had no other choice.

Angel saw Garnet when he came into the gully, and smiled when she saw him sit down on that rock. Looking around, she saw Les coming toward the gully, and felt it was time for her to move into position, so she could be ready to move if it became necessary. She climbed the slope and was able to look down and see she had a clear field of fire. Angel checked to make certain her pulsar was set on stun. Now it became a wait and see situation.

As Les approached the opening to the gully, he drew his weapon and made the setting to stun. His heart was racing and he was tense. These feelings were a bit strange to Les as he had been able to overcome them so many times before. He began breathing deeply and consciously forcing himself to relax. When his heart had slowed, he started for the opening.

Garnet heard footsteps and got to his feet and drew his weapon. He was facing the opening when Les Came in and stopped. They stood with their weapons leveled at each other and just stared. Angel was looking down on a scene that had suddenly frozen. Neither man made a move, and she felt it was time for her to act. She raised her pulsar and fired. As Garnet collapsed to the ground, Les couldn't comprehend what had happened. Had he unknowingly fired? He looked at his pulsar and wondered if that was the case, until he heard someone coming down the slope into the gully. He was still in a state of incomprehension as Angel came to him and holstered her pulsar. He stared at her with a disbelieving look.

"Thought I would repay the favor, Les." He just stood and regarded her as though he was in a dream. She leaned forward and kissed him. He looked at her and blinked.

"How did you get here, Angel?" She smiled and tilted her head.

"I've got a very fast stealth ship the rangers loaned me. I've been following since you left Earth. I had a feeling it would be difficult for you facing your brother." His arm holding his weapong slowly lowered to his side.

"My brother," he said, and looked down at the unconacious Garnet. He looked back to

Angel.

"How did you know?" Les asked. Angel straightened her shoulders and regarded him with a serious look.

"When I felt you were holding something back, I decided to do what you did – I went to the records. When you brushed off Garnet's mention of you as brother, on that video disc, I knew you were going to have a problem, and had the chief get me a stealth ship from the rangers." She got a bright smile and patted his arm.

"Let's get him to your ship, Les. After you turn him over to the rangers, I'll show you my ship." He nodded and began pulling Garnet to his feet.

[265]

Six months later, Les came into Angel's office with a broad smile and confident walk. She looked and her eyes widened when she saw his expression.

"What's put you in such a good mood?" she asked. Les sat down and rested his arms on his legs.

"I just had a communication from the warden on Forten," he replied. "My brother is taking to rehabilitation like a duck to water. He should be able to leave Forten in a couple of years. He's working in a chemical lab and teaching inmates general chemistry. But the best news is, when Garnet escaped from Forten, a Brock Deavers went to the dean and confessed that he framed Garnet on the plagiarism charge because he was afraid Garnet would come after him. The university has notified the warden that when his rehab is complete, he can have his teaching position back." Angel got a pleased look. It wasn't very often, in their profession, that such a good ending happened.

"I'm glad to hear that, Les. I know it means a lot to you." He nodded.

"In a week or so, I'm going to Forten to visit him. Want to come along? I would appreciate a fast ride in that new ship of yours." Angel smiled and nodded.

"I would like that, Les. I'm curious to see the change in Garnet. And I will give you a ride in the stealth ship. That way you can understand how I was able to follow you without either of you suspecting anyone else was around." She stood and came to the front of the desk.

"Now that life is back to normal," she said. "Let's concentrate on our relationship."

He stood, smiled, and embraced her.

"That's the best offer I've had in a long time," Les said, and kissed her.

THE END

HELLCHASER

www.ingramcontent.com/pod-product-compliance
Lightning Source LLC
Chambersburg PA
CBHW022006010726
47494CB00003B/911